PRIVATE NOVELIST

ALSO BY NELL ZINK

The Wallcreeper

Mislaid

Nicotine

PRIVATE
NOVELIST

FICTION

NELL ZINK

ecco

An Imprint of HarperCollins *Publishers*

HarperCollins books may be purchased for educational, business, or sales promotional use. For information, please e-mail the Special Markets Department at SPsales@harpercollins.com.

FIRST EDITION

Designed by Shannon Nicole Plunkett

Library of Congress Cataloging-in-Publication Data has been applied for.

ISBN 978-0-06-245830-8

16 17 18 19 20   OV/RRD   10 9 8 7 6 5 4 3 2 1

For Avner Shats

CONTENTS

NELL ZINK IS NOT TOO KEEN ON THE

Beatles; I am a devoted fan. This is just one of the many things we don't have in common. We come from radically different backgrounds and might have never crossed paths were it not for Zohar Eitan—a musicologist and poet—and a rather unlikely chain of events involving his sabbatical, a fictitious poet named Elad Manor, and the Swiss writer Robert Walser.

How then, you might ask, did I become the sole, exclusive reader of this now-celebrated author, a job I kept for so many years? (It took Jonathan Franzen nearly fifteen years to jump on the bandwagon!)

Sheer blind luck, of course; but what made Nell Zink decide to become my Private Novelist was probably the fact that we do, after all, share a few common penchants: coffee drinking, atheism, a fondness for obscure and dubious scientific theories and certain prog-rock bands from the '70s, and a general admiration for the natural world—enough to spark a long-term epistolary affair, lasting to this day. It gave rise to at least two novels (that's all I'm allowed to disclose at this time), now made available to the general public.

Like an astronaut landing on Venus with insufficient gear,

stunned by the heat, glaring sunlight, and native manners, Nell landed in the land of Israel near the end of the last millennium; she roved the country, transmitting to her few carefully selected readers insightful and beautiful passages pondering her experience. Naturally, at some point it became apparent that she should write a novel. And so she did. She named it—as explained in the novel itself—by referencing my own novel, published in Hebrew shortly before, *Sailing Toward the Sunset by Avner Shats*. She addressed it to me, a chapter a day, and my curiosity and amusement soon turned to awe and astonishment in the face of her writing: so much so that I felt compelled to translate it into Hebrew, thus creating the monstrosity titled "*Sailing Toward the Sunset by Avner Shats* by Nell Zink, translated by Avner Shats." It should, however, be made perfectly clear that the two novels have nothing in common. Well, almost nothing.

Nell, as the world now knows, is a formidable writer, and her English is out of my league. I had the unique privilege, which not all translators enjoy, of being able to ask silly questions regarding common American idioms that were Greek to me. Nell halfheartedly toyed with the idea of publishing what became known as *STTSBAS*, but the one agent she turned to, as I remember, said it was "unpublishable"; in the years that followed we came to have another thing in common: dormant literary careers (see chart). Sometime in 2005, Nell suggested she accept a challenge: I was to name a setting and a list of items and characters, and she would write a novel incorporating them, because "I have nothing to do and need some practice writing English." This might strike some people as odd, but only those who do not know Dr. Zink. (Yes, she holds a PhD in something or other. You don't really know her.) The result was *European Story for Avner Shats*.

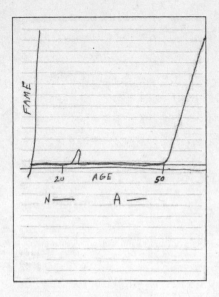

I am of Jewish-Polish descent, traditionally a guilt-ridden tribe, and so I feel guilty about not having done enough—anything—to let the world know of Nell Zink. Shamefully, even after her work was discovered by my betters, I tried to lower her expectations. To calm my conscience I can dig up this old e-mail:

Admit it: you're amazing . . . at least consider publishing it on the net. It's not fair to keep it inaccessible to other readers.

There it is.

—**Avner Shats, Haifa, December 16, 2015**

SAILING TOWARD THE SUNSET
BY AVNER SHATS

A NOVEL IN E-MAILS*

*One chapter per day in December 1998. New spell-checked edition, including all the egregious weaknesses of the original and its many errors of taste, prepared in 2011.

CHAPTER 1

IT HAVING BECOME APPARENT THAT I
should write a novel, my next concern became which novel I
should write.

An obvious choice was Avner Shats' recent debut, *Sailing
Toward the Sunset*. A plot summary presented on the occasion
of Shats' receipt of an empty envelope purporting to contain
an unidentified sum of money, in a room hidden deep in the
recesses of the Hebrew University and lined with waxy lem-
onwood paneling, a sum I know to have been $5,000, already
spent by Shats at the time of his smiling acceptance of the
empty envelope—the occasion was a ceremony commemorat-
ing his receipt, several months before, of the Peter Schweipert
prize for literary genius—but I shouldn't give away the plot
for several pages yet.

"Again and again," the novel begins, "my tea draws a [?] on
the internal bay leaves of my mind." The choice of the bay leaf
as a symbol for the unconscious is an interesting one. Bay or
laurel, *daphne* in Greek, as was explained to me by a linguist
of the Bar-Ilan University, is understood to be the name of a
daughter in Hebrew, in English, and even (most important
for her in-laws) in Dutch. The passage continues: "[?] of the

smoke . . . moving . . . excited [well]—I sit on a wooden chair made of red plastic jelly, waiting for the light, by a table whose [?] are heightened, but will not succeed in dividing the tools from the curling smoke."

I was reminded of Shats' novel the same night when, after the ceremony, the Baleno having delivered us to the Justy, the Charade being held too small for the task (I am told it is the mission of the writer to love words for their own sake), Zohar and I (*Zohar* meaning "splendor" or "glory") drove westward several hundred yards across Mount Scopus to the British military cemetery. The turf is deep and dry. Leaving the cemetery, we proceeded to the home of a distinguished Hungarian lady. Toward midnight her sixteen-year-old son told me about the Hungarian language, which resembles only Finnish. "I suppose if I hadn't been born Hungarian I would never have troubled to learn it," he said, more or less, "but I am glad to know it, as Hungarian poetry is the most beautiful imaginable."

Having mastered Hebrew in a year, the boy was learning Farsi. Open on the table was an English translation of the poetry of Hafez. I have always been a little suspicious of exotic poetry, much of which, the translators admit at some point or another, they fabricate. I feel sorry for all those who write in languages now dead. Who will defend them? The book contained two sets of translations: one into weak rhymes, the other word-for-word into clinical English. Since I can't remember an example, I'll make one up.

COLUMN 1: DOGGEREL
I think that I shall never see
A poem lovely as a tree.

COLUMN 2: ANCIENT WISDOM

To envision thought, impossible—
Words in sequence exquisite, the tree, too, exquisite.

I use the example of Joyce Kilmer's "Trees" because it contains a reference to breast-feeding (in the second stanza, "A tree whose hungry mouth is prest / Against the earth's sweet flowing breast"), of which I am reminded by the unfortunate subject of the ridicule I directed against translators of Rilke not long before we left the Hungarians' apartment, deep in the night and stuffed with tea and cake. Rilke made use of many arguably tasteless metaphors, all of which his translators routinely ignore in favor of grand metaphysical images, even in bilingual editions where the original and translation stand side-by-side as though German were already dead.

Rilke, to those who can read him, was what they call a "breast man," as, apparently, is Shats, to whose novel I will now return. The Hebrew language, dead to me—well, not quite dead, as you can see from the ancient wisdom I was able to cull from the first paragraph of *Sailing Toward the Sunset*—is certainly impenetrable to my mother's Internet browser, located in Oswego, New York, which is where I first saw its text. The character set was what my friend Alberto Bades Fernandez Arago habitually calls "Martian." But to one side, regularly replacing each other in the sprightly pictorial GIF animation which has supplanted mathematics as the universal language, were a tiny black pirate flag and a pair of human breasts. (I think a third element completed the sequence, but I've forgotten what it was.) Every time the flag appeared, followed by the breasts, my mind ceased functioning and I could only think, This looks like the cover art for *Pussy, King of the Pirates*, Kathy Acker's collaboration with the Mekons, an English rock band.

I think it was she who first began publishing other people's novels as her own. Other people had thought of writing short stories about people who did so, but, before today, only Kathy had the balls to do it herself.

Possible implications of the Shatsian GIF are as follows:

Implication #1: Shats did not write Sailing Toward the Sunset.

Where did he acquire it? The possibilities are many, but I will concentrate on the obvious and most likely one: He translated it from a language dead only to himself. Were the language dead to other people, the fraud would quickly be discovered. Not all readers are as credulous as those of Rilke.

Implication #2: His original may or may not have consisted of fifteen thousand rhymed couplets.

Implication #2 would be a lot to ask, yet the translator of Hafez admits that, in his original, every single line rhymed—twice as many rhymes, on average, as in the couplets relied on by Shats, Goethe, Alexander Pope, and others. Or, if you figure it another way, with Hafez's poems generally running to twenty lines or so, ten times as many.

Question: Now what are the odds, exactly, that these rhymes were graceful, effortless, and natural?

Answer: We can identify a practically infinite number of potential poets, whom I will designate by the variable p.

```
Rem p is number of poets good at rhyming
Let p = 0
Do while (r = "lousy") AND (p < = 10000000000)
p = p + 1 'cycles through all of human history
r = "lousy"
```

```
Loop
Print.Txtbox.txt "No one has ever consistently"
Print.Txtbox.txt "produced graceful rhymes, except"
Print.Txtbox.txt "maybe Heinrich Heine."
```

This program, which represents an extremely sophisticated advance in artificial intelligence since it exactly duplicates the thought processes going on in my head right now, will produce a conclusion baffling to anyone who has read Heine in translation, yet perfectly acceptable to those who have only heard rumors of his exceptional mastery. This trade in rumors of greatness is the most conspicuous feature of today's upmarket trade-paperback scene, which I fervently hope to penetrate with this, my second novel, *Sailing Toward the Sunset.*

(Titles cannot be copyrighted, nor can ideas, but only their expression.)

On a bookshelf in my parents' house, near the door where books often gather as driftwood on their way to the library book fair, I found a copy of *Possession* by A. S. Byatt. The cover of *Possession* showed a woman who would have been pre-Raphaelite had she not been soft and round. She appeared to have acquired her pre-Raphaelite tint through the application of auburn filters to something more pink and Viennese. The plot involved beautiful British academics in a detective story. Did or did they not ("they" being certain dead poets) have sex? All characterization is achieved through descriptions of clothing. *She wore a short, dark green raw silk kimono over black pants and a jade pendant on a satin cord,* a characterization reads in full, more or less. It is to be inferred that she is fat and forty-five, at which point the reader's attention wanders quickly back to the young, slender protagonists. I.e., the book was trash. As I skimmed it my face was contorted by sneers, and after skipping to the end to make sure the heroine really was the direct descendant of the vigorously adulterous dead poets and heiress to their fortunes, I resolved to write a novel myself. The result now lies before you, based not on a rumor of fifteen thousand perfect couplets in a dead language, but instead on the plot summary generously provided by an unknown interlocutor at an inscrutable ceremony high on Mount Scopus:

AN ISRAELI SPY MEETS A GIRL FROM THE SHETLAND ISLANDS. HER NAME IS MARY.

Other details were presented at a dizzying speed that precluded my knowing what they are.

The great reader Ms. Jumbo Loopy Chenille admitted to me that she had been saving a copy of *Possession* to read as a special treat, taken in by the cover and by a prize the book had received (the Booker). I begged her not to read *Possession,* but instead to borrow my copy of *The Waterfall* by Margaret Drabble, now out of print. In return I was lent her copy of *Dictionary of the Khazars.*

I intend to consider taking *Dictionary of the Khazars* as another model in my effort to re-create, from ideograms half heard and half remembered, *Sailing Toward the Sunset.* The Khazars, I have been warned by Shats himself, really existed. The *Dictionary of the Khazars* consists of an introduction and three alphabetized sections, one for each major Western religion to which the Khazars may or may not have converted. In it all the exotic and magical qualities of the Near East are remembered and preserved, somewhat as in the cabalistic magic scenes of *Fanny and Alexander* where Ingmar Bergman, who never ceased regretting his participation in the Hitlerjugend, demonstrates that a well-trained, ultra-Orthodox man can cause a bedridden elderly woman to burst into flames at a distance of several miles. When I read the book, I assumed that the Khazars had never existed, and was a little disconcerted to learn that they had.

The Hungarians, as I am reminded, quietly possess the most beautiful poetry in the world. To me they are at least as mysterious as the Khazars: Somewhere in Central Europe, or Eastern Europe—their empire borders Austria and is not far from Vienna (maybe it is Central Europe after all)—I can say with confidence only that it is a land rich in Siamese cats. I once spent ten days in Vienna with a medical student (he was not learning Farsi, but his girlfriend was from Iran and, to facilitate sex, he had formally asked her father and brother for her; he had no intention of marrying her, and I've always wondered how it turned out), and he told me that in Hungary Siamese, which go for hundreds of dollars in Austria, are cheap as dirt. Why would he lie about something like that?

His Hungarian Siamese was in heat. After failing on several occasions to satisfy it sexually with a cotton swab, he had taken to feeding it half a birth control pill once a week. The very week I visited, he had forgotten, and it crawled around a millimeter from the floor howling in a human voice. "How come nobody synthesizes this hormone and sells it?" he would say thoughtfully, pushing the cat out to the balcony and closing the door. "Pimps could use it to break women's spirits."

The other "most beautiful" poets I can call to mind are Leopardi and Pushkin. Were I rewriting *Possession* instead of *Sailing Toward the Sunset*, I might begin with a reference to

Leopardi or Pushkin. The function of books like *Possession* is to remind the reader of certain challenging material encountered early in the course of a liberal arts degree. Under other circumstances, with another audience in mind, I might begin with a Trident missile striking a glass-bottomed boat in the Gulf of Aqaba, geese fluffing their feathers against the bitter chill of the rocky interior of Bhutan, a circle of goldenrod bordering a pool of sticky liquid that happens to be leaking slowly into the Rhine near the falls of Schaffhausen, and the diplomatic crisis occasioned when these three things turn up together in the first six pages of a sensational bestselling new novel tentatively titled *Sailing Toward the Sunset.*

The missile didn't actually hit the boat—just nipped it, denting one gunwale by about an inch, but that was enough to crack the glass. "Meep!" cried Sissy the friendly dolphin, watching in horror as Red Sea water, oozing with phosphorescence, stained all our sneakers and began to creep up our socks. The rest of the passengers were spellbound, following the missile's slow ascent and descent as it arced upward, eclipsing the morning sun, on a course that I calculated would take it approximately to my apartment on Basel Street in Tel Aviv, give or take fifty feet. The skipper turned the boat around and made slowly for Eilat while I handed out life jackets. Clad in the typical plastic sandals and bikini of the native Israeli, he was not nearly as uncomfortable as the rest of us, and thought to entertain us, as Israelis often will, by turning up the radio really, really loud.

"Traffic on Ibn Gabirol has been diverted to the Namir Road due to a suspicious object," the announcer eventually said. I resolved to return to Tel Aviv as quickly as possible, and when we reached shore I took my pay from the cash register and ran down the street to catch the bus. Only ten hours

later, I was home. The sight that greeted me there was not
for the faint of heart. Where my coffee table had been, only
splinters remained, and Zohar's latest manuscript, which had
taken hours to print on the cheap new color printer I blamed
him for buying, lay smoldering on the floor. The missile was
gone—no doubt Shin Bet had seen to that. What would the
claims adjuster say?

I called Zohar in Bhutan. A faint rustling sound, as of
geese's wings, accompanied the signal as our conversation
raced around and around Earth from satellite to satellite. As
is well known, Israelis boast one of Earth's higher rates of
penetration for cellular and satellite phone service, second
only to Finns, and Zohar was no exception. Seeking a little
peace and quiet to perfect his academic discipline, he had hit
on the idea of spending the summer in a frigid mountaineer-
ing hut on an isolated pass not far from the dangerous border
with Sikkim. The dead trees, some dead already for hundreds
of years, were festooned with prayer flags, which looked to
the untrained eye a bit like the banners around a used-car
lot, only paler. The cold, dry air instantly embalmed anything
Zohar tried to discard, and he could not dig the frozen, rocky
ground, so he relied on the sparse vegetation, which resembled a sort of razor-wire heather whose tiny flowers were the
ivory gray of moths' wings, to cover the little piles of garbage
that had sprung up around his hut. He seemed relieved to be
summoned home.

Far off, near the Rheinfall, where colored panes of glass in
a small booth double for the colored searchlights of Niagara,
a pool of sticky liquid oozed and oozed, and in the booth an
Israeli spy and a girl from the Shetland Islands lay curled up
together, sleeping quietly. It was around four A.M., and they
had hitchhiked that day from Feldkirch. Her name was Mary,

and whether she knew that he was an Israeli spy, I don't know. She was ordinary looking, and he was ennobled only by his possession of certain distinctive eyeglasses, which Zohar calls "vain Ashkenazi glasses," oval with wire rims. Mary had noticed that he could read without them—perhaps that was her first clue that he was a spy. They had met the day before at a roulette table. She was drinking, and losing heavily . . . he took her elbow and offered to buy her another drink. Into it he slipped a tablet of vitamins B1 through B12. She saw him do it and asked why.

"I don't know," he said somewhat bashfully. "I was brought up to think men should be mysterious and aggressive both at the same time, which is a bit of a contradiction, since mystery involves a holding back, a withdrawal, so I had this idea of giving women vitamins without their consent and then maybe giving them a hard time if they don't like it, but actually you're the first one to notice." He was a living embodiment of Israel itself—its violent machismo, its shy longing for general approval. While he spoke he tried desperately to remember everything he knew about the Shetland Islands. Ponies, that was it. Extremely small ponies. But how small? He punched a quick query into the web browser he wore on his wrist, disguised as a wristwatch, and came up with a world record height, fully grown, at the shoulder, of three hands one inch—that is to say, thirty-two centimeters. How could such tiny animals work in coal pits? What brute would expect something like that to pull a wagon loaded with slag or ore or whatever it is they have in mines, or even a very small cart with just oranges, or even eggs? His heart filled with pity, and as Mary looked up, she saw his look of tender sorrow and realized that they would definitely sleep together at some point, probably very soon, assuming he wasn't with somebody. She took a look around.

"Did you ever see *The Secret of Roan Inish?*" she asked. "That's a really great movie, about islands in Ireland where they believe some women are actually silkies, these seals that put away their skins for a while and take on human form."

"Are you one?" the spy asked. His name, as you may have guessed, was Avner Shats. No, really it was Yigal.

"Actually I'm one of those mermaid people, and every step I take is like walking on sharp knives. Maybe I should lie down." She led him to her room upstairs. As she turned off the light he noticed a large, furry, damp skin hanging over the back of a chair.

Yigal had trouble sleeping that night. He was worried about the turn his spy operation would soon take. He got up to inspect the sealskin. It smelled musky and the inside was thick with cold, gelatinous fat. His operation called for the utmost in discretion and daring. He had to locate the heir to the Israeli throne and kill him.

The next night, as they lay oblivious in a booth near Schaffhausen, a Trident missile had fallen through my coffee table, shuffling a few papers, and detonated in Yigal's office. The significance of this was not immediately clear, but was widespread and started a sort of chain reaction, complicating Yigal's life in ways he could not have anticipated. For one, he had kept his insurance policies in his desk—not a bright idea. But the complications were slow in emerging, and had little effect on his state of mind as he lay dozing on the slippery concrete next to a beautifully ordinary-looking Shetland girl.

"Ordinary looking" in romantic fiction of this kind denotes a certain understated classic beauty. Mary's flaw was her hair, which was on the frizzy side and what they call "dishwater blond." Her skin was slightly yellow so that the red spots she got when running around outside in cold weather made her look better instead of worse, and she had stubby fingers. But none of that really mattered anyway, since she was really a silkie, and had quietly shipped her sealskin ahead to London by way of the concierge.

CHAPTER 2

IF THERE IS AN HEIR TO THE ISRAELI throne, it follows that he must be located where all other such long-lost items are located: the Great Library of Alexandria.

There is a certain sort of drunk who, once loaded on martinis, begins to reminisce about the Great Library. "Of all the works of Euripides, we have only those beginning with the letters *A* and *B*," the drunk says, a long ash from his cigarette falling to his right knee. With the heel of his hand, unconsciously, as from long habit, he rubs the ash into his pants. When I was an undergraduate, these drunks were already in their fifties, and unless well-fed and cared for by long-suffering wives, they were not destined to live much longer.

In the late 1970s a younger generation of drunks, heavily influenced by a book called *The Origin of Consciousness in the Breakdown of the Bicameral Mind,* began to take their place. The book proposed that modern man, beginning around the time of Camus, had achieved a level of self-consciousness previously impossible. The *Aufhebung* came about not in the traditional manner of pure spirit coming to know itself à la Hegel and Marx, but by actual mechanical means: The brain's two halves had been brought into communication for the first time by the growth of a little wad of tissue.

The first person to introduce the bicameral mind theory to me was not a drunk per se, but rather a tall, fat, bearlike schizophrenic, whose endorsement could recommend the theory to no one. He would sit in my dorm room for hours at a time, attempting to train me in ESP. Still, before long it was common knowledge among younger scholars that the ancient Greeks had not possessed self-awareness in any form. The professors explained it like this: In the works of Homer, people are always getting limbs chopped off, and they don't seem very upset about it, somewhat as though they weren't quite sure whose limbs those had been in the first place. A limbless Greek would just lie there wiggling in a state of naive confusion until his *psyche,* which just means "breath," demonstrating that the Greeks didn't even have a word for self-consciousness—more evidence that they lacked it—left his mouth for good.

The approach could be fruitful for our understanding of Homeric epic if we equate the siege of Troy with the electric current to a cage floor, as in the following commonly performed psychology experiment: If you put a rat in a cage with an electric floor and shock him every time he presses the lever that used to release his food, he'll just stand there pressing the lever and shrieking in pain until you stop. However, if you cut his brain down the middle and start over, he'll be able to let go of the lever right away.

Some say that the attics of certain Eastern monasteries contain treasures yet unknown, and were they accessible to scholars, the Great Library's loss might not be felt so deeply. Many questions that now trouble scholars could be illuminated: Why, in Genesis 1:2, is the "wind" of God said to "brood" on the water like a chicken? Who did the ancient Greeks resemble more, rats or robots? Which race really descended from the Khazars, and who is the current king of the Jews? What went on in Euripides' works whose titles began with gamma, delta, etc.?

The notion of lost, irreplaceable cultural treasures always reminded Yigal of a book he had seen one night in the window of a shop on Allenby: *Runts of 61 Cygni C,* "where one-eyed runts play endless games of sex." When he returned the next day intending to buy it, it was gone, and he suddenly realized that his girlfriend, for whom he had intended it as a birthday present, would not have found it nearly so funny. For years afterward, he was haunted by memories of the slim, yellow, small-breasted runts hiding among spears of pampas grass, their long-lashed eyes big as dinner plates.

In accordance with his training, he set about his mission by applying the techniques of disinterested scientific analysis: The likely pretender to the Israeli throne, he reasoned, would be a direct descendant in the male line from the last really popular king. Allowing for mutations here and there, the Y chromosome ought to be the same. Now, as the Tomb of King David lies just outside the Old City of Jerusalem, guarded only by a lopsided stack of paper yarmulkes on a table, obtaining a DNA sample was not a big challenge for an experienced operative like Yigal.

After that he wasn't so sure what to do. The logical next step, to collect a swatch of hair from every living male on earth, would surely compromise project secrecy. But a confession to his superiors that he had no chance of success would compromise job security, and I think it was this last concern that accounted for Yigal's lying so peacefully in the wet, a little hungry after a meager dinner of chocolate bars, on the floor of a booth above the misty falls of the Rhine.

Mary stirred in her sleep and woke briefly. She gave him her cheek to kiss, then suddenly rolled over, poking him in the stomach with her elbow and covering her legs with his coat so that he now had no blanket at all. He stood up to look out at the falls, his clammy hands jammed into his pants pockets. Suddenly he took out his wallet and began counting his money. He kept remembering the sealskin.

As this reconstruction of *Sailing Toward the Sunset* begins to meander, I realize I should be making a greater effort to remain faithful to my original, whose second chapter begins:

> I entered the swimming pool, whose floor gleamed with cleanliness. A literary atmosphere, in slow stages, in the room [illegible] lined with white suede. . . .

Meanwhile, on his knees, Zohar struggled to untangle the motorized front cable of his 1971 Land Rover, currently lodged firmly in the wet borax of a valley floor deep in the trackless interior of Bhutan, where to his weary eyes the flats appeared to stretch on indefinitely. Yet he knew these were the most forgiving of the many toxic marshes he must cross before reaching a serviceable airstrip, itself only the first stop of dozens on his way to Kathmandu, should he survive. Air service in Bhutan is by U.S. Army surplus C-130 cargo plane; there is no heat or pressurization, and the passengers may sit, if they choose, only in wooden folding chairs, several of which are stacked against the walls. Most prefer to huddle in their sleeping bags on pallets, walking around the aircraft not being advisable due to the chance of slipping on the rafts of spelt grains and quinoa that litter the floor by the millions, generally aft during takeoff and generally forward during landing. For sanitary reasons the transport of live animals is forbidden.

The idea with the cable is that even if you're stuck in a foot of wet salt, or, like Zohar, in a mixture of borax, gypsum, and quicklime, you can pull yourself along pretty well by wading out a few dozen yards in front of the Rover and pounding in a steel post with a sledgehammer. Then you throw the cable over it and crank yourself forward. Crossing Bhutan in this fashion could take a good long while and end up looking a lot like the movie *Lifepod,* or my other favorite, where the nineteenth-century Swedes try to reach the North Pole by balloon, but Zohar didn't have to cross all of Bhutan—just enough to reach the airfield.

The Swedish movie ends with the prime mover, the one who seduced his sweet and gentle best friends into dying slowly of cold and trichinosis, standing alone on a desolate beach and screaming. He knows his body will never be found, because there is no one left to pile rocks on it.

It really happened—thirty-three years later someone found all of it: the piles of rocks and packets of undelivered letters and undeveloped photographs. For months (the balloon didn't last very long) they headed north on pack ice that was drifting south. They wanted to see the North Pole. Then winter came. There was nothing to eat but polar bears. When the ice began to drift again in the spring, there was a big argument. The leader wanted to float south and look for whaling ships, but the others wanted to die on land so that the letters would be found one day. Then their wives would see that they really loved them, and that they regretted their terrible mistake.

Back in Tel Aviv, the Trident had disrupted phone service and I couldn't get a dial tone until late morning. When finally

I was able to get online, I found a message from Shats that had been waiting for me since the beginning of the summer, before I went down to Eilat.

I had gone to Eilat for the same reason everyone else goes—to make a quick buck. Nowhere else in Israel can endless days of sweltering heat, ruled by a sun which raises red, then purple, then yellow blisters under the shoulder straps of visiting Scandinavians and toasts darker skins to a mottled pattern of ashen wrinkles, be turned so easily into tax-free, black-market day labor. Towering luxury hotels line the beach, but behind them in the foothills is a demimonde of cosmopolitan flophouses whose inhabitants earn just enough to soak themselves inside and out in beer between bouts of petty squabbling over cots and towels and switchblade duels over drugs and women. They gather every evening around the hostels' blaring TVs to compare notes on the best ways of coming into money.

"Cucumbers," I was told (they are paid by the bushel and can be quite large), but I chose instead customer service in the eerie submarine realm of Sissy and her ilk. In my years as an adept of the Dolphin Star Temple in Mount Rainier, Maryland, I had learned the importance of dolphin-like movements and attitudes in the attainment of true spiritual harmony, and my first glimpse of Nachum, helmsman of the glass-bottomed skiff later damaged by the missile that wiped out Yigal's hard drive, was enough to convince me that he alone, of the Israelis I had met, truly understood dolphins. His skin was the shiny, streaked burnt umber of Naugahyde bus upholstery, yet through it a network of broken veins showed pink as coral, proving that it was not in Nachum's nature to be dark brown but rather the result of his conscious control of the inner workings of his own body. I apprenticed myself to

Nachum as to a master, learning like him to think only of the
moment, of my own delicate skin and its need for moisture,
and of fish. Whenever Nachum felt too warm, he would dive
from the boat into the Gulf of Aqaba, framed by the distant
white apartment houses and palm trees of Jordan, emerging
after a minute or two to let the clinging droplets cool his skin
for as much as five seconds at a time before they dried to a
salty protective crust. The tourists and I, shaded by hats and
with legs like stalks of rhubarb above our bobby socks, would
applaud as he pirouetted through the crystalline water, his
playful splashes dappling the rainbow slick of oil that trailed
behind us like a streamer and luring Sissy, and sometimes her
entire family, with a faithful impression of many fish dying
together in agony. "Meep, meep!" we would all cry together
in an ecstasy of interspecies communication. "I want to have
my baby in the water with the dolphins," one young woman
or another would invariably say, which struck me as an unin-
formed wish, since even a whiff of urine can draw great white
sharks from miles off, but I never objected aloud.

Mary would certainly have laughed audibly, with her characteristic stifled giggle, one hand almost covering her mouth.
She woke again and looked up at Yigal.

"What are you doing?" she asked, offering him a small corner of his own jacket as an enticement to lie down.

"I just remembered something," he said. "I have to be in Tel
Aviv by Friday." He looked at his watch.

"Are you cold?" She bunched up his coat, handed it to him,
and shivered. She missed the thick, cozy layer of blubber that
now lay neatly rolled on dry ice in a Styrofoam picnic cooler
in the hold of a ferryboat by Ostend.

He watched a bat fly over as he turned out his pockets, looking for something. The sky was turning blue with one brown

edge. Finally he wrote a few words on the back of a business card and set it facedown by Mary's head. "Call me if you get to Tel Aviv sometime." He walked away, thinking he might take a room for several weeks in Biel. Mary began to cry.

Thus it happened that Mary learned of the Trident missile impact almost two weeks before Yigal did.

Shats' message was about chapter one. I want to tell you about the breasts. I'm not really a breast man. My favorite part of the female anatomy is the . . . , he wrote.

Being busy trying to write, Shats continued, I never thought about what it's like to be someone else's subject matter. Turns out it's kind of fun, especially when the other writer avoids describing me as, say, a fat-assed smug. . . . Also, I like being a hero in a novel where I wear rounded glasses and sleep with a silkie from Shetland (the missing element in the GIF animation is a seal). "Yigal" is my brother's name, and Yigal Schwartz (rhymes with Shats) is the literature lecturer who got me the $5,000 prize.

But I'm really tired of discussing my book, he added. I was afraid I'd have to talk about it in the media, but apparently I'm safe, no one takes much interest. I was told someone reviewed the book on the radio and killed it. He said something like, "Behind it all there's just a big empty void." I didn't hear it. I was wondering beforehand whether I'd like to read the reviews. I thought yes, but now I'm not sure. I prefer not to know.

I replied by sending him chapter two.

CHAPTER 3

YIGAL'S FIRST RIDE DROPPED HIM AT
the entrance to Herisau, in Canton Appenzell. A stone foot-
path led into the fir trees by the road, and thinking a moment's privacy might be nice, Yigal walked down it. After
a few feet the path was covered with needles, and the trees
closed overhead, linking their boughs arm in arm, like a zip-
per, Yigal thought, until it was almost dark. In the gloom his
bare white penis seemed to glow like a firefly, and when he
shook it, it was as though someone were waving a handkerchief, trying to get his attention, from a long way off. Nothing
he did made a sound. Every noise was swallowed by the immense pillows of needles and twigs stacked around the tree
stems and pierced here and there by squirrels' entrances,
exits, and tattered flakes of pinecone, forming a landscape of
bumps and hollows as regular as an Olympic mogul run, in
which the trees stood like drinking straws thrust into the tops
of sand castles.

He thought of Kafka's shortest prose piece, "For we are like
tree trunks in the snow, which the lightest push could top-
ple; but look again, even that is an illusion," and decided to
walk a bit farther before returning. The path was blocked by

spiderwebs, in which sat huge black-and-orange spiders. Yigal
gently pushed them aside with a fallen branch and stepped
around them. Under the needles he could still feel the stones.
He took off his sandals and dug down with his toes until they
touched the warm slate, which had stored the heat of the noon
sun under its blanket of dry straw. He crept forward, listening
closely, and heard a car pass on the road behind him. Then
the trees unlocked their arms, the sky was visible overhead,
and Yigal found himself facing an immense granite obelisk,
surrounded by shaggy green grass, on which a voluminous
text was printed in German, French, English, and Italian. He
stood before the English side, which faced the sun, relieved
to know English so well, since the French side, on the north,
was indecipherable under a layer of moss that was presently
in bloom, raising tiny wet cups to the sun and sheltering a
puddle filled with tadpoles and liverwort. He began to read:

NEAR THIS SPOT
ON CHRISTMAS DAY 1956
ROBERT WALSER
POET OF LOVE, OF LONG WALKS
AND OF THE WHITE-COLLAR PROLETARIAT
WAS FOUND DEAD IN THE SNOW
AFTER TWENTY-THREE YEARS IN HERISAU'S
PUBLIC HOSPITAL
FEIGNING CATATONIA AND WRITING IN SECRET
TO SAVE MONEY

IN 1914 HE RECEIVED
THE AWARD OF THE WOMEN'S SOCIETY
FOR THE ADVANCEMENT OF THE POETRY
OF THE RHINELAND—THIS STONE IS RAISED

TO HIS MEMORY BY THE WOMEN'S SOCIETY FOR
THE ADVANCEMENT OF THE POETRY OF THE RHINELAND
ON THE HUNDREDTH ANNIVERSARY OF HIS BIRTH
APRIL 15, 1978

— HONORED SIRS! —

I AM A POOR, YOUNG, UNEMPLOYED CLERK NAMED WENZEL,
IN SEARCH OF AN APPROPRIATE POSITION AND HEREBY TAKE
THE LIBERTY OF ASKING POLITELY IF PERHAPS IN YOUR AIRY,
BRIGHT, FRIENDLY OFFICES THERE MIGHT BE SUCH A THING
AS AN OPENING. KNOWING THAT YOUR ESTEEMED FIRM IS
LARGE, OLD, PROUD, AND RICH, I CAN'T HELP BUT THINK
THAT YOU MUST HAVE SOME EASY, PLEASANT, ATTRACTIVE
LITTLE SPOT INTO WHICH I, AS INTO A SORT OF WARM
CUBBYHOLE, MIGHT SLIP UNNOTICED. I AM ESPECIALLY
WELL SUITED, IF YOU MUST KNOW, TO OCCUPY EXACTLY
SUCH A SOFT, WARM HIDING PLACE AS IT WERE, FOR MY
NATURE IS DELICATE, AND MY ENTIRE BEING IS THAT OF A
QUIET, MANNERLY, AND ABSENT-MINDED CHILD, EAGER TO
ENJOY THE HAPPY CONSCIOUSNESS THAT OTHERS THINK
IT DEMANDS LITTLE, WANTING ONLY TO BE PERMITTED
TO TAKE TEMPORARY POSSESSION OF SOME INSIGNIFICANT
CORNER OF THE WORLD WHERE, IN ITS SMALL WAY, IT MAY
PROVE ITSELF USEFUL AND COME TO FEEL SOME VAGUE
SENSE OF SATISFACTION. A SWEET, QUIET, TINY PLACE IN
THE SHADE HAS BEEN MY LIFE'S CONSISTENT AND NOBLE
DREAM FROM EARLY YOUTH, AND IF THE ILLUSIONS WHICH
I NOW ENTERTAIN WITH REGARD TO YOUR WEALTHY FIRM
ARE NOW GROWN SO STRONG THAT I MIGHT HOPE FOR
THE DELIGHTFUL LIVING FULFILLMENT OF MY OLD YET
ETERNALLY RENEWED DREAM, YOU WILL FIND IN ME THE
MOST DEVOTED SERVANT POSSIBLE, WHOSE CONSCIENCE WILL

NOT REST UNTIL EACH OF THE TRIVIAL OBLIGATIONS YOU
LAY UPON HIM IS COMPLETED PRECISELY AND PUNCTUALLY.
PLEASE UNDERSTAND THAT I CANNOT TAKE ON SIGNIFICANT
OR DIFFICULT RESPONSIBILITIES, AND DUTIES OF A WIDE-
RANGING NATURE WOULD TAX MY BRAIN UNDULY. I AM NOT
ESPECIALLY INTELLIGENT—BUT MORE IMPORTANT, I PREFER
NOT TO CALL ON MY INTELLIGENCE UNLESS ABSOLUTELY
NECESSARY. I AM, AS IT WERE, MORE A DREAMER THAN A
THINKER, MORE A ZERO THAN AN ACHIEVER, MORE STUPID
THAN CLEVER. BUT SURELY IN THE MANY BRANCHES
OF YOUR IMMENSE INSTITUTION, IN WHICH I IMAGINE
VAST COMPLEXES OF UNOCCUPIED DESKS, THERE EXISTS
SOME SORT OF WORK THAT CAN BE ACCOMPLISHED WHILE
DAYDREAMING. I AM, TO SAY IT OPENLY, A CHINESE, A
PERSON WHO PREFERS THINGS TO WEAR A SMALL, MODEST,
UNFRIGHTENING ASPECT OF LOVELY SWEETNESS, AND TO
WHOM ALL THINGS LARGE OR OVERLY DEMANDING APPEAR
HORRIBLE AND TERRIFYING. I KNOW ONLY ONE NEED—TO
FEEL SECURE ENOUGH SO THAT I MAY SAFELY THANK GOD
EACH DAY FOR THIS DEAR, BLESSED EXISTENCE. I HAVE
NEVER EXPERIENCED THE DESIRE TO SHINE PUBLICLY. THE
DESERTS OF AFRICA COULD NOT BE MORE FOREIGN TO ME.
MY HANDWRITING, AS YOU CAN SEE, IS QUITE FLUID AND
DELICATE, AND YOU DON'T NEED TO IMAGINE ME AS BEING
COMPLETELY WITHOUT INTELLECT. MY MIND IS QUITE
CLEAR; IT MERELY HESITATES TO TAKE HOLD OF TOO MANY
THINGS AT ONCE—ABHORS IT, IN FACT. I AM HONEST, BUT I
RECOGNIZE JUST HOW LITTLE THAT MEANS IN THIS WORLD
WE LIVE IN, AND HEREWITH, ESTEEMED SIRS, I WILL CLOSE,
IN ORDER TO AWAIT YOUR RESPONSE, FAITHFULLY DROWNING
IN DEVOTION AND REVERENCE,
—WENZEL

The path circled around the monument and led downhill. He followed it down a few stone steps to a sort of pit where a spring was indicated by a pipe sticking out of a crumbling brick culvert, and took a drink. At eye level he saw something like a hand sticking out of the leaf mold and debris. There was a bronze statue of a man, Robert Walser he supposed, lying facedown at full length with its left hand stretched toward the spring. The model was young, with a high forehead and full lips, and was depicted fully clothed, in a crudely patched tweed suit with army boots and a Tyrolean hat. The eyes were cut deep to look intelligent and expressive, while the smile seemed deliberately weak and silly. The face was creased with premature wrinkles as from suffering and worry and bad food. There was no signature and the statue did not appear to have been touched in a long time. A tree root had grown around a trailing shoelace, and the statue was tilted awkwardly as though it might eventually fall into the spring. Yigal gave it a good hard push to make sure it was still bolted down, and walked into Herisau to get some lunch.

The memorial to Walser actually had nothing to do with the Women's Society, etc., but was placed there by his daughter, who lives now on Panorama Street in Haifa—in fact, she is Shats' neighbor, and sometimes sees him on Saturdays at the Arab kiosk when he goes out for milk. She walks very slowly, with a cane, and he always says hello when walking up behind her, so as not to startle her. Her mother, a married Pomeranian Jew, met Robert Walser in Berlin in 1912. They were together several times in his apartment at No. 1 Spandauer Berg, Charlottenburg. By the time this book is published, she will have died, never having told anyone the secret, which she discovered while reading her mother's diary in 1960, four years after both her mother and Robert Walser were dead.

Robert Walser is my absolutely, totally and completely favorite writer, whose works I despair of translating, though
I'm pretty pleased with my rendition of "The Cover Letter,"
loose as it is. I've stopped recommending him to people who
don't read German. Even the snobbiest Knopf edition, with
the introduction by Susan Sontag, has painful errors in first
lines, and somehow everyone got the idea that he was a dark
and pained expressionist, probably by seeing the misleading
movie (*Institute Benjamenta*) of his uncharacteristic first novel
(*Jakob von Gunten*), so that they turn his pleasing and delightful coinages into portmanteaus that remind me mostly of *A
Spaniard in the Works*. Like Shats, he worked as a clerk and had
beautiful handwriting.

The public library in Herisau had two first editions by
Walser, *Jakob von Gunten* and *Die Rose,* lying with a photograph
in a glass case. They had been placed there in 1978 and never
disturbed since. The photograph showed a dog belonging to
the owner of Herisau's pub. The dog's name was Brahms. He
died in 1985.

"Where's the nearest casino?" Yigal asked the librarian.
She advised him to go to Bern. He took a flyer for a weaving
course off the windowsill, read several words, and dropped it
in the umbrella stand as he left the library.

As a young man, Yigal had often remembered Kafka's assessment of the four main components of the resting mind,
"Hatred, Rage, Shame, and Torture," with a sense of their perfect appropriateness. But as Yigal had aged, he had lost the
capacity for hatred. Even when he killed a man, he felt only a
sort of mild disgust. His rages had become stereotyped, one
so much like another, and all so like his father's, that one day
they had just stopped, choked off by the friction of tedium.
He had lost all sense of shame, sometimes not looking in the

mirror for days at a time, and, far from torturing himself, he was likely to eat half a gallon of chocolate ice cream at a sitting. His habit of visiting casinos stemmed from a mature preference he called, by way of contrast, "Whores, Gambling, and Cocaine." Generally it meant having a few drinks and watching people he didn't know, but sounded better. A brief demonstration follows:

Q. DID YOU EVER HAVE A MODEL RAILROAD?
A. NO, I WAS INTO WHORES, GAMBLING, AND COCAINE.

Q. —

I was going to write a few more questions, but suddenly it occurred to me why exactly I demand that Yigal stand around in casinos watching people: It's because that's what Daniel Deronda did—that's how he met Gwendolen Harleth! He met her at a roulette table. She was drinking, and losing heavily, flushed with emotion, playing away her family's last dime, pawning her jewels to play again—Daniel saved her. I love Daniel. I personally have seen a Swiss casino only once, from the side of the road. I've never met anyone who read *Daniel Deronda,* but the novel accounts for the regular appearance of "George Eliot Street" in the older Israeli towns.

With the introduction of *Daniel Deronda* I realize I have strayed further than ever from my task of re-creating, from limited and unreliable memories, Avner Shats' novel *Sailing Toward the Sunset.* Even worse, the mention of the rival hero Daniel draws attention away from the real focus of my work, namely, the subject author, for whom these chapters are written and e-mailed each morning.

The novel in letters has a long history in English literature.

Scholarly consensus holds the first English novel to have been *Pamela, or Virtue Rewarded* (Samuel Richardson, 1740). The heroine spends five hundred pages locked in a room, waiting to be raped. The hero even climbs into bed with her dressed as the housekeeper, having gained entrance by promising her some food, but she fights him off again and again, and ultimately wins the big prize: his hand in marriage. *Pamela* proved that light reading can be rendered suitable for young ladies, sparking a literary explosion that has lasted to this day. Richardson never intended to write a novel. He wanted to publish a manual of letter writing, but got carried away.

As Kafka said, "A letter is like a sheep, pretty soon here come the rest of the sheep" (I'm paraphrasing slightly), or later, "For we are like sheep lost at night in the mountains, or more precisely, I am like the sheep who is following the other sheep who are lost at night in the mountains."

This chapter is like the second sheep in line behind the sheep who is following the sheep lost at night in the mountains.

In my possession is an advertisement of a service, active on the Upper West Side of New York City during the 1980s, which promised to send the subscriber all Kafka's letters to his fiancée, Felice Bauer, in order, and at the rate at which they were originally sent (two or three per day for several years), for under $1,000, including an attractive storage binder. I swear this is true.

Kafka burned many unfinished manuscripts before his death, but he could not stop his intimate confessions from entering the public domain and becoming, by virtue of their authenticity, his most popular works. When we read a work written for publication, we allow a stranger to direct our behavior and narrow our focus. When we read that same stranger's diaries and letters, our reality is widened and enriched.

It is this voyeuristic urge present in all of us, along with the vogue for books recalling survey courses in comparative literature, which I hope to exploit by promoting, as though it were a novel, this series of elaborately coded personal letters to Avner Shats, written daily for several weeks in the month of December, 1998.

Yigal strolled into the casino at Bern and dropped SF 5,— into the slot machine nearest the door. Immediately it returned SF 15,—. He reinvested SF 5,—, cleared SF 25,—, and bought a whiskey sour from a woman dressed as a milkmaid. They talked. She persuaded him to buy four keno tickets, and at 7:15 he pretended he had won. A blinding light shone in his eyes as the imaginary cmcee handed him the envelope stuffed with cash, and he heard scattered applause. In the darkness behind the spotlight he could see someone trying to get his attention by waving a handkerchief.

He felt too drunk to drink anymore, and walked out to the street. A taxi pulled up, then pulled away. He sat on the curb, took off his undershirt, and threw it into the gutter. Then he remembered his plan to go to Biel.

Mary, to do her credit, didn't go straight to Yigal's apartment from the airport. First she walked out into the blazing sun of the runway and shook her head from side to side, hard, as though she had just emerged from the North Sea and her ears tickled. She passed through customs smiling and wriggling with joy after the confinement of the flight. Then she stood under the bus shelter, soaking up the brilliant light with her black, curious eyes. The poured concrete of the parking garage soared overhead like an iceberg, yet everything was wonderfully warm. She squatted down and traced a fingertip

along the pavement. Through the calluses she could feel a fe-
rocious heat, and she laid her palm flat. The sidewalk was like
the top of a coal stove, but pale gray as the arctic in winter.
She pursed her mouth and gave a mysterious approving look,
then sprang into the bus. It was one o'clock sharp, time for
news, and the driver turned up the radio really, really loud
until a deep, soothing voice filled the cabin of the bus with
chiming, incomprehensible sounds. Outside she could see
a hot, hard, dry landscape drowning in brightness, the dry
brush casting shadows so dark every field looked like a check-
erboard. The bus turned toward a residential neighborhood
of short white buildings selling ice cream under blue umbrellas, like an aquarium. Mary began to hum a happy song.

When she got to the beach, she had a little swim. She had
booked a room at a small place on HaYarqon near the American embassy, but didn't think she was going to need it, and
she didn't, since whoever cleaned up after the impact had left
Yigal's door unlocked. I first saw her from above, through the
hole in the floor, as she was shuffling through his personal
papers. They were in Hebrew. She looked frustrated. She had
already been working for an hour by the time I thought to ask
her what she was doing. I had assumed she was from some
competing intelligence agency, perhaps the one that had sent
the missile in the first place. She made us coffee in Yigal's
kitchen and told me the whole story.

"So Yigal knew you were a silkie the whole time?" I asked.
"I don't like that part, it reminds me of this thing my friend
Pat Sweeney talks about, where if you look closely at a lot of
novels they just add up to fantasies about fucking these easy,
available women whose feelings never get hurt, especially science fiction novels—there's so much science fiction about the
ethical issues that arise in a man's mind when he finds the

first really convenient sex of his life is with a robot or an alien
or something. Pat calls them sheep-farm books—Mary?" She
was crying.

"I know what you mean," she said. "Like in *Runts of 61 Cygni
C,* where these astronauts land and they start fucking all the
time with these little one-eyed midgets, and they start growing big yellow penises. Then they go back to Earth and of
course it's destroyed, just like in *Planet of the Apes,* and they're
stuck with these little tiny brain-dead—but, I mean, Yigal left
me. . . ." She began to cry again. I saw what she meant. Instead
of hanging around to take advantage of the willing alien life-
form, Yigal had run off, which might mean, at least in part,
what Mary thought it meant: that he was a decent guy. On the
other hand, he was supposedly in Tel Aviv, yet not at his own
apartment.

With my help, Mary at last found what she was looking for:
a list of names and phone numbers.

Now, when you're trying to figure out what sex Americans
are, it helps to know their names. Say you're faced with two
identical fat boys in flannel shirts, one named Dixie and the
other named Doily—I'll give you 7 to 5 that Dixie's the girl.
In Israel, names are more help when you're trying to guess
someone's age. All Rachels are over sixty-five, for example,
but Tals, Gals, Yams, Sharons, Shachars, and even Zohars can
be either sex. Fortunately I had noticed that the current crop
of what in Hebrew are called "pieces" are all named either
Naomi or something that ends with a *t,* and as I expected,
Yigal's list had four Naomis, two Osnats, a Nurit, two Dor-
its, and an Orit, plus an Ilanit and an Ephrat whose names
had been crossed out. I wouldn't have known where to start
if Yigal hadn't highlighted "Nofar," a name I'd never heard
before, in yellow and circled it twice in red.

"The highlighted one is Nofar, which sounds to me like a girl's name," I said, dialing the number.

"Yigal?" Nofar said. "Is he a variety of"—I'm translating from Tel Aviv slang—"as-if *Yoram* like that, black hair as-if curls like those?"

"Yes."

"I don't know him."

Mary called an Osnat.

"Good afternoon, I'm Mary, assistant to Mr. Francis Ford Coppola. Your name was suggested to us by Yigal Paz. We need actors for some scenes in a café—women aged twenty to thirty, fit and attractive, vivacious, good walkers—to serve drinks. There may be a speaking part. Are you slim? How's your walk?"

"I'm tall and slender, with chestnut hair in long, luxuriant waves, a full, generous mouth, ample breasts, a tiny waist, pert belly, disorienting hips, luscious knees and ankles, and a PhD in Oriental studies, which while you might think it means I can speak Hindi or Japanese, actually involved a lot of time in England. But I can put on an American accent, if that's what Mr. Coppola wants."

"Osnat, it sounds to me as though you've got exactly what we're looking for. I'm so glad Yigal put us in touch with you. Have you heard from him lately? How's he doing?"

The woman sighed. "Yigal is so strange."

We waited, and she sighed again. Then she asked, "How well do you know Yigal?"

"Um, pretty well."

"You know about his hobbies, right?"

"No," Mary said. "Unless you mean sex."

Osnat laughed bitterly. "Not that—all men go to whores. I mean the gambling and the cocaine. Yigal has a good job, and they say he inherited a lot of money. Where does it all go? But the whores too, you're right, I just don't understand it. I've told you what I look like. I've known Yigal since the army and I always followed him around, and not once, never, has he ever tried anything. At first I thought he was gay. I used to . . ." I stopped listening. What Osnat was saying reminded me vaguely of something I'd read somewhere, a clue to something very important about Yigal. I walked around the room, fingering the books and light switches, reading scraps of paper, squeezing my eyes shut tight and opening them again, retracing my steps, struggling physically to remember this trivial fact which might already have escaped me forever, until suddenly it came to me and I opened the closet door.

CHAPTER 4

THE MODEL RAILROAD: IN YIGAL'S
closet was a disassembled model railroad, stacked upright
with the locos and rolling stock on display in cellophane cases
on a shelf, and as I looked at it I realized that Yigal's Israeli
identity had fallen to 49 percent and needs to be jacked up
a bit.

For one, there are no closets in Israel. All rooms are bare
white boxes with tile floors and small, high windows. Maybe
you know someone who runs a catering service out of their
basement—that's what it looks like. None of the furniture is
built in—it comes and goes with each new tenant, like props
on a set. Instead of closets, there are enormous wardrobes
ten feet tall.

Sometimes from the bus I see new apartment buildings
going up with big picture windows facing southwest, and I
imagine what it must be like to live in one between April
and October: The central air-conditioning whooshing and
clattering like a jet engine, dusty swirls of bone-dry air
cooled with difficulty to 80 degrees turning the proud owners' skins—already suffused and boiling in the infrared—
flushed and dandruffy until they take to keeping a bottle of

Oil of Olay with the remote control. The cat lies in the sun on the bare floor and breathes twice a minute. The dead fan palm has kept its shape and color, and no one knows it's dead.

Probably they have closets too, and when their fathers visit they look into the closets, shake their heads, and say, "What a waste of space. The walls are three inches thick, and it's half empty."

Yigal had many thoroughly Israeli qualities which I have failed to emphasize. For one, he loved the Beatles. Also, he loved olives, cheese, and cucumbers. Once a week he rolled up his pants, dumped a bucket of water on his living room floor, pushed it around for ten minutes with a squeegee, and soaked it up again with a towel. He had a feeling of lofty superiority vis-à-vis the sexuality of American men. His number one concern in life was not to be made a fool of, and having money in the bank made him nervous. He drove aggressively, riding the clutch.

It looked to me like he was modeling American steam— there was a beautiful articulated brass 4-8-4 and a half-finished water tower, the shingles still in rows in a tiny Ziploc bag. Hundreds of twisted wire trees with brown trunks and dull green lichen foliage sprouted from holes drilled in the plywood, and a small mountain lay on the floor, complete with rock breaks, brush, and a flock of minuscule goats led by a weency woman in a red skirt. They were walking toward a pond with a wire willow tree and slightly oversized fish frozen in green, murky shellac.

Mary came over to look.

"I don't get it," I said. "An engine this size on the Durango and Silverton? Goats? There are no hopper cars. What's this all about?" I took down a Pullman car. Inside were real velveteen upholstery and little brass lamps. A man's tall hat lay on one of the seats, barely the size of a pinhead in HO gauge.

Mary touched the pond. "It's not a model of anything. It's art. It's what happens when you take things you don't know or understand, and use them to make something you love."

I like books with long irrelevant sections much better than books with long, purportedly relevant sections that exist only to raise the word count into the one-hundred-thousand paperback-original range. Also, coherent novels are never long enough to stand alone. Murakami's *Pinball, 1973* and *Norwegian Wood* put together are probably shorter than the irrelevant material in *The Wind-Up Bird Chronicle*. Without the etymology and pedigrees, *Remembrance of Things Past* would be just a page-turner in *True Confessions*.

Also, Zohar tells me that *Sailing Toward the Sunset* contains numerous unrelated and "found" texts. For example, Shats assigned the production of his own disavowed poetry to his fictional spy, and parodied, in the form of a sexual orgy, the British Famous Five detective novels for children, with no apparent connection to anything else in the novel, one assumes.

I was further alerted that his website, members.tripod .com/~shatsA, includes an excerpt, translated into English, from the Schweipert prize committee's hagiography, and on investigation I saw that Shats had also included quite a few legible clues to the content of *Sailing Toward the Sunset*.

"Is mankind descended from the seals?" he asks. "Can one navigate at sea by universal energy?" Yet no one who reads these questions can hope to obtain their answers except by applying himself full-time over a period of years to learn the nuances of literary Hebrew, not only of today, but of several previous eras, according to the prize committee. I sincerely hope that my re-creation of *Sailing Toward the Sunset* will be complete in time to meet the demand for an English translation.

(Begin irrelevant interlude)

"SOMEDAY, L.I.C." BY NELL ZINK

When the mail fell through the slot after breakfast, I ambled with an air of self-conscious leisure to poke through it with the toe of my shoe. Then the mailman cranked his siren. I yelled, "I'm here!" and opened the door. He gave me a paper box, about a foot on a side, and drove on.

I didn't recognize the return address. Bomb, I thought, but it hardly weighed anything. Could have been ping-pong balls or popcorn. I opened it up with scissors. In the box was a thin plastic sack, thinner than dry cleaners' plastic, tied with a knot. It was empty, plump, not taut, as if it had been blown up tight and then lost a little air in transit. Of course my first impulse was to stab it, but I sniffed it instead. The odor was neutral—vaguely plastic and smoky, as if it had been a long time outside. I picked the brown wrapping paper off the floor and sat down again to my cup of coffee. I put the plastic bag on the windowsill next to a glass of tulips.

The return address was interesting.

Society for the Advancing Recognition
354-1,345 301st Avenue, #21159T
Metro U.S.A. ZRHHWEBN

That was only about forty blocks from my house. Whoever had blown sixty bucks to mail it to me might as well have walked. They had to be rich, or incapacitated, or very busy. A strange gift, I thought. I found some tape and stuck it to the refrigerator. I didn't puncture it, I didn't untie it, I didn't look at it again. In fact, I forgot it existed until two weeks later when the envelope came. "Congratulations!" the note read. "You have not destroyed Part 1. Please submerge Part 1 in a large basin of pure water and immediately add Part 2, enclosed. When the fusion is complete, the resulting stone will be yours to keep." Part 2 was a chalky blue tablet that smelled of chlorine.

So it was murder cooked up to look like suicide. My assumption was that I'd stand there holding the plastic bag underwater while they killed me with chlorine gas. The police would find me with the bowl, the tablet, the room reeking of poison, note that I lived alone and key in "Solitude" next to "Cause of Death."

So I did the sensible thing. I took Parts 1 and 2, a large bowl of water, and a broom out to the street. I meant to hold the bag down with the broom handle so I could keep my distance, but as soon as I put the bag on the water, it began to dissolve. As I pushed it down the escaping gas made the water turn golden and fizz like ginger ale. I threw the tablet in and the water was flung out with a loud, sizzling *pop*. When I opened my eyes again, there was the perfect-cut pink diamond, rocking back and forth in the bottom of the bowl. I picked it up. Deep inside it, I could see a tiny twentieth-century scene of cattle eating tall grass. I turned it a hair and saw another scene— six human children holding hands around an enormous tree. Then I grabbed the bowl and broom and ran inside.

There was a different picture in every facet, but the theme was clearly pastoral twentieth century or early twenty-first. You could tell from the colors and the clothes. Fifty-eight pictures for fifty-eight facets, each one beautiful and delicate and hopeful as the past centuries, with a tracery of flowers framing some, and leaves framing others, and if you pressed it right up to your eye and looked into the light, the scene came alive in three or four dimensions—the solemn children would seem to smile, the cattle would advance one step, very subtly and almost imperceptibly. It was a bit like something I'd once seen on TV. Except the one I'd seen was smaller, and darker, with a single motionless hologram. The guards carried machetes (guns were too routine, they didn't frighten anyone anymore) because, as the narrator pointed out, a hologrammatic diamond was worth at least $70 trillion. I presumed mine was worth more. I wrapped it in flannel and put it on the shelf with the noodles, and got it out every half hour to look at it. Around nightfall I realized that it was already precious to me. I sat down to write a thank-you note.

"Dear Society," I wrote. "Thank you so much for the beautiful gem. It is lovely. Thank you for thinking of me. Very truly yours, Cynthia." I folded the note and wrote the society's name on the outside. Then I put on my boots for the walk to 1,345th Street.

My neighborhood was not a nice one. Its chief drawback was the sewer towers. Some urban planner a hundred years before had thought of instituting permanently recycling antiseptic rivers for universal waste disposal. The towers were the entrances for household trash. They had airlocks to keep the gas down, but they all leaked. As a result, my rent was very low. The air smelled of raw sewage. There was no way anything could decompose down there under the lights. We were slated for renovation, but of course now that the neighborhood had gone down, no one but me lived there, so the renovations were always being put off. But I didn't mind. My rent was about a quarter of what it should have been for an entire house. I bought a fancy air purifier and never opened the windows. So anyhow, I cut over to 304th Avenue, where the sewers are sealed off, and took the elevated walkway.

It was a warm, humid night with good visibility. The microwave balloons were at full altitude in deference to the high ozone. I could see the towers of Metroform on the horizon, looming behind a monolithic apartment block, and backlit by the fading clouds. There was a light ashfall. I put on my hat.

The walkway seemed to have been abandoned—no lights, no footprints in the ash. Probably there had been some rumor that it was dangerous, and now it was. The tiles creaked as if unused to being stepped on. I enjoyed the warmth of my hands in my pockets and thought about my diamond. It was nothing more than a rock, but seemed warm as another human body. The cool shades of green and blue gave warmth. When I looked at them, I felt my own warmth, as I never had under our sky of orange and brown, with all those cultured red roses, yellow tulips, pink granite—everything designed to be warm and friendly, but in the end no more friendly than the sun at noon.

I thought about the hologram I liked best: a round pool of water, surrounded by trees and overhung with tall grass, with an empty boat floating in the middle. It was the only picture that made room for me. All those happy children, animals, flowers, bright insects; all that cool white morning sunshine—all those self-contained vignettes of the past seemed made to tease me, luring and excluding me at once. To lie in the boat, which rocked a bit when the light changed, on its circular pool—what higher completeness could there be? Tiny green leaves and blue overhead, blue underneath, flowered banks on every side, no possibility of going anywhere, just an invitation to me to lie drowsy and motionless and wait. Of course I wasn't ignorant that they might have mailed out millions of them—I don't mean that I thought I was unique, but that the work of art was uniquely moving, in the way you could spend hours and hours looking into it before slowly realizing my point about that little green boat.

When I got to 1,345th Street I took the stairs down into the darkness below. Night had fallen. It was an old business district. It took me a few minutes to figure out which lobby to use, but I realized the *T* in the address referred to the elevator bank. There was no 211th floor in the T elevators, so I rode to 210 and looked for the stairs.

There was an eerie moaning sound coming from the walls. The building was swaying in the night wind as air from the sea rushed in over the warm air of the city. The inversion happened every night and was, I had read somewhere, the reason there are no really tall buildings in the old coastal cities.

I walked around until I found a door labeled "S.T.A.R." It had a tiny, dark window of reinforced glass and a strong, cold draft whistling around it as the building's motion eased the door in and out of its frame. I looked through the window. The stairs went up to another door, also labeled "S.T.A.R." In my opinion, they were stairs to the roof. I didn't know where to put my note. Under the whistling door? Certainly not under the next door, outside. But maybe there was a mailbox. I tried the handle. The door was unlocked but wouldn't budge. I waited a few seconds as the structure flexed again, and then I was on the stairs. I walked up, holding the handrail and shivering. The 211th floor had been toasty warm (heat rises, I suppose) but the air circling in that stairwell was very cold. There was no mailbox and the door was locked.

I turned to go back to the lobby. I figured I'd leave my note at reception. Then I heard a loud buzz, as if someone were buzzing me into a grocery store. I jumped back up and leaned on the door. The wind ripped it open and I stood under a sky black as coal, perforated with spots of brilliant light. Around me everything was black too—there were walls fifty or a hundred feet high, I had no way of telling, all around me. I was alone in a narrow shaft, twenty feet on a side, with the freezing wind rising and falling powerfully, as if the walls were somehow permeable to wind but not to light. The roof under my feet was soft and springy. And over my head were stars. The stars are perfectly well known—I'd seen dozens of pictures of them taken from the Chinese mountains and the space telescopes—but it had just never crossed my mind that I might see them myself for the first time from a medium-sized building in the middle of Metro U.S.A. I looked up so long that a few new stars appeared to push the old stars off to one side. Then I set my thank-you note down—it could swirl in the wind up there forever, but it wouldn't blow away—and ran down the stairs to the warmth of the world below.

I had trouble finding elevator bank T again. Instead, I found elevator bank U, for floors 210 through 270. I hadn't been on the top at all. I pressed the request button and a car came. I stepped in to see that it had buttons for all the higher floors, but I didn't stay on. I went back to the S.T.A.R. office. The wind was still whistling around the doorframe as I crept inside. The upstairs door was still locked, but after I tried it I heard the buzzer again, and nudged the door. It opened in a blaze of light. Overhead at the zenith was the small summer sun in a sky of pale blue. All around my feet were trampled violets. The high walls were dappled in a pattern of pale and dark green, and the breeze was warm and ticklish. I could see the size of the enclosure very precisely—rectangular, and smaller than I'd thought before. I put my eyes against the dark, cool green walls and tried to see through the mesh. I could make out snaking pipes and cables, and accordion-pleated air-delivery tubes, and fan blades. When I looked up again the sun had moved. I heard a twittering sound like a small engine squeaking, which appeared to come closer as it moved toward me in a spiral and then away again. I leaned down to feel the violets. They were real, living violets, moist and green as wet lettuce. My thank-you note was wet. By slow stages, I lay down and watched the sunset—that is, I watched the sun begin to touch the upper edge of the wall and move out of sight, dragging a deeper blue behind it.

I had decided that S.T.A.R. was an artist, very rich, because if you could make hologrammatic diamonds like mine you'd be bound to get rich very quickly, who could afford to be so idealistic that instead of selling his pieces to the highest bidder he had started giving them to people at random. Or not exactly random—he'd held an auction in which the bids consisted not of money but of elements of personality, and by keeping Part 1 on the refrigerator, I had bid high enough to get Part 2. The sun was vanishing and the air was getting colder. A solitary planet appeared and the wind began to pick up. I felt disappointed and got up to leave. Then I noticed the circuit box. I opened the small black door and read the list of options: Adjust Day Length, Time of Day, Season, Altitude, Temperature, Wind Strength, Lamb (Manual), and Part 3. The screen shimmered in the gathering dusk. I was torn between Lamb (Manual) and Part 3. I didn't know that it was up to me to start Part 3, or maybe I'd already seen Part 3. So I touched the screen at Time of Day and picked high noon again. The air warmed and slowed, and the sun jerked back into the upright position. Then I touched Lamb (Manual) and heard a click, like a sliding bolt, as all the colored lights and the sun went out and I was left surrounded by impenetrable metallic mesh in a dim gray elevator shaft. I felt a twinge of claustrophobia, like someone trapped in a mine. Then the lamb appeared behind the mesh, and I saw the tiny door, just his size, that he was indicating with gestures of his head. I kneeled and opened it, and he stepped inside. When I closed the door the lighting reversed again and it was high noon. The lamb put his head down and began to eat violets. He pulled them up by the roots.

"I can see why they don't keep you in here all the time," I said. He nodded contemplatively and smiled a sweet smile. His hair was radiantly white and curly in infinite curls, one upon another, tracing along his back like one long endless curl. The square pupils of his auburn eyes contracted slowly as he looked at me. I felt all my pockets and found a sweet roll. I set it on the ground between us. He let me touch his neck. He was softer than air and warm as coffee. He ate the sweet roll with curious eagerness, and then returned to munching violets. I wondered just how long I could stay there with him before he would do irreparable damage to the installation.

"Come here," I said. "Are you really so hungry?" He sidled away and scratched his back against the wall. I got up and scratched it for him. He bleated happily and ripped out another violet. Then I lay down again and looked straight up at the sun, fixed at noon, while the lamb's soft feet moved in predictable patterns around me and his quiet calls alternated with the contented grinding of his teeth.

After a while he lay down next to me and I rested my arm on his back. Then I noticed the time. I had been three hours delivering my thank-you note. It was damp with dew and I

wondered if the ink had run. I found it where it had blown
into a corner and unfolded it to check. But it wasn't my thank-
you note at all. It was handwritten, like my note, and read,
"Please enjoy Part 3." I took out a pen and wrote, "Thanks
again!" and put it back. The lamb was standing by his little
door. I thought maybe he was thirsty, so I let him out. And I
didn't know if he was supposed to be part of Part 3.

When I touched the screen a friendly, engaging male voice
began to fall gently from above. "Welcome. Tonight's feature
is entitled *Holiday in Austria*. Please make yourself comfortable. If at any time a comfort break is required, please
say so and the film will pause. At the conclusion of the film,
please have a safe journey home." Then the lights vanished
and the stars appeared. One star twinkled brighter than the
rest, alternating blue and green, growing larger, and seeming
to rotate, and I realized it was Earth. Then I saw it wasn't
Earth at all, it was a picture of high mountains and grassy
foothills with thick, glaring white clouds, as white as the
lamb's white wool, racing across an eggplant-blue sky. Gradually the projection changed from round to square and the
music began—an odd, regular melody, almost mechanical
sounding. The viewfinder drew closer to the mountains and
swooped in on a little house with low, overhanging eaves.
Then, from far away, the bark of a dog, and a bell, and a
small, fat woman in a tight dress came out the front door
and greeted the dog, who bounded up to her and licked her
hands. You could tell that the woman was blind. Her blank
eyes wandered randomly from the ground to the roof, and
she held her hands down for the dog to lick, instead of trying
to find his bobbing head herself. The viewfinder drew back
and the mountains came into focus again, enormous and
gray, taller than the tallest buildings in Metroform, streaked

with white snow. Higher on the mountain I could see a tiny white shape struggling to keep its feet amid a flood of scree. The dog barked and bounced, and at last the woman understood. She had to climb the mountain at nightfall to save the lost lamb. She took a walking stick from behind the door and followed the dog up the hill. At times invisible through the canopy of fir trees, at times a bright speck in a field held in dark shadow by a passing cloud, she moved slowly upward. Her red shawl swept the ground. Then the lens focused on the tiny lamb. He was caught in a slow rockslide, aggravating the trouble by his movements of panic. The sharp edges of flinty stone seemed unsuited to the lamb's tender feet. He looked down in despair and smiled a brave smile of resignation as the camera drew away into the sky. The perspective widened and you could see the old blind woman, still following the dog, still miles beneath where the lamb was trapped, as the sun slipped behind a mountain and the valley turned blue black. The camera kept vaulting backward until the whole region—her village, the roads—everything was visible, and even farther, back into space, until the revolving Earth returned, becoming smaller and smaller until it was only another twinkling star in the blackness of the ceiling. Then a dim red light appeared behind me. "Exit," it read, blinking on and off.

"Hello?" I called out. "Hello?" There was no answer. The light over the door kept blinking, so I left the office and closed both doors behind me. I found the U elevator bank again and rode express down to the lobby. I felt depressed.

I walked around the block and came back inside. I rode up to S.T.A.R. Both doors were ajar and the stairs were covered with dirty footprints. Inside it was midnight and a freezing, swirling wind with particles of ice. I could hardly see a thing—my eyes squinted shut against the sleet and bitter air. I pressed Lamb (Manual) and waited for him. After I propped open the exit door to get some light, I saw him approaching like a dim new moon. He bounded down to the hallway, his knees wobbling unsteadily on the spun-metal floor, and when he looked up at me and bleated I picked him up for a minute, just to calm him down. I set my face in the soft wool of his neck. I offered him a saltine (my pockets are always full of food for no very good reason) and then I took him home.

"Took" is really the wrong word—he followed me. As far as I know, that's what sheep do: follow each other. Or he was too stupid to know that his home was back up the stairs. I don't think so. I took him because of the hungry way he had devoured all the violets, and because I thought the society wanted me to. The lamb in *Holiday in Austria* had needed rescue from some very dramatic trouble, and this lamb was no less high and helpless, on the 211th floor of a dismal skyscraper in an exhausted suburb of Metroform. I also imagined that as I lay on my bed, the lamb would lie beside me, fluffy and pricelessly beautiful, and together we would be happy. I hoped there was no Part 4. The diamond and the lamb seemed like enough.

The lamb liked his new home. I applied for a pet certificate and got vouchers for corn. I hoped he wasn't too hungry. Soon we'd settled in. He ate from my hands and slept by me. I cleaned up after him and bathed him. I bought organic matter and filled half the basement with it. I planted grass and violets. He liked to eat down there, but as soon as he could he'd come back up and climb up next to me on the sofa. So I was sure he liked me.

It's hard to describe just how beautiful he was. His mouth was set in a slight smile, blissful and quiet, and his pure-white wool was thick and soft over his entire graceful body. The hanging bell-bottoms of his fetlocks almost hid his tiny black hooves. He teetered around the house looking for salty things to lick—hands, crackers, soup plates, my sweaty arms after a long night sitting up wrapped in blankets. He bleated for me to pick him up, and I'd put him over my shoulders. His eyes were deep brownish red flecked with gold, and raised their sorrowful look like an offering to our happiness. Dancing, running, chewing on my fingers, dozing in his nest, wherever he was, no matter how childish his pleasures, his eyes said, I know what this is worth.

Maybe you think I should have taken the lamb to the country. But I just thought it's so cold up there, and so many people—nothing like Metro U.S.A., but still so crowded there are more people than buildings. Plus, they have to work. My family has always lived around Metroform and been paid to eat and breathe as little as possible, and furthermore, I'll be damned if I'll work. Besides, the country wasn't really beautiful at all. At least, not compared to the scenes in the diamond.

Every day I expected S.T.A.R. to contact me. I've seen the lake in the diamond. I'm living with the lamb. I made up a story: What ultimately will happen is that I'll either learn that the place in the diamond still exists, or that it doesn't. I'll travel the whole earth. Maybe I'll go to Austria by boat. With the lamb. When I get there I'll find the round pool, and I'll meet someone. Who is the artist? Who's in S.T.A.R.? What is their motivation? Is the diamond a priceless antique that's being hidden with me? Maybe the national treasure of some secret kingdom, or secret order. S.T.A.R. is the thief who took it away. S.T.A.R. could be a revolutionary who wants to restore the earth. The system is so huge and convoluted, there's no way to get gradual change, it would take a breakdown. Why me? I'm the only one left—the only thoughtful person. What does S.T.A.R. have to do with the lamb? S.T.A.R. doesn't understand at all; he thinks the mass deaths at the seat of world government will solve everything; the lamb's innocence disproves him. He'll want to replace their power with his power. He'll ask for my help. When we flee to Austria, I'll meet a wise, beautiful old woman. The woman will tell me wearily, because she knows she's not going to survive, to let the lamb eat the diamond. When he does, the world will end. In a flash, as my body dissolves, I'll see the eternal peace and stillness and the little boat rocking, or I'll feel myself rocking and see the cattails. Then the world will begin again. It's a special kind of bomb that doesn't destroy the minds of thoughtful people. The world dissolves without flame, like a dream being forgotten.

So I wrote a letter inviting S.T.A.R. to lunch, and gave it to the mailman the next morning.

When he arrived the lamb ran to him. He stood resting his hooves on the man's knees, and licked his hands. He seemed almost frantic with anxiety and love. The man picked the lamb up tenderly and held him like a baby. The lamb never looked at me. During our lunch he sat at the man's feet, and after he followed him out.

The man seemed glad to meet me, and asked me all sorts of questions, and gave me a set of beautifully embroidered pajamas, wrapped up in iridescent foil. I sat with eyes wide, realizing the lamb loved him and was his pet, not listening.

He said, "Can you hear me?"

I bent down to glance under the table. The lamb was sitting with his head on the man's shoe. I started to cry, and asked him to leave. I thanked him for coming to lunch.

That night I put the new pajamas on and lay down alone.

They smelled of lavender and were soft as cushions, with pillowy embroidery floss looping out all over. I lay on my side and cried until I felt dizzy.

I woke up in darkness. The lamb was with me in bed, but the room was gone, and I had a vision. I saw the world from space, and it was not blue, green, and white. It was black, yellow, and brown. So many people had died that there were only a million left, living like me in the cities, watching documentaries about the exodus to the poles and believing them. But we were doomed, like the great whales: So few were left, in so large a space, that we never encountered each other. Then I really woke up. The lamb was gone, and I was alone.

I walked to the window and looked out at the street. It was blazing noontime. The man was sitting outside on a rock under an enormous chestnut tree with leaflets like dark green umbrellas that cast a deep, fragrant shade over my entire block. He was cleaning under his fingernails with a toothpick. The lamb was asleep on the bench seat of the mail truck.

I opened the door and he looked up. "I recognize you now," I said. "You're the mailman."

"Sometimes," he said.

"Is this Part Five?"

"This is actually Part Ten," he said. "I was getting really impatient. Will you live with me in Austria?"

"Let me get my coat," I said. "It looked kind of snowy."

"You can borrow mine," he said, but I shook my head. I got my coat and hat, the diamond, and a violet from the basement. He tucked the violet into his pocket and we climbed into the truck. We drove thirty miles to Metroform without seeing another person or car. "What's S.T.A.R.?" I asked.

He put both hands on the steering wheel. "What do you know about freedom?"

"It's when you get to do what you want. Like me, right now."

"But you see, I already know what you want, because I articulated it for you myself. I've seduced you in the most wicked and shameless way, by telling you a story when you were alone and you couldn't help listening."

"I don't mind."

"S.T.A.R. is my family's waste management company. I guess we're best known for the secret tunnel from the Black Sea to the South Asian effluent containment bunker. Very rich, very evil."

"Do any of those places in the diamond still exist?"

"Those shots were all taken on my family's estate."

"In Austria?"

"No, in Western Metro. It used to be a famous park."

"Then we'll go to Austria. We'll live there in your cave full of holograms or whatever it is."

He smiled and held my hand. The lamb woke up and stretched himself. The sun was rising behind us, making flashes of white run across the sky as the skyscrapers' reactive armor fought off the solar wind. In a parking lot our ICBM was waiting.

(End interlude)

In Long Island City, addresses are assigned on a highly rational system. Anyone wishing to find 5-16 Forty-Seventh Road, for example, knows if he turns left off Fifth Avenue it will be the ninth house on the north side. Forty-Seventh Street is one block south, and runs the other way. The cold anonymity of the L.I.C. streets, where shopping bags blow like dead leaves past thousands of identical Greek superettes and shuttered Irish bars, and storm drains breathe an odor of sewage as in the fictional work above, always seemed to me a portent of our common future. Through L.I.C. runs Queens Boulevard, eight lanes wide and arrow straight from Jamaica to the East River, lined with delis, lunch counters, and shops, with a stoplight on every block, so that never a pedestrian is run over but with his entire family, seven in one blow, and always by a driver whose license has been suspended 127 times. Really. Read the *New York Post* for a week and try counting the Queens Boulevard dead, keeping in mind that they report only accidents involving babies in strollers or vehicles that jump the curb.

Yigal stood up, buttoned his shirt, and walked toward the center of Bern, looking for an open bakery.

CHAPTER 5

PAMELA WAS PUBLISHED IN 1740,
Tristram Shandy in 1759. Such infinite progress in nineteen
short years! *Pamela,* as we already know, is an embarrassment,
a bore, and a model for *Justine,* regularly forced on students
of English literature for its historic significance. *Tristram,* on
the other hand, is held to be a "bawdy" and "ribald" work like
those catalogs of "conquered" "strumpets," *Tom Jones* et al.,
and routinely ignored. How I loathe, in retrospect, the old-
maidenly prissiness, worthy of Samuel Richardson himself,
that could perceive soft-core porn in *Tristram Shandy,* effectively discouraging me from opening the book until well into
my thirty-third year of life.

On reading it, I discovered, of course, that it is a mildly
adult version of *The Pickwick Papers.* Uncle Toby Shandy, a retired army officer given to pet obsessions, spends his days re-
constructing famous battles in miniature with the help of a
witty and loyal servant. A groin injury has made Uncle Toby
hopelessly benign, gentle, and patient, winning him the un-
dying love of the widow next door who is, however, eager to
know the exact nature of the injury.

The same professors who knew just enough to label *Tristram*

Shandy "bawdy" and "ribald" were eager to teach from *Naked Lunch,* if only they could have gotten permission. Meanwhile, they taught Faulkner, the same as in high school. I.e., the problem with *Tristram* wasn't its being too grown up; it was too juvenile. They didn't want to listen to us giggle about the groin injury—they'd rather send us down to Yoknapatawpha County to watch the inbred morons accidentally drilling holes in their dead mother's face. *Naked Lunch* was more Faulkner, with a bigger drill. And the ineffable, unforgettable saintly sweetness of Uncle Toby Shandy, later transferred so successfully to Mr. Pickwick, became a forgotten relic, something no one alive today thinks English literature ever possessed, except me.

Mr. Chips, Mrs. Miniver, Lassie, Seymour Glass—these later types of ghastly saccharine horror have nothing to do with the mature and truly humble generosity of Mr. Pickwick, who does his best to organize worthwhile club outings for the entertainment of his friends while endlessly tolerating the same poor parasites (he doesn't work for his money, after all) and supporting the same poor drunks (he likes drinking too). After reading *The Pickwick Papers,* I accepted Mr. Pickwick into my heart as my personal lord and savior, and I never pass a wino without giving him two dollars. When people ask me for loans I just hand them the money, saying, "If I'm ever so down and out that I need three hundred dollars, I'll know who to call."

But I knew better than to mention Mr. Pickwick to Zohar when I left Philadelphia and had a sort of potlatch, dispensing thousands of dollars' worth of electronics, my bicycle, drums, guitars, amplifiers, and so on to my friends. I let him think what he wanted. Mr. Pickwick is the Israeli Antichrist, the original and supreme *freier* (sucker). A specter is haunting Israel—the specter of Mr. Pickwick. . . .

Yigal was a little tight, dirty, and looking for a bakery at 7:30 P.M. on a Sunday night in Bern. The odds were 5 to 1 against him (there was an open *Konditorei*, but on a street he'd probably miss), and around 9:00 he was looking for a ride out of town. Two hours after that he was being turned away from the youth hostel. If not for the Rastafarian junkies at the bear pits, he would have slept in the park. He woke up on an uneven wooden floor. It was early morning, almost dark, but he walked out into the village street and found a bakery, bright and warm, with thick cream for the coffee and loaves of bread as big as cases of beer. He ate onion pie and two poppy seed pinwheels.

Maybe, like Osnat, you are asking, at this point, "Why is Yigal so poor? Can't he stay in hotels and ride the train? Isn't he a senior agent for a black-budget super-secret all-powerful worldwide network of maverick spymasters?" But please remember that Yigal was traveling incognito. It isn't so hard— you can tell your name to anyone you want and say exactly what you're doing, but you have to remember not to use credit cards. Yigal was an experienced super-spy, so he remembered. He had lots of money left, but he had an idea he might want it for something before he got to Lindau. He was thinking of buying a tent. In Lindau he could pick up a lot of money he'd mailed himself in a cardboard box. There was a pleasant little jazz bar there, where they knew him, the Fischerin. They were always extra nice to him because they figured he was an ecstasy dealer.

At the edge of the village was a tall forest bordered by a deep meadow. He took a few steps into the wet grass, then looked down with a sinking feeling. How come I always forget? he thought. Every time I'm in Northern Europe it's the same damn thing. He slid forward, grimacing. The meadow was knee-deep in slugs, each under its own blade of grass, oozing a slime that wouldn't wash off—water would just spread it around—his boots would dry silver white. He had never seen the banana slug of the Pacific Northwest, but he knew a slug so conspicuous and easy to avoid could not possibly be more revolting than the endless millions, living and dead, under and around his feet in this one idyllic Swabian pasture. He had heard that New Zealand harbors a snail so large it fills the evolutionary niche normally occupied by . . . he tried to remember—he recalled vaguely that the New Zealand grasshopper is so big that it functions as a mouse, but couldn't remember what the snail does. In any case, it's a foot long, and he had no plans to visit New Zealand.

The desert is so clean and pure, he thought. I should take the M16 and drive down the Egyptian border to where the mountains look like bare, golden, freshly swept stairs. As a rotting log broke open under his foot, revealing a wet safety-orange slime mold, he thought of the dry, delicate geckos that used to run across his kitchen ceiling, and of miniature blue-black birds flashing like obsidian against the dusty green of feral geraniums in the backyard. Then he remembered that if he went home, he would have to report in. What will I tell Rafi? Rafi, it's like this: I've narrowed down the search to two families—two clans, that is—two countries: Laos and Iceland. I'm certain the heir will be found in one of those two places, in a remote cliffside cave where I can say I did it, collect the bounty and get the hell off this ridiculous project which is destroying my career and all my relationships. I just know if I weren't always traveling, Nofar would go out with me. I feel like a sailor. It's no wonder she won't give me the time of day . . .

Yigal found a logging road and stopped to scrape his soles on the gravel. He realized that the slugs must once have had a predator, now extinct. He imagined the unicorns using their horns to lift the meadow thatch and reveal the slugs below, then eagerly munching them with their strong teeth and coarse tongues. What horror the virgins must have felt when the unicorns laid their slimy chins and stiff beards in their laps, how they screamed for the huntsman to come quickly, then the purely decorative nature of the roast unicorn centerpiece, its inedible meat slippery as okra. In his mind's eye, he saw the male unicorns' vicious battles for possession of the richest meadows and creek bottoms, where long brown slugs grew thick and fast as mushrooms.

He closed his eyes and pretended he was somewhere near Be'er Sheva in a field of crispy weeds and Roman coins, then sat down in the road to check his e-mail. There was a long message from his old friend Osnat. Secretly he hated her a little. When a girl like that hangs around a man like me, he knew well, saying she thinks I'm sweet, it means she doesn't actually think of me as male. If she respected me a little, it would cross her mind that her behavior ought to be driving me insane. Doesn't it occur to her that calling a man at six in the morning to cry about some fucked-up love affair is a tease? Why does she dress like that?

Osnat wrote, Thanks for putting me in touch with Coppola's people. I'm helping them scout locations. Call me when you get into town. Yigal, I hope you're taking care of yourself—please play safe. . . .

This motherly tone, Yigal thought, makes me sick. He wrote: What Coppola's people? I forget things, you know. I may be coming home soon. Amsterdam always makes me miss the sunshine. I don't think I've been outdoors in a week. I'll call you.

It's true what she said about scouting locations—Osnat was taking Mary to every café in town. I went with them to Café Tamar. They sat talking for two hours while four young men, all with open notebooks, eavesdropped. I sat down with one and he froze like a rabbit.

"Are you a poet?" I asked.

"I'm a rapper, an MC," he said in a wee, soft voice. "I can work better in a place like this. It helps me to let the rhymes flow." He crossed his legs, above the knee. "That girl, she's poetry in motion."

"You're an idiot," I said, standing up. I tried the next one.

"What are you writing, poetry?" I asked.

"Not yet. It's sort of a manifesto. I think the poetry of today is corrupt, bankrupt, meaningless—there's nothing of significance left for it. We need a hard, merciless, thrusting poetry that won't take no for an answer." He fidgeted nervously with an empty sugar packet. I tried the next one.

"Is that poetry?" I asked.

"It's a letter," the man said. "My girlfriend won't marry me. I really love her, but she thinks because I'm already married, it's not worth it for her. Well, I'm a man who can think for himself, and in this case I think I have rights. Let me show you." He began to dig around in his book bag, and I moved on to the fourth and last.

"Are you writing poetry?" I asked.

"Yes," he said. "Here's my latest poem. 'Dogs are Shakespearean, children are strangers—'"

"That's Delmore Schwartz."

"You know it?" He looked disappointed. "Okay, how about

this. 'The heavy bear accompanies me, honey covers his face, awkwardly staggering around—'"

"Are all your poems translations of Delmore Schwartz?"

"No, right now, looking at your friend, I have an idea for a poem based on Ginsberg's 'Song.'" He began scribbling in the notebook. "The weight of the world is love," I saw over his shoulder.

I went back to Osnat and Mary. Osnat was trying to talk Mary into being tested for HIV.

Thousands of miles off, the only Israeli in Eastern Bhutan was toiling uphill on foot, humming tunelessly and thinking about Piano Sonatas nos. 21, 23, and 26. At my suggestion he was carrying a plastic bag filled with water from the radiator—otherwise he would have died. I'd located a llama-trekking party from Portland, Oregon, just 250 miles away over the Nepalese border, and with the GPS ripped out of the Rover after the axle broke, he was making good time. Only once did he admit weakness. "I'm getting a hole in my sneaker," he said ruefully, and my heart went out to my brave darling.

CHAPTER 6

DANIEL DERONDA IS A SORT OF
young, beautiful Jewish Mr. Pickwick. Critics actually say, "This
novel is unrealistic because no one is as adorable as Daniel
Deronda." Obviously, these critics are boys. I have a friend
who's every bit as nice as Daniel. Plus, he's never been married,
has a master's degree, a good job, and wants kids. He lives in
Washington, D.C., and you can reach him at [address redacted,
even though it's all still true].

Daniel lived with his mother, a narcissistic and sexy actress,
until he was two years old. She was a Sephardic aristocrat,
something that turns up again and again in English literature. The most fabulous and intellectual Jews in European
myth are the ones who escaped from Spain, late and in small
numbers, bringing with them the mysterious spiritual culture
of the ancient world—orange blossoms, fiery chariots, nu-
merology, the Alhambra, etc. The paler native Jews, shrill and
irritating, insist on trying to pass for white, and constant vig-
ilance is required to keep them out of our swimming pools.
Daniel attended Eton, then went off to college, but it wasn't
until he was twenty-two that it occurred to him that there was
something just a little tiny bit unusual about his penis. His

strange penis then leads him on a voyage of discovery that ends in cabalistic studies, intimate involvement with a beautiful Jewish singer, estrangement from his adoptive family, and ultimately the realization that he was born a Jew.

Actually, of course, George Eliot doesn't mention Daniel's penis. I think of it only because I am not Jewish, and if I were to have a son, he would not be Jewish, so I see no particular reason for circumcision unless he asks for it by name, but Zohar thinks an uncircumcised Israeli child would be beaten to death in the first year of kindergarten. There is nothing I can say to refute him—I don't really know how much time and energy boys devote to examining each other in the bathroom and punishing deviants—except to present to him the shining example of Daniel, whose unusual penis, far from handicapping him socially, helped make him the most popular boy in the world and the third most charming character in English literature.

At the end of *Daniel Deronda,* the newly married Daniel heads "East" on a journey expected to take several years, and drops out of the purview of George Eliot. However, we find him again at the First Zionist Congress, giving the keynote address to the Spirituality Special Interest Group and meekly consenting to model for a bust of Aaron. Later that night, he stands with his back to the buffet, scanning the crowd for his wife so he can tell her he's stepping outside for a cigar.

At last he sees her—Herzl's wife has her cornered, trying to talk her out of ten acres near Jaffa that Herzl wants for an experimental vineyard. "I'm keeping it in olives and lemons," he hears his wife say. "The Lord will save the Jewish people by bringing them to a land where a kosher diet can be fresh, nutritious, and high in fiber. Does Daniel look to you like I feed him nothing but cream sauce, port wine, and strawberry jam?"

"He doesn't look a day over thirty-five," Mrs. Herzl is forced to admit. "Maybe Theodor should talk to you, he has some digestive problems . . ."

Daniel blushes.

"Seals don't get HIV," Mary said to me as we rode home on the bus.

"Are you a seal? Be serious."

"I'm not exactly not a seal," she said. "I mean, ask me to hold my breath sometime. I'm not like most things, which are what they seem to be, and if you put them under a microscope, you see the same thing, only smaller. I'm different. I think it's like in Platonism where you have substances and accidents, and my substance is to be a seal. I think. My parents were seals. If I look like myself, it's by accident. When I'm a seal, I'm a hundred percent seal, but when I'm human it's not quite a hundred percent." I begged her to explain and she started over. "Silkies are ancient and immortal, right? But seals and people aren't. And in a sense neither are silkies. You can't be a seal forever, or a person forever. You'd get bored. I'm only like four years old, as a person I mean, I think."

"How can you be ancient and immortal and four years old?"

"I don't know, people pay attention to stuff like that, seals don't. Nobody cares. I mean, some seals get older, and some don't. And some become silkies, and some don't. I think I seem pretty young. I mean, like the way I can't defer gratification, and this confused way I talk and stuff. I know I look like twenty-five, but I wasn't a little tiny seal when I first came out—I was pretty big—"

"When was that?"

"It was in 1990. I had this crush on this totally cute guy who was a ski bum in Taos, so I came out, but it didn't work out, so I went back in for a while, but now here I am again."

"You lived in Taos?"

She shook her head. "No, no, no—Santa Fe. I think if we'd lived in Taos, it might have worked out. For him, anyway." She looked sadly out the window at Rabin Square hung with flags, and began to cry. "Where's Yigal?" she sniffled.

I had to admit, I had no idea.

The next day Osnat called to tell us he was in Amsterdam, whoring around on drugs. She and Mary went out to Café Siach to cry together.

Mary came back angry. "How can she say she loves Yigal, and then say he's going to get hepatitis and herpes? It's like she wants him to be punished. I told that bitch Mr. Francis Ford Coppola isn't going to be needing her services, we're filming in Salt Lake City."

"Look what I got," I said. I sat her down in front of the computer. I had thought to ask for his e-mail address from Osnat, and I already had an answer.

Dear Nell, don't mention things like Trident missiles in unencrypted messages. This part is for Mary. My dear Mary, I am still wandering around Switzerland, but you are in my apartment in Tel Aviv. Why? Yigal.

Mary wrote him some sort of reply.

I also had a disquieting message from Shats in response to chapter five. There was a low humming sound outside just now, he wrote, like some huge engine in the distance, and what sounded like occasional underground explosions far away. I went to the window and there's this blazing sunset, the sky was very gray and the sea dark blue gray, and on the horizon bright orange strips of light. A *satil*—a navy missile boat—was sailing southward along the shore, then changed course and started sailing toward the sunset. It doesn't make sense—the distance's too long—but it seems the sounds came from the boat.

Could it be, I wondered, that the stress of reading *Sailing Toward the Sunset* has unhinged Shats' mind as the labor of writing it seems to be unhinging mine? My friend Mary (no relation to the Mary in this novel) remarked that I seem frazzled, and whenever I leave the house I find the outside world fantastically large and three-dimensional compared with the tiny world of the computer screen. And, Shats says, his English is good, but not entirely second nature; I think he put it, To see Hebrew is to read it, but English still requires concentration. In short, it may be that he spends more time reading each chapter than I spend writing it. It is possible.

I fear I may lose artistic momentum, and even as I do, Zohar's joyful faith in me as an artist for art's sake reaches new heights daily. "You are working! You are obsessed!" he cries, taking the opportunity to, for example, eat all the blueberry jam, knowing I may not think of going anywhere near the kitchen for hours.

I asked him why the outside world seems so lovely now, as though I were naked at midnight on a golf course having eaten a big handful of psilocybin mushrooms, and he said, "The outside world is more beautiful than any art." He ducked into the Justy (I had come outside to see him to the car) and arranged himself for a trip to the *Helicon* editorial board meeting. "But your art is very cute. You are cute!" He revved it to 4,500 rpm and sped away.

In one sense I am delighted by Zohar's transformation. For years he had seen me only as art's detractor—the sourpuss sure to say, "Are you sure writing a poem requires staying drunk for a week with ninety-nine channels of cable?" Now I have taken the role of art's disoriented, preoccupied hermit, and he—my gentle patron.

Meanwhile, down in the Gulf of Aqaba, Nachum's new

glass-bottomed boat skimmed across the small, frothy waves, followed by Sissy and friends, out to approximately the point from which the Trident missile had emerged on its mission of dangerous vandalism. He was busy preparing a bucket of dead fish when he heard one of the tourists say, "Will you look at that!"

Below them was only darkness. But it was a solid sort of darkness, punctuated with rivets, a huge hulk, immense and black—the submarine, still there. "I'll be damned," Nachum said.

"Get the dolphins to go down and tell us what it is!" someone suggested. Everyone agreed that would be the best thing.

"Oh, I don't think so," Nachum said, turning toward Eilat. He called me twenty minutes later and made me promise to stay out of my apartment whenever I could.

"Just let me know when it leaves, so I can relax," I said. I told him to tie a float to it, one of those little fishing buoys with a flag. Nachum protested, but that's what he did. The next day he called to say it had moved about a hundred yards closer to Eilat. The next day, it was gone.

CHAPTER 7

IT WASN'T MARY WHO BROUGHT

Yigal back to Tel Aviv—it was a syndicated newspaper story he found in a bus shelter in Konstanz.

A SPECTER IS HAUNTING ISRAEL:
THE SPECTER OF "MR. PICKWICK"

Inhabitants of Tel Aviv are reporting sightings of a mysterious submarine—the first UFO (Unidentified Floating Object) of its kind. A British "house" DJ active in the port of Tel Aviv has dubbed the object "Mr. Pickwick," calling it "rotund" and "jovial," and the name seems to have found resonance in the popular mind.

All official sources are denying reports of the vessel, which witnesses say is approximately 100 meters long and 20 meters in diameter. "A whale," scoffs a bored clerk at the Ministry of the Interior. "Crude oil," says an idle receptionist at a customs office. "A mass hallucination," adds the press secretary to the minister of culture.

Ordinary Israelis are not so sure. "A Trident missile submarine, without a doubt," says Amit, 22, a lifeguard on Tel Aviv's Hilton Beach, relatively near where most of the sightings have taken place at Tel Aviv's defunct shipping port. "Definitely one of the black submarines," agrees Maya, 24, barista at Sheinkin Street's Café Kazeh, echoing the American penchant for sighting "black helicopters" connected with U.S. government covert operations.

No one yet claims to have circled or touched the craft. Fishermen in the port of Jaffa say it is unobtrusive. None we spoke to had bothered going anywhere near it. A few mentioned a proposal to string an underwater cable across the Yarqon River, to keep the submarine from blocking boat access should it choose to enter the shallow estuary.

"From what I've heard, it wouldn't even fit," one fisherman said, shrugging. "So let them try it."

A widely held opinion holds the submarine to be somehow connected with the coming of the Messiah, and the port is now home to a religious revival. Buses arrive hourly from all over Israel, and banners proclaim, "Welcome, Mr. Pickwick, Our Messiah and King."

Sociologists are speaking of a "cargo cult," formed in response to reductions in U.S. military aid. . . .

"It's funny," Zohar said, "but not as funny as the Mishna." He was referring, of course, to the section on a man's duties to his dead brother's wives when there are two of them, both orphans, and one is deaf and the other "small" (a midget? underage?).

I'm trying to remember what book I've read that the present book (*Sailing Toward the Sunset*) reminds me of, and it's not *Possession* or *Dictionary of the Khazars*. I'm afraid it might be *Moby-Dick*, because of all the jumping around.

It is every author's nightmare to provoke comparison to *Moby-Dick*, whose shoelaces he is not worthy to untie.

The poets I knew in my teens called such a feeling the "Anxiety of Influence." It's what happens when you read "A Child's Christmas in Wales" and get an overwhelming urge to write about your grandfather and snow globes. The term is also applied to the eternal recurrence of metaphors, similes, and rhymes. Its usual form of expression is "Everything has already been written."

Once I participated in a poetry workshop.

My poem begins:

Sea lions hunt all the time.
When they're not hungry, they hunt mali mali.
Mali mali are big black fish, round in profile.
They move glacially through the sunny upper layers of the
*   Pacific.*

The sea lions, after biting off a mali mali's fins, bat it around like a volleyball for a while before letting it sink to the bottom where, alive and helpless, it awaits their return.

My poem concludes as the sea lions

. . . whisper, while deciding at which end to begin, quoting
*   Artaud,*
"In the state of degeneracy, in which we live, it is through the
*   skin*
That metaphysics will be made to reenter our minds."

"They're called mahi mahi, and they're white," remarked my uncle Charlie, who had told me about them in the first place. "Otherwise, it's okay." Years before, he had described to me his harrowing experience watching a seemingly innocent episode of *The Undersea World of Jacques Cousteau* in which the events indicated above transpired, and since then I had retailed "the mali mali story" as frequently as possible, never failing to mention both my uncle and Jacques Cousteau. The story, as I saw it, was so compelling that no artistic failure on my part could lessen its power.

Also attending the poetry workshop, where most of the Anxiety-laden poets strove to combine the stumbling density of Hopkins with the double entendres of Nabokov, was a woman who said her favorite poet was Ogden Nash. Every week she read us her latest oeuvre, generally in eight lines rhymed ABAB CDCD, on the subject of springtime. I considered her hilariously thick, yet illiterate and stupid. How dismayed I was, years later in Washington, D.C., to meet her again and find that she had become an editor of *National Geographic*. In the intervening years she had acquired oval wire-rimmed glasses like those worn by Yigal and a collection of drab coatdresses, and the look of intelligence this gave her, combined with her absurdly sporty body, beautiful skin, piercing blue eyes, and long blond hair, had gained her a career for which others (me, for example—I had tried and failed to get a job at *National Geographic* as a clerk typist) were perhaps better qualified. "If everybody in editorial died tomorrow, we could still put it out for five years," one of her subordinates told me. He was a homely workaholic who had edited his college paper three years in a row.

In the Anxiety of Influence process, the great literature of the past, by confronting the author with his own mediocrity, destroys his self-esteem. In reaction, the author does his best to evoke this literature as little as possible, while still feeling he must equal it in quality. At his death, diskettes and notebooks are discovered. Each contains two or three short pieces no one has ever read.

Luckily, I suffer more often from an opposing feeling—the fear of failure to make clear exactly what my unconscious influences are and why I like them so much. Far from publishing a formal disclaimer to the effect that comparisons to *Moby-Dick* are unwelcome, I would encourage the reader to discard *Sailing Toward the Sunset* immediately in favor of *Moby-Dick*, the wit and profundity of which shame all other novels. I welcome any and all influence of my favorite authors, whom I am willing to meet halfway by confessing that if my work ultimately resembles that of Melville in any way, it is as much an accident as if Melville's work resembled mine.

Unlike the Anxious writers, I am free to evoke the great literature of the past as often as possible, and without inviting comparison, in the easiest possible way: I mention it, over and over. I am grateful to my models, *Possession* and *Dictionary of the Khazars*, for demonstrating the ease with which this can be accomplished.

I wish I had a copy of *Moby-Dick* right now, so that I could borrow a few of Melville's epigrams on the subject of the whale so nearly resembling the mysterious "Mr. Pickwick," which now nestled comfortably, as though it planned to stay for a long time, on the Mediterranean seafloor.

CHAPTER 8

BEFORE DESCRIBING THE ENIGMATIC

submarine, I should remind the reader that my aim in *Sailing Toward the Sunset* is not to create irresistible literary characters, but in deference to my models, *Possession* and *Dictionary of the Khazars,* to dispense with such fripperies in pursuit of a higher goal: the suggestion, through breathless innuendo, of an exotic and unverifiable past.

I turn to Shats' eighth chapter. It begins on page 213. The novel ends on page 234. This chapter is surely an especially dense one, whose every word carries an ambivalent and multilayered significance, as these twenty-two pages must ultimately carry three-quarters of the hermeneutic weight of the entire book. It begins:

> The angels [could be "queens"] of complaint
> came to Jamaica in the eighteenth century, and
> told the committee of virgins: the [?], symbol
> of reality and [?] of the bitterness of the power
> structure . . . the two deaths separated by eighty
> years. . . .

Hebrew words notoriously have multiple meanings, since each Hebrew word is based on a three-consonant root, and the twenty-three consonants (I don't think that's right, but it's something like twenty-three) yield only 12,167 possible combinations. As I recall, English has at least three times that many words, indicating that each Hebrew word must carry, at the absolute minimum, three English meanings. I.e., the sentence can also be translated:

> Deeply eroded ravines [could be "gutters"] of res-
> ignation came to Sicily in despite of the 144 eli-
> sions, and told the objectors: the [?], essence of
> truth and [?] the bad flavor of the fruiting tops . . .
> the five circles split into eighty fragments. . . .

Or:

> Cain entreated God for permission to lay down
> his weapon: but God said, one [?] has brought
> me here, I cannot be turned back . . . the wind
> [piped?] in Cain's ears, loess filled his lungs, he
> walked in the dust behind Abel, carrying a bag of
> newly grafted mango seedlings. . . .

The multivalence of the Hebrew vocabulary, I am told, makes it uniquely suited for poetry. (I have this on the authority of Amir Or, editor of *Helicon*.) Personal experience, on the other hand, gives me the sad impression that the Hebrew language is narrowly pedantic and precise. The title of Zohar's book, for example, *Shu Hai Practices Throwing the Spear*—"It's not a spear," Zohar said to me with an air of frustration. " 'Throwing the spear' is what we call that Olympic field event, the javelin. It's 'Shu Hai Practices the Javelin.' "

Okay, I thought, whatever. Guess that's bound to happen if spears fall out of daily use.

Mary and I went down to the old port to look at Mr. Pickwick.

The old port of Tel Aviv, with its dusty cats, scabby dogs, flaking concrete, deep and opaque berths for ghost ships, etc., is surely worthy of treatment in prose-poetry, that bastard child of television. The style of montage, of snapshots succeeding each other, is similar to the way an inexpensive documentary, where the tripod is carried from place to place while the camera is turned off, might be perceived by someone who is not really paying attention. Certain parties I have attended present themselves to my memory with the benefit of similar editing techniques—I know I was there for ten hours, but all I remember is:

> *A small fire of twigs. Why were we building fires?*
> *Standing on the dock, I look back at the house and*
> *sway. Matthew on an attic cot, shivering and moaning.*
> *He does not look up. The hippie-earth-babe chick he's*
> *seeing—damn her. Splashing of the oars as I am helped*
> *into the boat. Two fingers of peppermint schnapps, he*
> *is not expecting this, neither am I, on Doug McLeod's*
> *head. Can't he see I'm already drunk enough?*

Mr. Pickwick–related activity radiated from a yeshiva occupying one of the largest buildings in the port, next to the river. Dozens of buses were parked on the uneven gravel, and a crowd of men in black suits was milling around and sitting on beat-up garden chairs in the shade of the walls. We pressed through to the front, by the sea. "You can't see anything from here," Mary said, kicking off her shoes and beginning to unbutton her blouse.

I stopped her. No one should swim anywhere near the mouth of the Yarqon. We returned through the crowd to a sort of reception desk, where a few pictures of our King and Messiah were hanging decorated with Sukkoth streamers and tinsel. "You must be here for the disco," the staffer said sympathetically. He pointed us one building over.

As we approached we could hear the fast, monotonous, irritating high drone of techno music over the idling of the buses. A pimply, hollow-chested young man stopped us at the door. "Do you have tickets?"

"We're looking for information about Mr. Pickwick. Have you seen anything?"

"We're waiting here for Mr. Pickwick," he said, gesturing toward the interior. The pitch and volume rose in a whooping, tense curve, and I could hear yelling from the dance floor. "We think Mr. Pickwick will come soon. The tickets are seventy shekels, you can get them at the white shipping container on the other side."

"Thanks," we said, sidling away.

"I want to see Mr. Pickwick," Mary said, leaning on the seawall. "Can you watch my stuff?" She climbed over, gave me her clothes, and dove out past the rocks into the surf, suddenly looking very tiny and white in her black silk underwear. She didn't come back up. I waited two hours, then wandered home, feeling sort of stupid for waiting. I put her clothes in a paper bag with her other possessions (another set of clothes, a toothbrush of Yigal's) and set them by the door. I mean, I dug around for a while, but that's all I could find. I thought, This can't be all she has, there must be more. I cried a few tears, thinking of the lonely and vulnerable seal-girl adrift in a hot, dry world, then let her in the door around seven P.M. She was glowing with the exercise, fanning herself with a newspaper.

"I am so glad to see you!" I cried, hugging her closely, her damp bra leaving two spots on my shirt. "What was it like?"

"Well, it's true what they say, it's huge. It's completely black, metal. I went all around it, every side and the bottom, and there's not a mark on it, except, well, except something I'm not sure I should say—you know how dolphins are supposed to be really smart?"

"Sure."

"Well, they aren't so smart—I mean, they have a language and everything, they read and write, but that isn't what makes a person smart. I know you're a Dolphin Star priestess and everything, so I feel really bad about telling you this . . ."

"What? Wouldn't you rather I know the truth?"

"Well, you know the way the whole human race thinks dolphins are totally wise and, like, cosmic? And the seals sort of like it that way, it keeps you guys off our backs. So I'm not sure—do you promise not to tell?"

I nodded. "Yes."

"I hate dolphins." She sighed. "It was covered with personal ads. Really gross, explicit ones, the kind where they get really specific about who's going to put what where and how many—"

"Gross," I said. "You mean they were printed ads, or just written on there, or what?"

"Graffiti," she said. "Mostly. It's a new medium—ships with that antibiotic paint haven't been around that long. It's bringing the oceans closer together I guess, and everybody says it's a good thing, but nobody knows where it's going to lead. If this is any evidence—ick. It's so typical of those stupid dolphins to spoil everything. I need coffee." She started for the kitchen.

"Mary," I said. "So if dolphins are so bad, then what's really the wisest animal in the sea? Is it seals?"

"Starfish," she said without hesitation.

"Seals eat starfish," I objected.

"We do not! We venerate starfish!" She shook her head so that her wet hair slapped against the wall. "Starfish are wise. Starfish are gentle. We only eat fish and birds, though I personally never eat birds. No seal would ever, ever, ever eat a starfish." She emphasized each of the last few words by stomping her foot.

"I guess I was thinking of sea otters."

"Nobody eats starfish."

"But, Mary, it's true. Now I remember, the sea otters fold them up so all the sticky suckers are on the inside, and then they eat it like a Popsicle."

"That's it," she said. "You are not a nice person." She glanced into the bag with her clothes, grabbed it, and left. A minute later I heard the door of Yigal's apartment slam, and that's the last I saw of Mary until four days later.

This next scene actually took place in Yigal's bed, but I am informed by Shats that the vast majority of scenes in Israeli fiction take place in cemeteries, so we'll say instead that Yigal and Mary were holding hands as they walked on noisy gravel past the blazing white stones and skinny cypresses of the old cemetery on the south side of Tel Aviv. They rested for a moment in the shade under an aluminum canopy, and he fetched her a cup of water. Several aisles away a funeral was going on. The naked body of a middle-aged woman, wrapped in a sheet, was slowly vanishing under half a ton of sand. Yigal lay on his back, watching a reflection on the ceiling. Mary drank with her head on a pillow, dribbling water down her chin. He turned toward her and asked, "How did you get here, anyway? Swim?"

"No, I flew. On an airplane."

"What sort of passport?"

"Canadian."

"How'd you get that?"

"I bought it."

"What do you do for a living?"

"Nothing."

"So where do you get all this money?"

"You promise you won't tell? Don't be mad."

He kissed her fingertips and so on as though he had no intention of telling or being mad, but actually he was thinking about whores, gambling, and cocaine, and hoping her career involved gambling. Credit-card fraud was another acceptable alternative; arms dealing was something he was used to, spying a possibility, though he didn't think she was a spy any more than she was a silkie from the Shetland Islands . . .

"Well, it's like this, you know how silkies are sort of magical, and when you're sort of magical, there are things you can do?"

"Cut to the chase."

"Well, if I think really hard about money, I find it in my pocket. Most silkies just live off guys, but I don't think that's fair. To the guys, I mean, but also I think it's degrading to be always asking guys for money."

"So you find it in your pocket. Which pocket?"

"Usually my pants. The back pocket, here." She patted her butt.

"I understand." Yigal nodded. "I get money by mailing it to myself."

"Cool!" She seemed impressed.

"No, seriously, you think about it and it's there?"

"Sure. Like, right now, I am thinking about a hundred shekels for groceries."

"Why don't you think about fifty thousand shekels and buy a car?"

"Can you drive?"

"Sure."

She got up and went over to her pants. "Here. Wait, I don't think this is fifty thousand. Maybe fifty thousand won't fit in my pocket."

"You're right," Yigal said, counting the money. "This is only ninety-four hundred." He threw it to the floor and took her in his arms. "Skip the pants. Go for a million shekels in the laundry hamper."

Yigal was not a *freier,* so that after he lost hope of getting a straight answer out of this mysterious woman whom he liked so very much regardless, he just changed the subject, and not being a *freier,* he didn't immediately go and look in the laundry hamper either. He waited until the next time she was in the bathroom. He stuffed it back in without counting it.

After a decent interval (I think it took him two days), Yigal said: "Please marry me. I really hate my job." They had gotten out of bed and gone downstairs to Café Tolaat Sfarim.

"Of course," Mary replied. "If I didn't want to marry you, I never would have told you about any of it. I know you really love me. Otherwise you would just ask me for like a billion dollars and hit the road."

When I told Zohar about it, he said, "Tell that girl I need forty thousand dollars to buy a big white Lincoln Town Car." His voice was thick and slurred. "I'm cold. Where did you say those camel people are?" He was still seventy miles shy of the Nepalese border. "You tell that girl, tell that girl I need forty thousand dollars, buy me a Hummer. Baby, do you have a sweater I can borrow?"

"Hold on, Zohar," I said. "I'm coming to save you."

"Don't do that. It's only seventy more miles. Get there by to-morrow. Wish me luck, baby, I'm gonna need it. Got a glacier in the way. Ouch."

"What's wrong?"

"Hangnail . . ."

I waited a minute and finally said, "Don't keep me on the line while you play with it. Satellite phone time is expensive." We exchanged vows of love and hung up, but I was starting to worry. It occurred to me that getting Zohar home from Bhutan in time to teach the fall semester might be more complicated than anyone had thought.

CHAPTER 9

I WAS SLOW IN FALLING ASLEEP LAST night and awoke at six, unable to shake the uneasy feeling that I had somehow involved myself in something unutterably sordid, and that I was surrounded by death. I'm pretty sure this happened because Zohar rented *Taxi Driver*. The same thing happened a month ago when I saw a VH1 documentary about Studio 54.

At 7:30 I crawled from the bed to the computer and found an especially dense and challenging message from Shats. The ostensible subject was the old port of Tel Aviv, more of a marina, really, it turns out: The port could never handle ships, they would anchor at some distance, and boats would come and go, loading and unloading passengers and cargo. He portrayed the people of Tel Aviv standing by the quay and singing as Zim Ship No. 1, *Kedmah*, lured their flimsy dinghies to certain death in the pounding surf, July 1947.

My mother had this to say: Frank called last night. They dropped a seventy-million-dollar crane over the edge in some deep trench, so they are back in Mobile being repaired.

My brother Frank, a ship engineer, lives in Seattle and works on a very large boat out of New Orleans. The boat, a gigantic coracle approximately four miles in circumference, carries immense towers of steel to the center of the Gulf of Mexico, where, wiggling and heaving, it drops them into trenches, then pops four hundred feet into the air, relieved to be rid of the extra weight. Workers such as my brother grip their coffee cups tightly in preparation for a bounding, vertiginous return to New Orleans by hydrofoil. Even the work schedule is larger than life: Rather than time their work by the sun as other workers do, they work by the moon, "twenty-eight days on and twenty-eight days off." Already in the four hundredth hour of a shift, the workers are bleary-eyed, rigid automatons, hardly aware whether their coracle is moving as scheduled toward the meteor-craters of the Yucatán or merely spinning in circles. Has the seventy-million-dollar crane broken loose, or was it cut loose this morning, in response to orders no worker can be sure he did not hear in a dream?

Such a ship could not dock in Tel Aviv, any more than Mr. Pickwick could sail up the Yarqon. Only a few wooden rowboats come and go, rocking in the shadow of a single heroic statue—*The Hebrew Worker*. A magazine shop lends an air of commerce to the scene. Other ports, in Haifa and Ashdod to the north and south, are made to submit to the indignity of a more than symbolic function.

Yigal did not go down to the port. Instead, he went to his office. A brief euphoria after his engagement to Mary had surrendered to the realization that he could not quit his job. Most especially, he could not quit his job and then appear to be living very well without it. His assignment was frustrating, even impossible, but it was the only thing standing between him and certain death.

"Laos and Iceland?" Rafi said. "Take a look at this report about the carousel in Central Park."

Yigal scanned it. "This one's two years old. I'm telling you, he's not in New York."

"You're right, he's not—he's at Rye Playland, since April. I'd like you to talk to him. That's not much to ask, is it? Just talk to the guy. And be careful. How are you fixed for money?"

"Not too bad, but I could use a little extra this month— some nuclear missile landed in my office, so I'm thinking of upgrading my hard drive, plus I need to buy some paint. Also, my fiancée wants a car."

Rafi handed him $5,000. "You're not cutting down on your travel, are you? Because if you are, you won't be working in this office. You'll be in purchasing in Holon. Medical supplies for the veterans' hospital. Have you considered changing apartments?"

"I like my apartment." Yigal shrugged, his boss shrugged, and the meeting was over. As he walked home, he formulated a list of questions.

1. What's in the submarine?
2. What is Rye Playland?
3. Will another missile fall into my apartment, or is my apartment the safest place in Israel?

When he arrived back at Basel Street, he came straight to my place, and I got out the tarot cards.

"This is a sort of cute tarot," I said. "It's all these smiling, happy dolphins—look—"

"Even the hanged man?"

"That's actually a very positive card," I said, handing him the deck to shuffle. "That's why he's leaping and splashing that way. It means change."

"Dolphins don't have necks." He gave me the first card.

"Eight of urchins—eight of urchins—let me get my book." I struggled out of the lotus position and grabbed the Dolphin Star handbook. "Hmm. This is interesting. It's actually a little essay about the biology of dolphins. I hate it when they do this—it's how they cover their asses, like if they actually said what was going to happen in the future and got it wrong, I'd sue them or something." I handed him the book.

"Unlike seals, who feel love every day of the year but conceive their pups only in the fall, dolphins have insatiable sexual appetites year-round." Yigal took off his glasses and rubbed his eyes. "Whatever," he said, handing the book back. "Next card." He pulled the lobster.

"The lobster means safety."

He nodded and pulled the three of barnacles, symbolized by a pack of young male dolphins abducting a female from her pod.

"Travel. Give me three more cards and lay them out in a row." He withdrew the seahorse, coral, and the ten of shrimp.

The book was explicit. "Ten of shrimp after the seahorse means a ride on the Derby Racers. 'The Derby Racers,'" I read aloud, "'is a monumental revolving, domed structure located on the grounds of Rye Playland in Rye, New York. Unlike a conventional carousel whose figures move up and down, the Derby Racers figures move forward and backward. The vast, deep rumbling sound created by the revolution, on wooden rails, of this large building more than one hundred years old is the most impressive achievement of Western civilization, the first and last wonder of the world.' Coral—that's just sex, pure and simple. I don't know how that fits in. This is interesting." I tried to read further but Yigal took the book away.

"Nell, there's a card called 'Leviathan' symbolized by a big black blob waving a trident." He looked upset.

"I didn't write the book. Are you saying the Dolphin Star Temple had something to do with it? Because if you are, forget it. That thing went right through my coffee table." I took the book and put it back on the shelf.

"One more card?" He held up the four of shrimp.

"Four of shrimp is ambiguous. It means either mechanical difficulties—could be the plumbing, could be bursitis—or an explosion and fire." Yigal shook my hand and left.

I realize now that my free-floating anxiety might stem partly from having written so much dialogue yesterday and today. I'm not good at it, and I don't claim to have an ear for colloquial speech. Writing dialogue is an unnecessary risk and an inefficient way of telling a story. (All my best stories are in one paragraph, with no dialogue at all. The only exception is in the story about the anaconda, when he says in a plaintive manner while dying bankrupt in the prison hospital of self-imposed starvation: "I can't eat small things, and I can't eat dead things—without money there's just no place for me in this world.")

But if efficiency were my goal, would I be devoting a month of my priceless youth, which can never be regained, to the re-creation of a novel already written? For four long years Shats labored to make straight in the desert a highway for this second version of *Sailing Toward the Sunset,* stealing time from work and family to create an entirely original literary masterpiece. In order to follow in his still-warm footsteps, I quit my last full-time job in 1995 and haven't worked a day in the last fourteen months. Were I efficient in any way, I would have re-created Shats' book of short stories, his reviews and feuilletons, his diary and letters, and his bank statements by now. Ashamed of my indolence, I will pass to another topic.

When I first began work almost two weeks ago, I made extensive notes regarding the topics to be covered. Now I find that two have been omitted completely. They are:

1. The Hart Senate Office Building
2. Poe's "Tamerlane"

Outside the Hart Senate Office Building in Washington, D.C., is a long brick sidewalk, where I often walk on my way from Union Station to my friend David's office. Washington is a beautiful and peaceful city, most especially in springtime and in this particular section, Capitol Hill. The humid air telescopes the long view down the Mall toward the Lincoln Memorial and the row of reflecting pools into a single wide-angle panoramic painting. In May thousands of tulips in red and orange engulf the Capitol itself, but in April the predominating color is the pale green of new grass brushed with the delicate frosty pink of apple and cherry blossoms, those still on the trees, and those that drift from the trees into soft, feathery heaps, covering lawns and filling gutters with pale petals that keep for weeks in the cool shade of the oaks and tulip poplars. I wander through the drifts of flower snow, throwing soft handfuls upward and letting them fall until they cover me, and occasionally lying down in them, at which point I probably look like a complete idiot, and it's no wonder I'm unemployed.

Anyhow, outside the Hart Senate Office Building is a big parking lot, and between this parking lot and the building is a strip of plants a block long, so beautiful and diverse that I suppose it must have been designed to represent the fifty states and must be subsidized by all fifty. No one ever looks at it but me. It sits in an ugly spot where no one ever goes who is not in a hurry. Besides, in Washington, D.C., such things are ordinary.

Inside the building is a strange sculpture. A black mountain range sits on the white granite floor, jagged peaks upward. The heavy black plates of steel are at least twenty feet tall. From the ceiling hang the clouds—the same heavy black plates of steel, but rounded. The clouds twirl slowly and threateningly. No one walks on the floor anywhere near the sculpture, which sits in the center of the lobby out of the way, but senators who go from one office to another must look out and see it. The building was the first ever to have an open but fireproof atrium. Were fire to break out, water would pour from the edge of each balcony in a solid sheet, creating a temporary wall. The sculpture would sit in a choppy sea of dirty water thick with shredded paper and blue-green carpet lint while the impotent flames raged on in the offices, trapped behind an artificial Niagara.

Poe's "Tamerlane" is a long poem, but I used to know it by heart. Tempted by Ambition, the shepherd Tamerlane hopes to make his girlfriend a great queen. His empire complete, he returns home to find her dead.

I have no words, alas! to tell
The loveliness of loving well!
Nor would I now attempt to trace
The more than beauty of a face
Whose lineaments, upon my mind,
Are—shadows on th' unstable wind:
Thus I remember having dwelt
Some page of early lore upon,

With loitering eye, till I have felt
The letters—with their meaning—melt
To fantasies—with none.

In despair, Tamerlane compares his wasted youth to the sun, and his maturity to the moon, less harsh, beautiful, but cold. He protests,

And boyhood is a summer sun
Whose waning is the dreariest one—
For all we live to know is known,
And all we seek to keep hath flown—
Let life, then, as the day-flower, fall
With the noon-day beauty—which is all.

I used to carry this very small book (Poe didn't write much poetry) everywhere with me when I worked in offices. Memorizing it was an accident. I discovered that I almost knew it already, so I just worked on the gaps. Then I stopped carrying the book. Reciting it to yourself from start to finish takes a good ten minutes. All I seek to keep hath flown, I thought every Friday as I deposited my large paycheck.

Later, when things got worse, I thought more of "The Raven"—"Is there—*is* there balm in Gilead?" Gilead probably isn't far from here, come to think of it—it's probably a stoplight with a falafel stand, like Armageddon.

Back downstairs, Yigal asked Mary if she'd like to help him set up the model railroad. She spliced all the track and he hooked up the signals and the whistle. They darkened the room and watched the engine, whose heavy flywheel made its starts and stops gradual, dramatic, and forceful like those of a real train, circle behind the mountains over and over, first one way and then the other. The engine had a real Mars headlight, and there were lights in the passenger cars, where tiny hand-painted passengers sat diffidently looking out at the warm evening. Mary and Yigal lay on the floor and watched it from eye level. The next day, they left for New York.

CHAPTER 10

"ISN'T IT STRANGE HOW AVNER'S book resembles our story exactly, although it was written long before?"

It was 8:30 this morning when Zohar turned to me and posed this question, his curly hair disheveled by friction with our irregular nest of cheap, lumpy pillows and his sweet smile framed by a bulwark of ferociously masculine stubble. His appearance was charming in the extreme and I thought of taking off my shirt, but instead I asked him what on earth he was talking about.

"It's just the same. A spy is sent on a stupid mission to a foreign country and brings back a girl."

I had not been aware that Zohar was a spy.

"Who do you spy for," I asked him, "Elite?" Elite is Israel's leading chocolate producer. I surmised that Zohar's work had involved monitoring competing products worldwide, and that the "stupidity" of his mission had something to do with the quality of American chocolate.

Refusing to name his employer, Zohar assured me that when the narrative of Shats' *Sailing Toward the Sunset* begins, the Israeli spy has already persuaded the girl from the Shetland

Islands to live with him on a permanent basis. They arrive in Israel ready to settle down in chapter one.

Briefly, I considered starting over, but then I realized that the addition of a lifelong commitment to the story of Yigal and Mary would not alter it in the least. Mary's reluctance to be fully comprehended, Yigal's continuing fantasies about Nofar, his panicked flight, the sublimation of their cognitive dissonance into marathon sexual activity, the rationalization of a mindless Dionysian compulsion as an economic partnership—these are well-known aspects of lifelong commitment, and my treatment of them as aspects of a shallow and probably doomed flirtation does not affect their fundamental nature.

Therefore, on the arrival of Yigal and Mary in New York, I will send them almost immediately to city hall, where they will be married in a ceremony lasting several minutes.

An Israeli marriage was practically impossible. Only religious weddings can be performed there, Mary was not a Jew, and Yigal's low profile did not permit large bribes.

Seal marriage may have played an important role in shaping Mary's conceptions of the institution, but she did not mention to Yigal that her usual routine was to submit for two weeks a year to whoever seemed largest. It was dissatisfaction with the seal system, after all, that had led her to seek a better life on land.

Shats and his wife, Orly, and daughter, Ayelet, visited us last night. We walked on the beach near the Roman city of Apollonia, where Orly spoke of geology, of embryology, and of the aurora borealis—in Hebrew, the "Northern Zohar." Shats described the brightly glowing lagoons of the Sinai. Later, he told us how some anthropologists had once decided that mankind descended from an "aquatic ape."

I had heard something to that effect myself. Why else would we be smooth and hairless as eels? Why else would we have breasts at the top instead of at the bottom, if not to keep our children from drowning as we wade in search of marsh-mallows and cranberries? Our abundance of subcutaneous fat helps insulate us against the chilly waters of the Eocene swamps, while the unique human confusion of the esophagus and trachea, which allows us both to speak and to choke on food, has an important function of some kind—a function of . . .

There was a moment of silence. Shats tried hard but, like me, he could not remember the underwater function of the human larynx. We looked searchingly into each other's eyes, struggling to find there some insight into the trivial, absurd breathing habits of our damp, naked, nonexistent ancestors (biologists had heaped ridicule on the theory), and it was perhaps this tender moment of shared regret, stolen in the aftermath of a dinner party for which I cannot quite claim success (people seemed to be poking at the food as though they thought it was weird), that led Zohar, at approximately 8:40 this morning, to say, "Avner is in love with you!" (He had tried "You are in love with Avner" on several previous occasions to no avail.)

"Give me one piece of evidence," I demanded.

Zohar was unable to think of any, and I concluded that his claim had the same origin as his occasional declarations that he is moving to the planet Mars to live there with the parakeets Pouf and Poufa—a sort of waking epilepsy, a random firing of disused neurons. On the other hand, his failure to justify the statement may well have originated in a quality Shats and I share—you might guess "discretion" or "asexuality," but I refer the reader instead to our lovingly maintained sense of personal innocence and forthrightness. Many less privileged people attempt this feint, but they forget that, unlike Shats and I, they are least innocent when they are most forthright.

It occurs to me that the elephant and the hyrax too have breasts at the top, but instead of hypothesizing that they used to walk upright, I will return to a question posed by Shats himself several chapters ago: "Is mankind descended from the seals?"

The obvious answer is "No," but his posing of the question reveals an interest in wrongheaded pseudoscience I feel I have unwittingly echoed, to good effect, in several chapters of the present re-creation of his novel. My own interest in quasi-plausible nonsense was fostered early, partly by *Smithsonian* magazine's regular features on, for example, the genetically engineered "rat-cow" and the probable appearance of the natives of Jupiter (dense, amoeboid), but mostly by my uncle Charlie. I recall his explaining to me in 1971 or so why dinosaurs are extinct: Although they had evolved to be birds, they could not overcome their fear of heights. His crowning achievement was the all-encompassing theory that immediately predated his conversion to Presbyterianism:

EVERYTHING IS THE SAME SIZE,
BUT SOME THINGS ARE FARTHER AWAY IN THE FIFTH
DIMENSION.

I remember standing on a college playing field and deducing that the world itself, which appears very large, must on this theory be very close to me in the fifth dimension—and it was. My explanation of the phenomenon "horizon" was truly refined, but I've forgotten it now.

Now it is noon, and Zohar has spent the morning catching

up on his reading of this, his second exposure to *Sailing Toward the Sunset*. His criticisms are invaluable:

"Is Yigal very fat?"

"No, why do you ask?"

"Because he can eat half a gallon of chocolate ice cream in a sitting."

I take a didactic tone. "Zohar, skinny people can eat lots of ice cream if they want. They just don't eat much else that day. It's not like the way you used to eat an ice cream, then lunch, then an ice cream, then another ice cream, then dinner, then ice cream . . ." He grows bored and leaves the room, returning in a moment to ask:

"What is your relation to Yigal?"

"I'm his upstairs neighbor."

"You didn't have an affair? Did he go to Switzerland before or after I went to Bhutan?"

"I don't know."

"Then how do you know what his penis looks like?"

The fictional Zohar was too busy to remember that he had left his wife to the tender mercies of an introverted, easily embarrassed professional assassin. Crouched in an ice cave only two hundred yards from their position, he waited for the Bhutanese border police to break camp. Days were wasting, and he knew the llama-trekkers would pass nearby only once. The guards were drunk day and night on hot yak's-milk liquor mixed with honey wine, but they slept standing up, leaning on their rifles. All around, the snow was stained with the blood of the lemmings and chinchillas which were their only food. Zohar's patience was wearing thin. Squatting in a tiny room made entirely of ice, too low for him to stand up and too narrow to lie down, he had whiled away five long days and nights pondering the intricacies of the *Great Fugue*, when suddenly he heard a whistling *ping*. A bullet had struck near the entrance of his hiding place, releasing a shower of ice crystals which stuck to his face, melted, and became uncomfortably wet. Zohar's tolerance was at an end, and he stepped from the cave, raised the GPS in the air, and yelled, "Mossad!" The border guards drew close in curiosity, their rifles raised. "Mossad!" Zohar repeated firmly. "Israel! Mossad!" Comprehension dawned, and the terrified Bhutanese dropped their guns and ran at top speed down the mountain. Correctly, Zohar had guessed that word of the Israeli secret service's recent descent into incompetence and chaos would not have reached the isolated puppet regimes of the Himalayas, but as he crossed the mountain pass he cried bitterly in shame at having drawn the guards' attention to his déclassé Middle Eastern origins. His only comfort was that he would—probably—never see them again. Looking to the sky, he sought in its vast reaches oblivion from the horror of what he had been driven to by excruciating necessity. Then, lowering his eyes to the sunny plain, he saw the line of llamas, their gay Peruvian halter-tassels whipping in the cold breeze. Zohar jogged down the rocky incline, dialing as he went. They turned their heads, smelling salt (his boots were still covered with salt) on the wind, and you can imagine the looks on the faces of the American advertising executives and lawyers, led by a temp administrative assistant in marketing, as Zohar's solitary figure advanced upon them from a near-vertical wall of ice, talking on the phone.

"That's great!" I told him. "Don't let them get away!"

He folded up the phone and introduced himself, and within moments he was allowed to join them. After weeks of walking across a frozen wasteland, Zohar was again walking across a frozen wasteland, but this time with big, hairy, decorated animals to keep him company. He called me again in a panic when he found out that the llama trek cost $250 per day, since his travel per diem is only $100. I reminded him how cheap the rest of his trip had been.

Yigal and Mary took their time exploring New York. Yigal had an especial interest in the G, L, and 7 trains and related maps in the public library. Mary was eager to spend hours looking carefully at Max Ernst's *Two Children Are Threatened by a Nightingale,* the quillwork on Native American slippers, and the Paracas Textile. They met every night in Chinatown for dinner. One day they went together to the Cloisters, and another day they walked over the Brooklyn and Manhattan Bridges. Finally, one morning, Yigal said it was time to catch Metro North to Rye.

They arrived at Rye Playland in separate cabs. Yigal walked slowly from arcade to arcade toward the Derby Racers, waiting until he saw Mary at a distance. Well rehearsed and armed with a pistol, she was to provide cover, but instead she was crying inconsolably not far from a Whack-A-Mole. Yigal ran up and put his arms around her. "My sweet," he said, kissing her face over and over, "what's wrong?"

"It's a polar bear game," she sobbed.

He looked up and read the label twice to be sure. "No, sweetheart, these aren't seals. They're moles. Look at their noses." He turned her again toward the sick, corrupt, and reprehensible game of murder and violence. "They have pointy little noses and big pink paws."

A child approached, seized the rubber mallet, and put a token in the slot. The moles descended, then emerged briefly and unpredictably, like seals at their breathing holes, but still they could not evade the quick, violent swats of the angry child, whose concentration created an atmosphere of

frightening stillness in the midst of the pounding and beep-
ing of the game. Yigal led Mary away. "They're moles," he said
again.

There was no one in line for the Derby Racers. Yigal and
Mary looked on in awe as the empty ride slowed heavily and
majestically, like a planet dying on its axis, then presented their
tickets and chose horses. As the building gathered speed, both
were conscious of steadily increasing ecstasy, of great power,
of the strength of art unfettered by commerce, of freedom
from the limitations of the body, of the flimsy nature of the
ephemeral structure around them, whose readiness for collapse seemed only to increase its splendor, and of its awesome
beauty. There were no mirrors, no painted figures—just the
race of the horses, their mouths foaming, and wooden railings,
and at the center a small man who, Yigal could see, was biting
his nails while chewing gum. This, Yigal knew, was the man
Rafi wanted.

Mary stayed on her horse for the next round while Yigal
made his move.

"*Lamerchakim mafligot hasfinot,*" he whispered.

"Rafi can suck my dick," the man replied. He shook the hair
out of his eyes. "I told that motherfucker several times there's
nothing left. What does he want, a DNA sample from every
man on earth?" He pushed his glasses up the bridge of his
nose and began digging around in a desk while Yigal fingered
the hypodermic in his pocket. "Hang on, let me show you . . ."
He took a medallion and a black-and-white photograph from
the drawer. "Take a look. This came off the last guy with any
connection to the case, and this is a picture of what he looks
like dead."

Yigal looked down with interest. "Wow, you're right. This
guy is so clearly dead. I never saw anything so sloppy in my

life. What's this thing again?" He looked more closely at the medallion.

"From the British Museum. Believed lost with the *Dakar,* now commonly known to be in a desk in Rye Playland."

"Can I have it?"

"Sure. Forwarding address?"

"No, thanks. Wow," Yigal said. "This is cool." He stepped back onto the revolving platform and found Mary. "Look, Mary, this is something really old."

Mary studied it. "It's strange. I know it's supposed to be a wheel, but from certain angles it looks sort of like a skull—what are you going to do with it?"

"It was stolen from the British Museum."

"Look at the other side—it's a seal and a woman's breasts. You should send it back to the British Museum and get them to say what it is."

"I have a better idea. Put it in your back pocket and pretend it's not there."

"Okay." She waited a moment, concentrating. "It's gone! Do you want to ride again?"

Actually, it wasn't gone at all. Mary had liked it and wanted to keep it. She thought Yigal was silly to throw it away.

CHAPTER 11

YIGAL'S REASONS FOR HIS ACTION

were as follows: The *Dakar*, purchased in 1968 in England by the Israeli navy, vanished without a trace on its maiden voyage. Mr. Pickwick seemed to be connected with both the Dolphin Star Temple in Mount Rainier, Maryland, and his apartment on Basel Street. An ancient relic of the House of David bore the image of a silkie.

This structure seemed to Yigal like a house of cards. If one element was removed or changed, the whole thing would fall, and then instead of having to understand the power relations of the disparate elements, he could extract the card he wanted and be done with it. The hypothesis Yigal wanted to test by depositing the medallion in the silkie ATM could be summarized in one word: monotheism. Are the House of David and cash advances to silkies handled by the same guy? A positive answer, Yigal thought, would be a real convenience.

Just a week before, Yigal, a logical positivist, would not have regarded the question as meaningful. Now, like Hamlet, he was somewhat more open-minded. Unfortunately, it did not occur to him that the medallion might be a mass-produced

popular item worn by silkies as a brief fad in the 1890s, with
no connection to the House of David at all, unless you include
its role as evidence that the last remaining heir, instead of
marrying a Jewish woman, had married someone about as
unlike a Jewish woman as a person can get, namely a silkie;
and that this closely guarded fact, which effectively put an
end to all hope of a Messiah, came out only at the woman's
death, when the medallion was found on a fish-gut string
around her neck. Her five grotesquely deformed children
had died in infancy, but their graves, under a row of lilac trees
in the Jewish cemetery in Fishguard, were empty. Had the
bodies been removed for religious reasons and reburied in
unmarked graves outside the walls? How did an Israeli sailor
come into possession of the medallion, and who ordered his
murder?

I'm not saying that's what happened, but it didn't occur to
Yigal, which shows that the luxury of married life was beginning to soften his intellect. Yigal was conscious that he might
be missing something very important and obvious, but he
couldn't imagine what.

I was having a busy week. Activity at the port was increasing,
mostly because of a phenomenon I could easily explain, but
didn't care to: a constant traffic of dolphins over, around, and
under Mr. Pickwick. This had brought out, in addition to the
religious and disco elements, every young mother in Tel Aviv.
An intimidating riot of strollers blocked access to the seawall,
on which toddlers were perched, their mothers holding their
waists and telling them, "Look! Look! Dolphins!" The dolphins leaped obligingly from wave to wave. Spinner dolphins,
common dolphins, spotted dolphins, bottlenose, a pair of
young minke whales—everyone was there, and the crowd was
getting thicker and thicker.

It reminded me of the practice Pierre Louÿs, in his turn-of-the-century soft-core freak-book *Aphrodite*, attributed to the ancient Greeks: Women, wearing whatever flattered them most, which in the case of hot post-adolescents meant nothing at all, would loiter near a certain Athenian wall on which men were in the habit of writing their own names, the names of women, and a price per woman. When a woman saw her name connected with a man and a price she could accept, she would stand under it for a while, waiting for him.

I always wondered what *Aphrodite* was doing in the Modern Library, usually a squeaky-clean repository of family classics. The heroine of *Aphrodite* was the most beautiful of the professional courtesans (strange how inoffensive that word sounds) and a nymphomaniac bisexual. Her beauty is darker, more full, more exotic than that of the Greeks— accordingly, it comes out after a bit that she is a "Hebrew." She mesmerizes men with her native love poetry, "My tummy is a baby goat," "My head is terrible like an army with banners," etc., which according to Louÿs leaves Greek erotic poetry in the dust. In the end she dies painfully, imprisoned for impersonating the goddess, but not before a sadistic Greek takes her portrait in marble in the throes of a love I will not discuss or describe. The book was a gift to me. I read it and forgot about it until, years later, I found it and threw it in the trash.

Many people think it is wrong to throw books in the trash. They think because they happen to love some books, they should love all the others too. Their relation to books, regardless of their content, is one of respectful stewardship buoyed by paranoia, and they would see my disposal of *Aphrodite* as a criminal combination of censorship and infanticide. These are the people who give all their worst books, which they would not read again, to charity. This is surely why much of my most disturbing childhood reading was done at Girl Scout camp, where I read *The View from Pompey's Head,* a long novel about the one-drop rule (the protagonist discovers that he is black), two years in a row and memorized a manual for seducing teenage boys—I remember how it said I should sit: left elbow on back of chair, right hand on left knee, left leg crossed over right leg to produce illusion of maximum thigh-plumpness.

It is a common practice in America today to write outraged, grief-stricken articles about library administration, on the lines of "Crouching by the back door like a demonic hungry hell-toad was an immense garbage dumpster filled with— can you imagine the horror—books!" They do not stop to imagine the tears of boredom in the dusty eyes of the bibliographers who are charged with determining, before each book is discarded, that it has never been read, has never been cited, was obsolete at publication, and will cost eighty dollars to deacidify.

How do people come to love books for their own sake?

My theory is that the process begins in early childhood. A child who is reading a book quickly becomes conscious that he has never been quieter, and has never appeared more intelligent. He need only look up for a moment to see that his parents are swimming in effulgent self-satisfaction and pride. Long before he can read himself, he finds that allowing himself to be read to makes his parents more docile, gentle, and patient. "Junior loves books more than anything," they proudly say as he chews on a corner of *Pat the Bunny* following a performance. Mentally, they see him surrounded by books—a lawyer, a professor. . . . In his teens he discovers that reading has the power to liberate him from other chores. "I can't do that now," he calls out from under a blanket, "I've got ten more pages." The parents see a lawyer, a professor. . . . They forget that he is reading one of the later, less coherent sequels to *Tarzan of the Apes*. Jane has been kidnapped again—will Tarzan arrive in time to save her from being used sexually? Who is most effective in a fair fight—apes, Bantu, or little tiny white people ten inches tall?

I read only the first twenty volumes. I kept them in a special pink box with a handle, like a lunch box. Every afternoon I practiced in the woods around our house. My goal, to climb from one tree to another without touching the ground, was quite limited and specific, but I never attained it. It was a mature white pine and hardwood forest where most trees had their first branches about thirty feet up.

Around this time, I was known to perform strange feats of strength in the president's physical fitness thing (I can't remember what it was called), some Nixonian program to toughen up the youth of America. Asked to hang by their hands with their chins over a bar, other little girls would drop after five seconds, but I stayed for a minute, until I was asked to let go by the teacher. I did something like seventy-five sit-ups, with my legs straight on the floor. My weak event was the six-hundred-yard walk/run, perhaps because Edgar Rice Burroughs had emphasized brute strength over aerobic fitness.

Mr. Pickwick remained motionless in the water. The authorities still denied its existence. It was almost forgotten in the general joy over the "gamboling" and "playing" of the toothed whales in all their variety, their constant comings and goings, their eager departures for assignations, and their hurried returns.

Last night (I assume the reader has no difficulty detecting shifts from fiction to nonfiction, but in case there is some confusion, an explanatory note: everything I write about Avner Shats and *Sailing Toward the Sunset* is 100 percent true) I went with Zohar to the Tel Aviv Museum of Art to hear a performance of avant-garde classical music. It turned out to cost sixty shekels, so during the first half I took a walk to Dizengoff Square to see the revolving multicolored fountain shoot flames while loudspeakers blared *Swan Lake*. Suspended on an aerial plaza over Dizengoff Street, the fountain, which bears an inscription to something like world peace, may be the least tasteful object in the world. I looked up at it, laughing and smiling, for several minutes and then returned to the concert hall, where the intermission was just starting. Zohar introduced me to a number of composers, novelists, poets, visual artists, and men who said they were all of the above or some lesser combination. I told each of the men that I was writing an English version of *Sailing Toward the Sunset* by Avner Shats, based not on the Hebrew original but on rumors and hearsay. Despite the supposed artistic sophistication of each of them, all became confused. None had heard of Shats' book. I am pleased to think that in the carapace of their dependence on mass media I was able to pry open a crack through which each was afforded a glimpse of Shats' work, despite the fact that it still has not been reviewed except by the radio personality who consigned it to the abyss.

CHAPTER 12

BEFORE I WROTE ABOUT ÖDÖN VON
Horváth's novel *Youth Without God,* I thought I should check
that it's available in English. I know it's available in French,
because the only mention I've ever seen of it was as *Jeunesse
sans dieu.* Von Horváth, an Austrian, was known for broadly
cynical and harsh socialist satires like the play *Faith, Hope, and
Charity* and the novel *The Eternal Philistine,* literary equivalents
of the caricatures of George Grosz.

Youth Without God (1937), his second-to-last work, is written
in rhythmic one-sentence paragraphs, like a poem, although
it is mostly about intrigue among little boys. The book concerns a teacher's conversion to resistance, prompted at first
by an aesthetic concern: the coldness of his students. They
test themselves dispassionately, seeking new experience for
its own sake, and they dismiss and satirize everything they
see. He knows that everything he does (camping trips, the
books he reads with them, the essays he assigns) is intended
to harden them for war, and he does his best to help them
prepare. But he winces a little, involuntarily, drawing the attention of "the Club," four boys who meet secretly to discuss
banned books. Club members must swear never to express

contempt in any form. After the teacher loses his job, his home, and his reputation, he begins to wish openly that he could find God. Finally an elderly baker tells him: "God is in our house. He lives with us because we never fight." God, the teacher realizes, is a real experience, but a delicate one, which even the mildest dishonesty or ridicule will scare away.

Von Horváth died in Paris in 1938. He was walking to his hotel from an appointment about the film rights to *Youth Without God* when a tree branch fell on his head.

Anyhow, I thought the fastest way to the English version of *Youth Without God* might be Amazon, for which I hear nothing but praise. When I entered the Amazon site (for the first time) and searched for the exact title, I received the following truly ingratiating response, worthy of the younger von Horváth:

CLOSE MATCHES FOR THIS SEARCH:

A Night Without Armor: Poems by Jewel Kilcher (hardcover)

Siblings Without Rivalry: How to Help Your Children Live Together so You Can Live Too by Adele Faber and Elaine Mazlish (paperback)

Don't Go to the Cosmetics Counter Without Me: An Eye-Opening Guide to Brand-Name Cosmetics by Paula Begoun with Bryan Barron (paperback)

Ancient Secret of the Fountain of Youth, Vol. 1 by Peter Kelder; foreword by Bernie S. Siegel (hardcover)

How to Survive Without a Salary: Learning How to Live the Conserver Lifestyle by Charles Long (paperback)

Without Remorse by Tom Clancy (mass market
paperback)

I'm not making that up—it said "close matches." Would it
really be so bad if somebody burned every copy in existence
of each of the books above? Don't they all sound like they
started life as articles in *Woman's Day*? I'm not trying to promote wasteful bonfires in public squares—the whole process
could easily be accomplished without publicity, as was the
suppression of *Youth Without God*. I favor the use of books to
generate electric power. Tel Aviv (this may come as a surprise
to my American readers) is bitterly cold in the winter—that is,
it rains every third day while the temperature hovers around
60, and no one has central heat. The net effect is like that
of the boarding school in *Jane Eyre*. *Without Remorse* could be
used to provide two minutes' complimentary energy to every
Israeli, which he could use to fill a hot water bottle and tuck
it under his shirt.

Mary naturally assumed that Tel Aviv would always be
toasty warm. The heat of the summer, which reminded her
of a potter's kiln, seemed unlikely to give way any time in the
foreseeable future, and no one had told her about the winter,
which, after all, is quickly over.

Her sealskin lay in a furrier's storage locker, like so many
other sealskins before, but she had not forgotten it. She had
a habit of putting it on now and then, unlike other silkies
who would abandon theirs for good, letting themselves blend
gradually with the mass of humanity. She liked keeping her
options open, and never burning bridges.

She was desperately curious to know the origins of the
strange medallion. The next morning she went to the Jewish
Museum, approached a curator, said, "Umm," turned, and

left the building. In the afternoon she walked slowly between long, dark display cases in the Met, hoping to see something similar. In the evening she sat in bed, absentmindedly switching channels, and the next day she went to the New York Public Library, where Yigal was spending all his time. She didn't see him (he was down in the maps division, and she was in general reference) and she strode up to someone and said, "Hi! I'm trying to figure out what this is." The librarian, who felt rather irritated after spending twenty minutes with a man in search of the very best pancake recipe, was pleased to speak with someone like Mary, who kept her distance and didn't smell funny. He led her to the huge black catalog books in deep recesses along the walls and asked, "Do you have some clue what you're looking for?"

"What do you think?" Mary said, handing him the medallion. "I heard it might be connected with the House of David, the Jewish kings, but to me it looks like a seal with breasts."

"Are there silkies in Wales? David is the patron saint of Wales."

"Silkies are Irish," she said. "But I guess they could get around, if they wanted. How did a Jewish king get to be patron saint of Wales?"

The librarian shook his head, reminding her that one question was enough, and started her ordering books on ancient coins. Two hours later, she had:

1. A depiction of a leopard that made it look like a seal
2. Ditto, depiction of a lion
3. Ditto, a camel
4. Ditto, a wildcat
5. Etc.

Wouldn't everything be simple, she wondered, if all of them were really intended as seals in the first place? The wheel was a symbol of Saint Catherine of Alexandria, but the breasts could signify the Roman virgin martyr Agatha. . . . She considered her options and ordered a book on Egypt. That night at seven she'd made up her mind: The medallion was fourth century Egyptian. It depicted, in a sad and clumsy way, Saint Catherine and a sphinx. In other words, it was extremely boring and disappointing.

Mary felt she should get rid of it before Yigal noticed she still had it. It was probably worth something to someone, and it seemed a shame to throw it in the trash, but she couldn't sell it, and besides, Yigal might expect her to be able to get it back on a moment's notice. So she did the only thing she could: She stopped by a post office, and she mailed it to me. Her letter was open and candid.

> This is something I want you to keep for me. I think it's Saint Catherine and a sphinx, but apparently Yigal thinks it has something to do with the heir to the Israeli throne. He gave it to me to send away, so now I'm sending it away.
>
> New York is great. Yigal spends a lot of time reading about the subway. We go to museums. We had sushi—yum!
>
> I can't wait to meet Zohar! I hope he gets back soon!

Zohar was sleeping peacefully under thick felt blankets at his last stop before Kathmandu. After a bath and a shave, he'd turned into the most popular member of the tour group. All of them—yuppies desperate for just a whiff of the old odor of culture and sophistication they remembered from college, driven to acquiring it in the crushingly efficient way natural to people with twelve days' annual leave—were in awe of Zohar. Here was a man who existed to analyze the piano works of Beethoven, whatever the price—a man who would endure any hardship, who never took a day off, who would never be finished, always driven, always unsatisfied, always moving on, a solitary cowboy on the high plains of the Beaux-Arts, who had arrived at insights too deep to be shared with dilettantes like them, which didn't keep them from hanging around to buy him drinks every night, just so they could hear him say things like "I hate all classical music." He was having a great time, except in the mornings. There is no Turkish coffee in Nepal. To the Americans he only said mournfully, "That's not coffee." Each of them, especially the single women, privately resolved to visit Israel in the near future.

CHAPTER 13

YIGAL'S AGNOSTICISM BEGAN WITH A
gift from his parents on his eighth birthday: *The Wind in the Willows*. God makes way for "The Piper at the Gates of Dawn," and as far as Yigal could tell, it was a big improvement.

He bought a copy for Mary at Scribner's across the street from the library. I admit it's a Rizzoli now, but for the purposes of this novel, it's still Scribner's. The book delighted her. "This is just like the ocean! Who is this guy?"

You can tell a lot about the author of *Wind in the Willows* by reading it, but Yigal hadn't given it much thought, so he said, "I don't know. The author."

"He must have lived in the ocean for a while. These characters are so much like people I used to know down there. This frog is just like a sea tiger."

"Sea tiger?" Yigal was imagining something large and furry with stripes, since a seal in Hebrew is a "sea dog."

"It's a sort of squishy green thing about a foot long, with spots. What I mean is, sea tigers are always trying to take advantage of people. Actually they eat them, but you know what I mean. They sting, but they're easy to avoid."

"Do they talk?"

"No, no. They have personalities, but they don't talk. Even rocks have personalities. They just sit there, and that's doing something. It's not at all like a bird that flies around, or seals playing."

"Who in the ocean do I remind you of?"

"You're like an albatross. You keep moving all the time, and you sleep on the sea." Yigal frowned. "I mean, you don't seem to like your apartment very much. You're always traveling."

"Trident missiles fall on my apartment." He took the book from her and leafed through it. "Do you want to go to England?"

"No, I want to go to Tel Aviv, where it's nice and hot."

Yigal closed the book and said, "I don't."

"But that's where you're from. It's your home."

"And? Doesn't it seem like I'd want to get away? What bird spends its life sitting on the nest where it hatched? You left the ocean."

"Only for a while. I'll go back, there's nothing more relaxing. Besides, I might have to. I think I'm pregnant."

Yigal jumped up, then sat down again. He was swaying a little, as though she had hit him on the head with a board. "What? Already? How did you manage that? Are you sure?" He dropped the book, and his face contorted in anguish. Then he remembered that he might have had something to do with it, and he knelt to stroke her tenderly. "Dear Mary, this is sudden, but I'm so happy and proud—"

"Why?" Mary asked. "It's just a pain in the neck. I've never been pregnant when I was human, but it's got to suck. I mean, walking around, carrying all that weight all by yourself. But I love you, so I won't go back to Shetland until the very end. Then I'll be gone for maybe eight months till I can get it weaned and swimming."

"There's something I don't understand," Yigal said. "You mean our child is a seal?"

Mary laughed, then looked very solemn as she said, "Yes, I imagine it will be a seal. They're always seals."

"Couldn't it be a silkie like you? It could be a seal and still look and act completely human." Yigal was starting to seem really upset, like maybe he was wishing he'd listened to all the things his mother had told him about really getting to know a girl for at least two years, and meeting all of her family. For the first time since the army, he wanted to talk to his mother, but he realized there was nothing he could say. She had always told him what would happen if he married a girl who wasn't Jewish—the shouting, the recriminations, eventually one day she'd call him "Dirty Jew!" and pack up and go back to her parents—or something like that. Also, he recalled, this non-Jewish girl would be too skinny and give no milk. His mother always gave him advice of questionable usefulness, but he imagined it must have been really great stuff to know in Russia in 1942.

"Nobody's born a silkie. Being a silkie is a—a sexual preference. If you develop a taste for human guys, well, then it can happen."

Yigal was actually crying.

Mary tried to cheer him up. "It might only take three or four years. Seal pups grow fast. I'll take her to a harbor with cafés, where she's sure to see lots of cute waiters and stevedores . . ."

"So in four years," Yigal sobbed, "I might get to see my fifteen-year-old daughter—what if it's a boy?"

"There are no boy silkies," Mary said. "At least not to speak of."

"So he'll be a seal. Why didn't you tell me this before?"

"You're kidding, right? How can you be mad at me? I told you everything!"

"Like hell you did!" Yigal grabbed a towel off the rack and stuffed it in his backpack. He was muttering obscenities to himself in Arabic. Mary turned on the TV. After he left, she curled up in a little ball and cried herself to sleep.

Zohar was talking to journalists in the bar of the Hilton in Kathmandu. "It was nothing," he said. "Don't forget, for the first two thousand miles I had a car."

They all sat scribbling in their notebooks. One asked, "What did you eat?"

"I depended on an Israeli invention, the world's most compact and nourishing food, nutritionally complete and aesthetically satisfying, color coded for mnemonic purposes—pink for breakfast, green for lunch, yellow for dinner—so that even in the utmost extremity of deprivation, the Israeli is able to eat regular meals. I am referring, of course, to the world-famous 'Kokos,' pioneered by our industry, if I am not mistaken, in the desert town of Be'er Sheva in 1961."

"Can you show us what you mean?"

Zohar pulled a pink Kokos from his pocket.

"Breakfast," a journalist said, nodding.

"Yes, it was just about breakfast time when I saw the llama caravan pause at a glacial stream eight thousand feet below me on the icy steppe."

"Ooh," the journalists said in unison. Zohar took out an Israeli Swiss army knife, made in China, with the awl and can opener broken off, and cut the Kokos into six pieces.

"Astounding," a journalist said, chewing thoughtfully. "Do you like pancakes?"

"Yes," Zohar replied.

"That's great, great," said the journalist. "Our readers really go for a guy who likes pancakes."

"Although I am known chiefly for my prose-poetry, my first loves have always been those of the common people, such as your readers: pancakes, olive oil, Peter Handke, Krembo, Raymond Carver, Tetris—are you getting this down?"

"You're going a little fast. Who's Krembo?"

Zohar realized he was losing their attention and said, "It's a sort of pancake."

"Great, great," the journalists responded. "Another bourbon? How'd you get out of Bhutan? Mr. Eitan? Where'd he go?" Suddenly, Zohar was nowhere to be found. Even the last slice of Kokos had vanished. Zohar was seated comfortably in a taxicab, on his way to the airport for a flight to Bangkok.

Then I had a sudden insight: What if Shats' *Sailing Toward the Sunset* employs less complex, easier Hebrew in the middles and ends of chapters than at their beginnings? Most authors start writing in a high, dense literary style and slack off gradually—why not Shats?

I opened his book at random and was instantly rewarded with a perfectly comprehensible passage about some guy named Taylor, who is hitting on some girl. "You could take off your clothes and sit on my lap," he suggests to her, in his mind, before beginning to speak. The Hebrew is alarmingly straightforward, and I can put no other interpretation on it.

The guy named Taylor was standing behind Mary in line at a liquor store on Madison Avenue the next morning around eleven. He was an up-and-coming toothpaste executive in a blue suit and a yellow tie. She turned around and looked hard at what he was buying. "Why so much rum?" she finally asked.

"It's this stupid office party we have every year for the interns—the Equinox Luau."

"Wow, that's dumb." She looked down at the bottle of champagne in her hand. "I don't know why I'm buying this. I'm pregnant." She set it on a corner of the counter and put the twenty-dollar bill back in her pocket.

Taylor, who had been in the middle of thinking, "You could take off your clothes and sit on my lap—" but had suddenly stopped, said, "They have milk too, in the back." Mary fetched a carton of milk and stood in line behind him. "Go ahead, I'm not in a hurry. I have the whole afternoon off to get ready for this stupid party."

"What else do you have to do?"

"This is it."

"Want some help? My husband just abandoned me in a cheap hotel and I'm feeling sort of lonely. I couldn't get a flight back to Israel before the day after tomorrow."

"Do you know where he went?"

She shook her head. "England, maybe? Or he might be riding back and forth on the L train, or the 7, or maybe the G." She set down the milk and wiped her eyes on her sleeve. "It's so sad."

Taylor paid for her milk, picked up his case of rum and stepped outside to hail a cab. "Listen," he said, "I've got to go, but I wish you the best of luck. My advice is, you go back to the hotel and wait for him. I'm sure he'll turn up. Taxi!" He turned toward the street.

"My husband leaves me alone and pregnant in a strange city, and you think you can make it all right by spotting me $1.49?"

He was embarrassed, and lowered his voice. "That's not

exactly what I was thinking. But now that you point it out, I guess that's what I did. Would you rather pay me for the milk?"

Mary opened the milk and poured it into the gutter. White and slightly viscous, it gathered particles of soot and gravel and a green note of antifreeze as it flowed to a crack in the cement and out of sight.

Taylor watched it in silence. He was not actually an insensitive guy. "Sorry," he muttered. "Do you have money for food and the hotel until your flight?"

"I have plenty of money. I was just lonely . . ."

Taylor, who like all sensitive guys was made terribly uncomfortable by pathos, put his hand in his pocket and fiddled with his organizer.

"How would I look with lighter hair?" she asked suddenly. "I mean, like ash blond?" Raising her eyes from the milk, she had noticed a salon on the other side of the street.

He was taken by surprise. "Terrific," he said. "I mean it." He was relieved to be able to give her something she wanted, even if it was a trivial compliment about a hair color she didn't have. When he got into his cab, they both were smiling. He really felt much better, and took a card from his inside pocket. "Listen, if you do your hair, call me, I'd like to see it. I'll buy you lunch."

CHAPTER 14

SHATS APPEARED SHAKEN BY RECENT
events. He wrote:

> While reading chapter ten, specifically the parts
> describing our visit and aftermath, I decided it would
> be safer to regard everything in *Sailing Toward the
> Sunset* by Nell Zink as pure fiction, a novel with stories
> about fictional people, who may or may not resemble
> real people I know. However, your assertion in chapter
> eleven, "I assume the reader has no difficulty detecting
> shifts from fiction to nonfiction, but in case there is
> some confusion, an explanatory note: everything I write
> about Avner Shats and *Sailing Toward the Sunset* is 100
> percent true," undermined my comfortable position. I
> will maintain this pretense, however, for the time being
> at least.

He then refers to a list of literary figures provided in the
original *Sailing Toward the Sunset*. Half are fictional, and one
is the poet Zohar Eitan. But, he adds, Zohar might as well be
fictional, since no one has heard of him. With this insight, I
think Shats hits the nail on the head.

In a sense, I am a fictional literary figure already—the novelist Nell Zink. This novelist will come into real existence for most people the day *Sailing Toward the Sunset* appears in a shop with cardboard around it, and will cease to exist the day it is remaindered.

The fictional Avner Shats is not a character in either version of *Sailing Toward the Sunset*. A former scuba commando, Shats published his first story, "Gill-Slit Neoteny: Challenge for Genetic Engineers or Invitation to Hubris?" in the *Congressional Register*, July 14, 1981. Following a prison term for piracy, he spent six years in Liberia assisting General Butt Naked (now the evangelist Milton Blahyi) in his effort to satisfy Satan's appetite for human blood. After Naked's conversion to Christianity, Shats returned to Israel, attaining a master's degree in literature from the Hebrew University in 1996. He now lives with his wife, Ronit, and eleven children on Moshav Modi'in. He has published four novels, *Race for the Bottom, The Manganese-Nodule Murders, Belly-Up!,* and *The Shark Inside Me,* and the 1997 collection *Tentacles,* whose title story won the PT-109 Award of the Naval Institute for best nautical adventure under one hundred tons.

Furthermore, to my dismay, the lucid, readable Hebrew I mined so proudly from the interior of *Sailing Toward the Sunset* was not in fact the work of Shats, but of David Pupco, his collaborator in drafting a political thriller.

Bemused by my mistake, Shats writes, [Taylor's] wife left him . . . for consuming South African pineapples, thus breaching political correctness codes (it was in the eighties). That was my addition. She also refused to blow him (Pupco's). He really is sensitive, I guess. I think in the original plot he was killed, but I didn't include it: I just used him for the obligatory porno part every thriller must have.

The next day at noon Mary, with noticeably lighter hair, in a ponytail to keep it from being too distracting, sat opposite Taylor in a dark niche in Little Italy. She looked dandy, and they were both glad that Taylor had been right.

"So you think you look too good for him now?" Taylor asked, twirling a carnation from the vase on the table and leaning on his elbow.

"He's had better-looking girls than me before. You should see this girl who's in love with him now, Osnat—she's like Cindy Crawford."

"What's his secret? You said he's nothing special—I want to know how he attracts these girls."

"His job, I think. Or the self-confidence it gives him. Also, he doesn't have regular hours, or any hours at all really, and girls like that. Actually, except for a couple minutes last week, I don't think he's worked since I met him."

"What does he do?"

"He's a hit man. Why do you look angry? Isn't that a funny job for a nice guy like Yigal?"

Taylor leaned across the table and took her hands in his. He had drunk two glasses of Chianti. "Mary, please don't go back to him. I mean, don't fly to Israel tomorrow. I think maybe this is the luckiest thing that's happened to you since you met him. I don't think you, and your baby, should be following this criminal who's abandoned you. I think you're terrific. Way too good for him."

"You think so?" Mary asked.

"You say he kills people for a living."

"Well, he tries to avoid it. Nobody really knows who he's supposed to kill anyway, or if the guy even exists. It's a weird political thing. Maybe he never killed anybody in his life."

"How long have you known him?"

"About a month."

Taylor appeared to be doing math in his head. "And you're sure this is his baby? Is there someone else? You can tell me."

"There's nobody else. I love Yigal."

"Why don't you stay in New York, just for a while, and keep checking for messages at the hotel, and let me help you?" He took her hand again.

"Because Tel Aviv is so nice and warm. Hotel rooms have those little forced-air heaters that don't really work unless you turn them up so loud you can't think, and the bathtubs are gross."

Taylor turned his head away and looked at a picture of gondolas, then turned back and said, "You could stay with me for a little while. You can sleep in my office and turn up the heat as high as you want. I know this sounds dumb, but there's something so unique, so special and sort of childlike about you, and I hate to think of you running back to someone, just because you think you have nowhere to—"

"I know, I know," Mary said. "Don't get upset."

While Taylor was amazing himself by inviting a pregnant stranger, whose husband was a professional killer, to stay in his apartment—it made him feel almost as glamorous, he thought, as professional killers must feel—Yigal was sitting in a rented car in a state park in northern New Jersey taking hits off a bottle of Bacardi 151, and I was on my way to the port to watch the sunset. There was a lot of commotion down by the water, and I couldn't get close enough to see anything. I was pushing forward through the crowd when everyone suddenly turned and began running toward the road, crushing me against a wall so that my head got slammed twice and I scraped up my shoulder. I was bleeding from three places by the time the stampede thinned out enough to let me near the seawall. When I got there, whatever had happened was over.

I asked a religious guy what it was.

"Nobody knows," he said. "All I saw was something going up, like a rocket. It was black and white."

"Damn it," I said, but when I got home, nothing was out of place. I turned on the radio—nothing. I tried a religious station, and again there was nothing, no news. Then I went up to the roof to take down my laundry, and there I found the Trident warhead. It had bounced off the mattress Yigal and Zohar dragged up there in April, and landed in a barrel of rainwater.

I e-mailed Yigal right away.

Yigal—
Another attack, lucky this time, it's in a barrel on the roof. Please tell me what to do with it. Maybe you can keep it from happening again or you're going to be looking at a lawsuit from me and the condo association. Take good care of Mary.

Readers of political thrillers enjoy technical details, so I should point out that the submarine, Mr. Pickwick, was a unique futuristic prototype with no moving parts. It was made almost entirely of a gelatinous substance from which the missiles slipped like spoons from a bowl of cold consommé. The exterior was sheathed in a continuous ribbon of osmium sealed with caoutchouc and wooden dowels. Like the golem of Prague, it took its motive power from a name. However, in this case the name was not that of God, but of Moshe Dayan.

Yigal woke up before it was light and slipped out of the car to retch. Frightened, a doe and two bunnies crept back into the underbrush. They had wanted to give Yigal a message of universal love and hope, but in the end they were too timid.

He drove slowly out of the park to a Wawa store and drank a great big coffee. During the night, he had decided to volunteer for more hazardous duty, something with plague germs or Kurdish guerrillas, but after the coffee he sat in the car and looked at the rental company's map of New Jersey. Three hours later he was in Atlantic City, up $15 on blackjack. By nightfall he had won $80 and was buying drinks for a secretary from Red Bank. He spiked them with B vitamins, but she didn't notice. They talked about the weather and gambling until she asked if he was Italian.

"No, I'm Israeli."

"I'm Jewish too! Come over and meet my friends."

"I don't think being Jewish is the most important thing to have in common." Yigal finished his drink and signaled the bartender for another. "I think it's more important to be human."

"We're all human under the skin. What really matters is communication, and it's so easy to communicate with someone who shares your way of life and your traditions."

Yigal realized he was sliding off the barstool, so he stood on the floor.

"Are you okay?"

"Maybe I should go to bed," Yigal said. "I feel dizzy."

"How many drinks have you had?"

"None at all, compared to yesterday. It's my wife. She— forget it."

The secretary backed away one step and said, "Where is she now?"

"I don't know."

"You poor man!" She threw her arms around him. "You need some cheering up!"

"No," Yigal said firmly. "I need to be depressed. I need to find a deep hole, fill it with mud, and climb in headfirst."

"What a wet blanket."

"I need to lie under a fallen redwood in the Olympic rain forest, while banana slugs crawl all over me." Yigal was struggling with his wallet, trying to pay and leave.

She must have misunderstood, because she slapped him and said, "You son of a bitch." After a brief walk under escort, he found himself in front of the casino with the secretary and all her friends. His pistol had fallen out of his jacket and was lying there on the sidewalk. He picked it up and ran toward the parking garage.

Meanwhile, as Mary walked from the bathroom to Taylor's office past his open bedroom door, she glanced inside to say good night, and saw that he was lying on top of the bedspread, wearing striped pajamas. His fly snaps were open and he was gently petting himself. "Sorry," she said, closing the door.

"No, it's okay," Taylor called out. "Come in, I want to talk to you."

"What about?" She sat down on the bed.

"Oh, Mary," he said. "If you would just touch it."

"No, thanks."

"Or put your mouth on it." He reached out for the back of her neck, trying to incline her head in a certain general direction.

She stood up quickly. "What gave you that idea? If you try anything like that again, I'll leave and I won't come back. I ought to kick your ass."

He snapped up his pajamas and sat upright. "I'm sorry. I

thought it would be fun. You know, nothing ventured, nothing gained. I apologize."

"It was incredibly rude."

"I said I'm sorry."

She left him alone and closed the door. He lay there masturbating for a while, thinking about his wife. For eight years he had loved her, supported her, helped her get work (she illustrated gardening books and seed catalogs) and worked very hard to be as romantic as possible and to please her in bed. In his whole life, he had loved only her. She had left him very suddenly. She said it had something to do with South African produce, but he knew it was the fatigue, escalated by repetition into a sort of agony, of the scene with which he unfailingly managed to destroy their most intimate times together and both their egos: When they felt closest, when he really felt that they belonged to each other completely, he would always feel compelled to take advantage of the situation by asking her, very hesitantly, if by any chance she hadn't overcome her revulsion, which was so instantaneous and physical that Taylor couldn't help perceiving it as a sort of mortal insult to him, though he knew it wasn't intended as one, to oral sex. Every time he posed the question, it drove a wedge between them, which seemed all the greater because of the perfect closeness that had to arise before he would even dare to ask it. In the end she left him and moved in with her sister, saying she couldn't stand his hypocrisy.

Mary lay in the dark and thought about her husband. She wondered where he was.

Yigal happened to be lying on the floor of the rental car while police shone flashlights all around him. He was lucky to be drunk. It's more comfortable to be drunk if you have to lie across the hump in the floor of a Lumina and crush your ear against a bristly plastic carpet while noticing bits of dry mud in your mouth, especially when Atlantic City police with lead-weighted flashlights two feet long are after the illegal weapon that is still in your pocket. Yigal felt he had gotten his wish. At least, he hoped there was nowhere to go but up.

When he heard other cars starting and moving around, he slid to the front seat and looked in the mirror. There was some orange juice left in a bottle under the passenger seat, so he poured it over his hair and slicked it flat. He took off his jacket and his glasses. He pried open the inside cover of the car door, dropped in the gun, and snapped the cover shut. Then he drove slowly down the ramp and out of the garage, past the secretary from Red Bank, who was sitting in the front seat of a police car, talking to the policeman. He put on his glasses and was happy to be seeing details again, but instead of relief he felt only bitter scorn for the whole world. Idiots, he thought.

He stopped at a wayside in the Pine Barrens and pulled the car several hundred feet into the woods. The crackly pine-cones and the hard, sandy forest floor, the sort you can sweep clean with your hand until it feels smooth as fur, reminded him of the artificial forests in the Negev, except that in New Jersey the pines had grown all by themselves. He had read that by 1820, there wasn't a tree standing in America between the Appalachians and the sea. The soil was exhausted and everyone had to move west. If there were any justice, they would have returned to find a rocky desert ready to wear them out with backbreaking work, but instead they were awarded vast forests of loblolly pines. He was very quiet, imagining he could hear jackals. He lay down in the car, and while he slept he had a vivid dream.

He dreamed that Mary was begging outside the Port

Authority Bus Terminal. She looked at least six months pregnant and she pleaded with Yigal to return to her. As she spoke
she curled up smaller and smaller, until she looked like an
old woman or a crippled child. Yigal woke up grimacing and
remarked cynically to himself that the dream was an obvious
wish fulfillment and that he wished to punish her, but in the
dream he had picked her up on his outstretched hands like
a pillow, and taken her to a small, round swimming pool.
There, in the water, she relaxed and grew back to normal
size. The swimming pool looked familiar, and he realized
it was the one in the middle of Bosch's *The Garden of Earthly
Delights,* ringed with tall grass and filled with naked women.

Mary was in the cafeteria of the Whitney Museum, telling
Taylor her theory about *Runts of 61 Cygni C.*

"I see what you mean," Taylor said. "I guess I always secretly
wanted someone to be my runt."

"You mean your wife. You wanted your wife to be your runt."

Taylor looked ashamed, which was not surprising, consid-
ering the effort Mary was putting into making him feel bad.
Had he been less sensitive, he would have been delighted that
she was talking about sex at all, but he was sensitive enough
to know by now that he didn't have a snowball's chance in
hell. Two well-dressed, good-looking, bored, lonely, young,
idle, single curators were sitting at the next table, saying
things like "Neither of them has a wedding ring," and the-
orizing about Taylor's name; background; income; abdomi-
nal, lateral, and gluteal muscles; "package"; and apartment,
so it may have been unlucky for him that the first thing they
overheard clearly was Mary's saying, "You wanted your wife
to be your runt." Then they listened extra hard and heard
Taylor say:

"I still love her. I'd do anything to get her back." I think he was just trying out new ways to look better than Yigal, but the curators stubbed out their cigarettes and went back upstairs.

Mary said, "Then call her. You were unfaithful to her. It was indirect, because it was the make-believe runts, but you made her feel it, by bringing it up all the time—"

"You're right. I was horrible." He covered his face with his hands.

"Maybe she forgives you, now that she's seen what life is like without you."

"You're so sweet," Taylor said. "You seemed so vulnerable at first, but you're so strong."

This went on at length, but Taylor didn't seem to be making any progress, and after lunch they split up. Mary went back to his place to get warm. When he paused to remove a personal-ads tabloid from a box on the corner of Madison and Eight-ieth, thinking that he might want to experience oral sex at least once before he died, a taxi changing lanes while running a yellow light was nudged by a bus running the same yellow light while dodging a bicycle, and jumped the curb. He died instantly. Mary imagined that he had spent the night with his wife, and that she was responsible for their happiness, which was no less realistic than his imagining that she secretly longed to give him head. In the morning, she left him a congratula-tory note and checked into a better hotel.

CHAPTER 15

I REALIZE I HAVE BEEN NEGLECTING the great works of Western literature, so in the spirit of Yigal's remark, "Idiots," I will discourse on the subject of *Remembrance of Things Past*. Two facts about the work are well known: (1) the mature Marcel is thrown back into the past by the taste of muffins, and (2) the book contains secret references to Proust's homosexuality. For example, Albertine is really Albert.

Imagine my surprise, after passing the muffins around page 8, which apparently is as far as most people get, to discover that Albertine is a lesbian and that the volume titled *Cities of the Plain* (in French *Sodom and Gomorrah*) largely concerns the Baron de Charlus' relationship with his tailor. Marcel's first act when Albertine finally leaves him is to pay a tradesman for temporary use of his little daughter—is this, perhaps, a coded reference to pedophilia?

Still, I recommend *Remembrance of Things Past*. Marcel does not ask to be held to heroic standards, and there is nothing like the experience of reading a book that is truly long. Proust was a thorough psychologist, and I am sure he could have written a beautiful novel about Zohar's relationship with his portable radio. His boring dinner parties take as long to read as they might have lasted in real life, and characters mentioned briefly can reappear months later, in different contexts, displaying qualities unsuspected previously and continuing for hundreds of pages before vanishing forever. When, in the final volume, the vast array of social climbers meets to find themselves old and out of style, the effect is breathtakingly lifelike. His translator, C. K. Scott Moncrieff, maintains a lovely prose style throughout.

It is said that, to foster concentration, Proust sealed his windows with foil and refused to leave his bed. I have no such requirements. Having been raised to evade chores through reading, and helped by natural introversion, I am disturbed by noise above a certain threshold of volume and by little else. If I write while playing a CD, I do not hear it. I forget pots of rice, and the pitas I remove from the toaster oven sizzle as I drop them in the sink.

Significantly, it is the word "Nell!" which I find easiest of all not to hear. "Nell," in other words, is perceived on some level not as my name, but as something akin to the six-digit number my computer must send to the server at Tel Aviv University in order to enter and manipulate it.

When I was a child, I rushed to read *One Day in the Life of Ivan Denisovich,* impressed by the idea of a novel about the events of a single day. Unfortunately, unlike Proust, whose protagonist moves relentlessly forward after the muffins yank him violently into the past on page 2, Solzhenitsyn cheats. I.e., he allows Ivan to reminisce about other days.

I was much more impressed by *The Gulag Archipelago.* At times I envied the prisoners, who were given relative privacy and the chance to sleep eighteen hours a day. When one felt lonely, he would turn to his neighbor for a brief spell of chess or chemistry, then fall cheerfully back into a doze. Their transfer to the labor camp horrified me, and many years later, when I began to work for a living, I developed a mental game which permitted me to stay with jobs I should have quit on the first day: the Gulag Archipelago Test. Standing in a student cafeteria, sweating profusely into plastic gloves while a supervisor yelled, "Tighten up on that line! You girls better tighten up!" I would ask myself, "Is this as bad as building a railroad in Siberia in January with no shoes?" The answer was always no, and I would go on working hard until I was fired.

After reading Solzhenitsyn I would sneak out into the snow barefoot, just to see how long I could take it—generally, not long at all. With boots on, the process was more gradual and bearable. The numbness in my legs, moving upward by shades and turning into a dullness and blissful lethargy that affected my entire body, always tempted me to lie down and rest in the soft, inviting snow, but I kept in mind what my mother always said: "Never lie down in the snow." I would lie down for a few seconds, hurried and guilty, then jump up to run inside for hot cocoa.

Am I a masochist? I admit to an early habit of lying down in the sandy construction site near the cafeteria at the Girl Scout camp and pretending that I was in the middle of the Sahara, without water, unable to move, and soon to die; I still like indirect flights with long layovers, and last April, I resolved to tour the Great Sand Dunes National Monument in southern Colorado by flying into Kansas City. But even as a child, I was able to identify things I didn't like. I loathed 440-yard races, for example, and said frequently, "Running four-hundred-and-forty-yard races is an exercise in masochism." (I am sure I am quoting myself accurately—my family is the sort where people look at broken glass on the floor and say, "I would like to file a formal protest." Now all children talk that way, having learned it from TV situation comedy writers.) Sometimes instead of finishing the race I would throw myself to the ground, making sure to skin my knees badly for authenticity. In other words, I do not think my masochistic behavior was inspired by masochism, but by a desire for significance, and where is the significance in running faster than a few other rural Virginia high school girls? Significance came from emulating Solzhenitsyn, or the Count of Monte Cristo, or the sailors in the books my dad was always lending me, who endured weeks on rafts by catching seagulls and sucking them dry, or the one who survived two weeks' confinement to the bowsprit by carefully rationing a single pint of rum. A girl who plunges toward a cinder track, scarring her hands and covering her knees with blood just to avoid thirty seconds of asthma and the shame of coming in third, is worth six of a girl who plods obediently around the track in 1:15, in my view, now and, apparently, then.

Likewise, I believe that my actions with regard to the Great Sand Dune were governed, not by masochism, but by a creative urge. Direct flights and clean, comfortable hotels make for pleasant vacations, but drab stories. Trailers packed with living beef forced me off roads all over the vast reaches of the Great Plains. The Rockies loomed before me, frightening monoliths of black ice. Climbing the Great Sand Dune, I paused for ten or fifteen breaths after every step, as though I were on the last approach to Everest without oxygen.

I carried only water, a peanut butter sandwich, and Little Debbie apple turnovers. The ascent took nearly two hours and began with a punishing barefoot run across the glacial stream which encircles the dune, carrying sand from downwind back to windward, preserving the position of the main dune indefinitely. At the top, the wind was cold, the sand was unsteady, and I was met by an elderly couple with ski poles, but I didn't care, because what I had come for was the descent: 750 vertical feet of leaping and sliding through sand soft as puffy feathers, as if I were fifteen again (I used to leap down hills all the time), weightless and invulnerable.

Soon after, I was the only guest in the only hotel in still-frigid Pitkin, Colorado, where flocks of blackbirds sang pure, clear notes alternating with what seemed to be English, and a few days later, I was trapped in a snowdrift on a blind curve near the top of Monarch Pass. The masseur who rescued me laughed heartily when I said I regretted not driving over Red Mountain instead. "It's nothing but switchbacks," he said. "There's a big monument to the snowplow drivers who have died." I thanked him for saving my life. Only then began the true test of character: benign paroxysmal positional vertigo. (They call it "benign" when they don't think it started with a stroke.) After three thousand miles my eyeballs, grown used to the passing of scenery, now twitched uncontrollably from left to right at all times, and I was unable to walk. I could only drive. I hit the bottom somewhere east of Dodge City in an itchy bed in a thin-walled motel. The room was hot, and rolled like a daysailer in a nor'easter to the moans and erotic repartee of an ever-changing stream of whores.

For significance, offhand I would say it borrowed slightly more from *Lifepod* than from the Swedish movie about the North Pole expedition (I escaped alive). Missing was any trace of the Gulag Archipelago—my freedom was complete, almost too complete. Tales of imprisonment and slavery have faded from my inner life since I stopped attending school. Like most adults, I now embrace literature that celebrates futile journeys.

Accordingly, Mary set out the next morning to Brooklyn on the 7 train from Grand Central, then transferred to the G train.

The G moved slowly, wobbling and stopping at intervals, its flickering lights often failing completely. At first Mary only looked around at the weary faces of the people whose lives were spent on this forgotten train, which rolled shuttle-fashion from Brooklyn to Queens and back again, but after a while she thought, This can't be what Yigal comes here for, and she turned to look out the window. The tunnel walls crept by, opening here and there in a white niche for workmen to hide from the passing train, and every so often there was a glass-windowed office and a Christmas tree, gray as charcoal and draped with shreds of tinsel. She looked again at the other passengers, and then the lights went out. Outside, the walls had fallen away. Holding her hands around her eyes, she tried to let them adjust to the darkness, but they were too slow and the train heaved into motion again before she could see what was outside. She closed her eyes. The next time the train stopped, she was ready. They were in a mothballed station, sealed from above, with just the barest crack of daylight falling through a grating. The distant walls were very busy and irregular, as though something were piled against them, stacked up almost to the ceiling. She heard a door slam somewhere on the train, and as it began to move and the lights came up she saw someone walking, far away down the platform. She moved to the end of the car and tried the door. She stepped gingerly onto the metal plate over the coupler and leaned out over the swinging chain. When the train stopped she jumped to the rocks below. She could feel dense black dust on her palms as she crossed to the other side and walked down the tracks, looking for a ladder.

A man helped her up. "Thanks. Where am I?" she asked, wiping her hands on her pants.

The man turned on a flashlight and shone it in her face. "Hi," he said.

"Hi. Don't mind me, I'm just browsing."

"You're a silkie."

"What?"

"I can tell you're a silkie, despite what you've done with your hair. I bet you had no idea that anyone, even another silkie, could pick you out in this light, but I can, even though you're the first silkie I ever saw."

Mary laughed at him. He continued quickly: "'The skin, hair, and fingernails all of the same tint, the openings of the ears and nostrils precisely the same size. It is said that he who created silkies saved himself three minutes' labor in this way, for to him no labor is too trivial to be saved'—you can deny it if you want, but I know you're a silkie."

"I don't deny it. So there. How did you know?"

"You don't know where you are? Not at all?"

She shook her head.

"This station is part of the Institute of Demonology Libraries. Now do you get the connection?"

A little background information: By 1968, the height of the psychedelic drug craze, it was apparent to librarians of demonology that their collections, once merely misunderstood, were becoming dangerous. The attractions of rigorous study were outpaced for most students by drug-induced feelings of conviction, leading to widespread and deeply held Satanist beliefs. Orgies and human sacrifice ensued, and one by one the great demonology libraries were walled up—at Holy Cross, at Notre Dame—and their catalogs stricken from the record. The many branches of the institute represent only a fraction of the great lost treasures of the Jesuits, etc.

"Are you saying silkies are minions of Satan?"

"Not necessarily, but unlike the other minions they're very well-documented, so I started doing my dissertation on them. I got this job conditionally and then never finished it."

"Oh, I'm sorry. Actually, there is something I'm interested in. I used to have this little medallion . . ."

He led her toward a heap of boxes. "This is everything I have. Take a look. The collection's not cataloged—just organized by station. Everything at this branch was at Marymount."

"Can I borrow your flashlight?" She opened a box and peered inside. "Is this one just bones?"

"I think so."

She tried another box. It was full of coins, medals, statuettes, dice, spinning tops, bundles of sticks, packs of cards, and rotted kapok. "So you don't actually know what any of this is?"

"No." He looked into the box. "Sometimes I take it out and play with it, though."

She asked to see his collection of silkie material. He pulled out a box with a lid, then began removing folders from it. Mary picked each one up and put it down. "These are all in weird languages I can't read."

"I know. That's the problem. It took me eight years at Columbia just to get started. If you can read four words in a row, you're practically an eminent scholar, and after you publish, you wait for years for someone to get curious enough to check your work." He sighed. "I'll show you one of the places I learned to recognize silkies. It's written in heavily inflected early medieval Latin that was spoken in Spain and noted down in Arabic characters, in shorthand. It's pretty typical of the silkie stuff—a little tract called 'Women to Avoid.' "

He unrolled a crumbling scroll on his desk, held the flashlight over it, and began, " 'Women to Avoid. Of all the women, these women you must avoid. You must avoid the bear. Large, hairy, you must fear the bear. You must avoid the'—I forget what this is . . . I know—'the squirrel.' "

"Skip to the silkies."

"Hmm. 'The seal you must fear, above all women. Small, gold, both skin and fingernails. The hole of the ears, the hole of the nose, precisely alike.' See?"

"How many women have you accused of being silkies?"

"I don't meet women very often."

"Why not?"

"I don't know. You'd think more women would be drawn to this kind of scholarship, but demonology seems to be very much a male thing."

"Don't you go upstairs? Don't you go on dates?"

"I don't know, I just sit down here and read. It doesn't pay so well, so I live with my mom—"

"What have you got on Jews?"

"Oh, reams and reams. That whole wall over there." He pointed across the station. "The roof leaks on that side, it should all be gone in ten years or so."

"I know this is a personal question," Mary said, "but do you ever feel you're wasting your life?"

He grinned. "Isn't that just like a minion of Satan, coming down here to tempt me—don't you know you're the woman I fear most?"

"If I were you I'd fear the bear and the squirrel more," Mary said. "Are you sure I can't tempt you upstairs for some coffee?"

"Just a minute," he said, loosening his tie. He pulled out a wooden crucifix on a chain and held it toward Mary.

"Ouch! Stop that!" she cried. He jumped back in terror and she began to laugh. "Come back, I was kidding."

The librarian was still panting in fear as he led her up the stairs.

Somewhere, I won't say where but my friends know who I mean, there is someone who goes around saying that I live to torture men. Am I a sadist? Is it true that I cruelly force men to fall deeply and helplessly in love with me, and then crush them, body and soul, like bugs?

On this theory I am, like Mary, entirely ordinary looking, with what is called in Spanish a *cara de buena persona*, prompting men who would not ordinarily aspire to possess the ideal woman (which I am, all things considered, in spite of my appearance) to regard me as already practically theirs. Letting down their guard, they notice only too late the transfigurative power of the brilliance, wit, and sympathy I employ in elevating myself beyond their reach to celestial heights from which I can only look down smiling, waving, forever unattainable. If I were better looking, they would realize the danger from the beginning and take precautions. If they, on the other hand, were better looking, they would not bother with someone like me in the first place. Their own homely awkwardness becomes the snare that traps them: Fearing they'll never do any better, they are caught, like Dante's Paolo and Francesca, whirling in a vicious circle, but by themselves.

Lucky for everyone, I am divinely beautiful, and no man can look at me without becoming intimidated and depressed. Close relationships cannot flower in the atmosphere of universal self-abasement created by my very existence.

Mary, however, was not so lucky, and she was in real danger

of hurting the feelings of the homely and awkward demonologist. They sat drinking coffee together for an hour, Mary
doing her best to befriend him, hoping only to learn what
she could about the IDL and its possible connection to Yigal,
Mr. Pickwick, and the heir to the Israeli throne. Unfortunately, he seemed to know nothing but silkie folklore and
esoterica. She yawned and asked for the check.

Meanwhile Yigal knocked on the door of the Dolphin Star
Temple in Mount Rainier, Maryland. The high priestess an-
swered, clad in her steel-gray robes. She had just been per-
fecting a new dolphin-like movement.

"Yigal," she said softly. She walked backward, her gray gauze
streaming in the breeze from two electric fans, and knelt on
a silken pillow before the altar.

"Holy one," Yigal began, "things are getting confusing and
I need your help."

"Yes, my priestess in Tel Aviv told me of your trouble."
She nodded toward a picture of me on the back wall, deco-
rated with kelp. "You wish to learn the meaning of the card
Leviathan."

"Yes."

"Yet you never drew that card."

"No, holy one."

"How do you know it exists?"

Yigal said firmly, "I don't know the card exists. Let's just
say I want to know the meaning of the entry in the book.
You know why." She nodded and beckoned him forward to
the altar. He sat beside her on a cushion and raised his arms
in a dolphin-like manner. He closed his eyes and when he
opened them, she was holding out a different book, a very
small one that looked a bit like a CIA manual. He began to
read aloud:

The Leviathan is a unique futuristic prototype with no moving parts. Made almost entirely of a gelatinous substance, it is sheathed in a continuous ribbon of osmium sealed with caoutchouc and wooden dowels. Like the golem of Prague, it takes its motive power from a name—the name of Moshe Dayan.

The Leviathan was built for the state of Israel in 1968 with the help of a team of conservators from the Institute of Demonology Libraries, New York. Soon afterward, it was stolen. Some say the Leviathan is an all-powerful weapon, capable of spontaneously generating any amount of force conceived by its operators. The basic principle is simple: Any object mentally projected into the Leviathan will there, over a period of weeks, take actual shape until bursting forth spontaneously.

In the hands of a capable engineer, Leviathan could be an invincible deterrent, but there are indications that the group currently controlling Leviathan has only the vaguest notions of physics, mechanics, and weapons technology, leading the submarine to generate ineffective weapons which upon examination are found to be bereft of interior detail.

Both were silent for a long time. Yigal read the passage again, committing it to memory. Then he looked up and asked, "The dolphins?"

The high priestess shook her head. "I don't know, but I suspect them. A human group would have been controlled by now."

"Who wrote the book?"

"Allow me a question. Who has examined the interior of weapons produced by Leviathan?"

Yigal looked upset the way he sometimes did in the presence of Dolphin Star mysteries, especially ones that seemed to involve his employers. Then he remembered happily that there was a Leviathan-generated Trident warhead on his own roof in Tel Aviv, sitting waiting for him in a rain barrel.

"Shall I go, holy one?"

She nodded. He jumped up and was on his way.

CHAPTER 16

HOLDING THE EDGES OF THE RAIN
barrel, Yigal and I slowly tipped it over on its side. The water poured through holes in the battlements onto the awning above the café, and the Trident warhead rolled out.

"Here goes nothing," Yigal said, hitting it with a hammer.

A second later we were jumping back, saying things like "Ew!" "Yuck!" "What the hell is that?!" The nose cone of the rocket, which seemed to be made of a compressed calcareous material, had broken open easily to reveal a thick, white, gooey substance that oozed all over the roof. We had no idea what it was, but we both knew what it reminded us of. I ran for the hose, and we washed it down to the awning and into the street. We could see pedestrians running.

Over coffee we discussed the possibilities.

I was sure of one thing. "This is definitely controlled by dolphins. They've seen Trident missiles go up, obviously, and being dolphins, they assumed they had a sexual function—"

"Why assume it's dolphins? It seems to me that any sexually mature, but naive, onlooker might make the same assumption about the Trident program. After all, they only see it go up. They don't see it come down. The mode of delivery re-minds me more of the sperm packets used by mollusks."

"You mean cephalopods—octopus—that ninth arm—"

"Precisely. They're reputed to be very intelligent. The only thing I can think is that one of your undersea pals down in Eilat is in love with you, and they've been aiming at you all along, not me. They overshot you the first time, so then they tried something smaller and lighter."

I shuddered with disgust. "Anybody could have seen me in that glass-bottomed boat, and—from below—I was out there in shorts all that time—it could be anyone, coral, or a parrot fish! Or a sea anemone! I feel violated."

Yigal put his arm around me. "There's another possibility."

"What?" I sniffled.

"Twelve-year-old boys. Actually, I can see this up to seven-teen, eighteen—"

"No," I said. "I refuse to believe that. I don't know anyone under forty."

We sat in silence.

"Maybe it was something else," I ventured. "What about the one that blew up in your office?"

He shook his head. "That was probably the candy and flowers."

We spent the afternoon covering the roof with a double layer of plywood and a sheet of PVC.

The demonology librarian, whose name was Ian, took Mary's hand across the table. "How would you like dinner at my place?"

She smiled. "I'm tired, but before I go, there's one more thing I'd really like to ask you. Do you think, in all that Jewish material you've got, that there's anything to link anyone alive today with the biblical House of David?"

He laughed. "No way. That's what you call a loaded issue. Questions like that are fertilizer, if you'll pardon the expression. When you start to spread something like that around, you get forgeries, destructions, pages ripped out, words cut out, words written in . . ." He lowered his voice. "They also say there are some powerful curses. There's a story about the first generation of librarians, the people that worked at the institute when it started. They're gone now. Something made their bodies into a big blob of something like Jell-O. They say it blocked the G line for two days and they had to get it out with a Sikorsky Skycrane . . ."

Around five o'clock Yigal said, "I need a drink."

"That's so unlike you. Have you really started drinking?"

He stuck the roll of tape in his pocket and said, "Come along. First we'll get a bottle of rioja, and then I'll tell you about how I started drinking." He began in the elevator. "So, Nell, where did the dolphins get their ordnance survey map of Tel Aviv?"

"Good point."

He told me about his visit to the Dolphin Star Temple and concluded, "I see this as a power struggle between internal and external security. Shin Bet tried to use silkies to control the dolphins, and Mossad tried to win over the dolphins directly through the Dolphin Star program. But the silkies and the Dolphin Star priestesses are wild cards. Plus, neither of them has any actual communication with the dolphins. The silkies feel nothing but contempt for them, and you, well—"

"It's true, I wouldn't know a dolphin if it bit me on the butt." It was slightly humiliating to learn that I had been the clueless pawn of a global spy network, but I was proud to feel that my ineptitude had played a role in saving the world from the ultimate weapon of terror.

Yigal added, "I suspect that my mission isn't exactly what they told me. They had me going after Shin Bet's silkie contacts." There was a promotion going on, so we tasted six or seven reds before taking the rioja. "Let's just go walking and drink straight from the bottle," he said. "For confidentiality."

We strolled to Independence Park through the gray-gold twilight. A hotel blocked our view of the port, but we could see a trio of dolphins leaping through the waves, heading south. "I'd like to see them retain control of it," I said. "They're basically harmless, especially now that we've reinforced the roof."

"I'd rather find and remove the name so we can forget the whole thing." He finished the bottle and threw it down to the beach. "Now I want to tell you why I started drinking." The story about Mary took a long time. We sat down on a bench and he kept stopping in the middle of sentences to let people pass by. He stuttered, seeming shy and ashamed, and finally claimed he couldn't go on.

"Of course you're hesitating to tell me this," I said. "Your behavior is disgraceful."

"Really?" He looked up, suddenly cheerful.

"Of course it is. You're a loser and a shit."

"Then I have to take her back?"

"Absolutely."

Yigal hugged me. "I have no choice!"

I could see that his typically Israeli need to be as masculine as possible had been wriggling under the heel of a dilemma: It's very masculine to repudiate the woman you love and suffer alone for the rest of your life for the sake of pride and vanity, but it's also very masculine to sacrifice your youth and freedom to bring up her children. It was a hard choice for Yigal, but since he was a little shaky on whether the "children" in this case were technically "children" at all, he'd been leaning toward number one. All it took was a little light arm-twisting, and he was firmly back with option number two, which had the added advantage of confirming his common decency and securing his relationship with Mary, assuming he ever saw her again.

"She'll turn up," I said. "She sent me something to keep for her."

"What?"

"This little medal with a dog—or maybe it's a koala—and a wheel and some other stuff—she said she got it somewhere. Yigal?" He was crying again. "Be a man for a minute. How about this: What if they're not after me at all? What if it's someone after you who's trying to exploit someone who's after me, because he can't control Mr. Pickwick by himself? So they're working together to defend the Israeli royal family."

"Which royal family? The Dayans?"

"No," I said. "That can't be. I suggested it to Zohar, and he said, 'That's just too stupid.'"

Yigal shrugged and looked out to sea. "I've spent a month in New York looking for material on the House of David and getting nowhere. There comes a time when a man has to ask himself, 'What House of David? What are we really talking about here?' Nell, look at me, and tell me honestly, I'm not talking about nature now: Is there anything in human culture so stupid that it can't be true?"

I pondered his question. A woman walked past us, carrying a $300 Italian clutch purse made of patterned vinyl. "No," I replied.

CHAPTER 17

YIGAL SPENT THE NEXT TWO DAYS drunk, writing the following story based on something Kafka began writing in his diary in August 1914, "Memories of the Kalda Railway":

MEMORIES OF THE KALDA RAILWAY

A small railway in the interior of Russia: I was there only a year, long enough to learn two songs from the railway inspector. The songs were "Where Are You Going, Little Child, in the Woods?" and "Merry Comrades, I Belong to You." Tuneless, meandering songs, each a thousand verses long, sung endlessly to the unvarying southern horizon, which I faced each day, slowly rotating my chair to follow the sun's progress. The first was a lament—quiet, with deep vibration building up in the chest and occasional sobbing. It was about a lost child, after all. The second usually came after meals and was a high, barking wail of pointless joy. The train came seldom, of course. In the five months I was stationed there, I saw it twice. It came carrying the railway inspector; after two weeks, during which we did little besides drink, repeat the songs, and fall asleep at last in each other's arms, wrapped in our overcoats against the cold, it returned from Kalda to take him away again. When he arrived the only other passenger was a brown heifer. There was no conductor to close the doors, and when the nine empty cars pulled in, she came to the vestibule and hesitated, considering perhaps a moment on the grass while the engine took on water. I approached slowly, trying not to frighten her. She shivered and her nose seemed dry. My attention was seized by her deep brown eyes' rectangular pupils. I thought I could make out something inside—a reflected scene, but one that had nothing to do with my shed, the signal, the water tower, or the featureless prairie around us. I saw a tiny boat rocking on a river, with willows hanging over from the banks, and cattails all around. The sun was brilliant and a stone fly skittered over the water. Then the heifer closed her eyes. The locomotive bathed us in steam and pulled away. Then the inspector walked up to greet me. He offered me vodka and began teaching me the songs.

When after two weeks' oblivion I honorably left the service of the railway, I asked if I might first ride to Kalda, the end of the line, before returning home. There is little to see in Kalda: a tiny gray town of stucco and daub, a few small plazas, a broken bottle or two, where even the wind arrives tired by the thousand miles from the nearest hills. In Kalda (it was said), though the cirrus clouds race by above, taking just a minute to fly from one horizon to the other, the earthbound air is still. Black-clad women move slowly about, speaking briefly to each other on their daily rounds from the market to the laundry. Then they warm their vegetable diet, wild onions, in huge pots nestled in mounds of smoldering peat. They have nothing to sell and consequently nothing to buy;

the population is very old, dying even; all the men are gone, and the railway will soon shut down. This was the common wisdom regarding Kalda, which was held to be the remotest outpost of our civilization.

Yet someone there would receive a heifer. She stood blankly grinning as I looked into her eyes, and then as the train creaked into motion she listed gently from side to side, still watching me, generously, gently. In her eyes the boat rocked. As I turned to look for it my eyes filled with steam. Then she was gone, into slavery, or to be eaten, who knew. She was right not to seek freedom in the vast upturned bowl of the steppes. In name I was free—nothing held me there but the promise of a salary—still, as everyone says, the plains are a prison. A single shopping street in the city holds more humanity than the entire high plain. The destitute or insane person who might excite our sympathy quickly becomes an unrecognizable tangle of dry bone, immune to charity. The heifer knew this, and she voluntarily chose life in Kalda over confinement to the steppes (I am convinced of this).

I waited six months for the next train. The winter was uneventful. Snow covered the grass and starving legions of rats swept down from the north. The wind never stopped. Then, in the end, rain fell, the poppies opened their orange mouths, the sky took on a faint glow like dawn, and from an oblique angle, if one lay on the ground, the steppes appeared green. Soon I saw a weasel hunting for mice. Then the train came in a slow smear of colored smoke. After that I waited another week, teetering on the flimsy wooden rails.

This time there was a passenger, an elderly man with thick glasses and an unseasonable woolen hat. He read the same front page of a newspaper over and over while I listened to the rails, watching the landscape repeat itself as the shadows slowly moved around the car into nightfall. The cars never stopped lurching from side to side, and when I closed my eyes I felt that I was standing on a moored rowboat. Sleep was impossible with the constant motion. The dining car was at the eastern end of the train, due to the prevailing wind. Twice a day I fixed myself a cup of tea and stole a few biscuits from an unmarked, ancient tin under the cash register. I brought tea to the old man. He never left his seat except to piss between the cars. He was shy of doing it standing in the doorway, facing that endless horizon.

When we reached Kalda it was late afternoon, warm and silent. The old man turned away from the station and fought his way, wheezing with effort, alone into the tall grass.

I had only one night in Kalda before the train would leave again for six months, and like a sailor with one night's shore leave I was uncertain how to spend it. I could not stay even two nights without committing myself to walking back to the city, which was impossible. Perhaps with an oxcart to carry water I could have walked, but as far as I knew there was only one animal in Kalda. The station faced a dusty plaza ringed with low gray buildings. There was no glass in the windows, as if no one had used them for a long time.

I fell asleep. When I awoke the little heifer was nibbling my hand. Its cheek rested on my thigh and its lips curved upward in a smile. It looked up to me with eyes blank as tar. In the pupils nothing was to be seen, but in the glassy surface I could make out my own reflection. My beard was long, both gray and red, and my eyes formed dark circles. My face was sunburned in patches and my nose looked almost purple. I suddenly felt my lips and tongue, and struggled to wet my mouth with saliva. It and my eyes were gummy with dust. I stroked the heifer's head as she smiled and tried to lick my hands. The sun dropped below the horizon with a start and I realized I was cold.

There has never been an inn in Kalda. I moved a coin to my shirt pocket and began to think about asking for shelter. Looking around, I saw that someone was approaching us. She was all in black and carrying a heavy walking stick. The heifer's ears perked upright and she left off licking me for a moment. When the woman was very close to me, close enough to see that under my filth and fatigue I had the features of a young man, she threw back her hood. She had fine, dusty yellow hair that fell thickly past her shoulders and was tucked into her coat. She looked no more than twenty-five years old.

I started to my feet and wiped the grime from my mouth. The heifer nuzzled against my hips and drove the two of us back down the black, silent street through the dark to her house.

In the morning, instead of returning to the station, I went alone to the fields to mow last year's mustard and turn it under. To do otherwise would have been tantamount to murder. There were no young men in Kalda and no surplus that might have been sold to pay the fares for the old men and women to leave for the cities. No one was strong enough to walk a hundred miles, let alone a thousand. So the empty train made its way back and forth, and the people ate wild onions. With my help there would be potatoes.

Her name was Mary. Her mother seemed at first very proud and silent, but I learned much later that she had been the victim of a beating by her husband. It had left her unable to speak. Regardless, whenever she saw me she threw her chin into the air.

The heifer was Mary's. In mid-June, when the air was thick

with black flies and mosquitoes, she gave birth to a calf. She lived at the end of a short grass rope in the courtyard. Mary fought valiantly for the milk, but I think somehow the little starved cow reserved the best for her calf. The milk she gave us was thin and sour. Mary made cheese from it. She said that if she sold enough cheese in the city, she could make enough money to leave Kalda. I encouraged her, but thought she failed to understand urban commerce. Livestock can be sent alone to Kalda, and no one but its rightful owner will think of retrieving it, but cheese cannot sell itself. Still, I did not volunteer to leave her for six months for the sake of selling the cheese. I told her that I would be able to persuade the conductor to grant her a fare on credit against the value of the cheese, and we would leave Kalda together. Of course I would pay her fare myself. What could the cheese possibly be worth, after three months in the summer heat? We devoted long nights of discussion to the fate of the cheese. One night I remarked offhand that we could sell the cheese to whoever had sent her the cow.

"Isn't that your cow?" she asked with an air of studious wonder.

"Then it must belong to someone else," I said.

She put her arms around me. "I care for your cow because you are my husband. It is up to me to take care of all of us now, to make money so that our child will have clothing."

For the first time I was to be a father. I embraced her passionately. When the autumn arrived I was fit and proud. From working in the fields I had strong, callused hands. We went down to the station with Mary's mother and the sack of cheese. The train pulled in slowly. A young man, a passenger, was holding the rail and leaning far out from the train, shading his eyes. "Mary! Mary!" he called.

She ran forward to him, grasping her belly. "I can no longer be your wife," she said. Her mother grunted.

"I forgive you everything," he said. She began to cry. He held her tenderly. I walked to our house and untied the cow and her calf. They raced off into the tall grass.

When I returned by another way to the station, Mary and her husband were nowhere to be seen, and I bought a seat in second class. The inspector joined me one stop past my old post. When he heard my story he descended from the train to buy a bottle of the cheapest vodka. He taught me a love song, a wordless march with accompanying hand motions. We became so drunk that the stars wheeled below us like carnival lights reflected in a well. But even after a week the embraces of the inspector were of so little use against my pain that I leaped gently and secretly, without saying good-bye, to the tall-grass prairie near a river, in a fertile area dotted with towns. I followed a path through the reeds to a riverbank, where a little boat lay rocking under a canopy of willow branches yellowed by autumn. The boat had waited a long time through the summer rains and falling leaves, and had to be dragged in and overturned, cleaned, and left in the sun for a day. Then with my pay jingling in my pocket I began my journey downstream.

I paused at every opportunity to explore the country. In a medium-sized market town I visited a bookstore. Among the ancient and indecipherable texts was a book by the railway inspector, which he had dedicated to me. The margins were filled with notations in his own handwriting. The topic was the history of the Kalda railway.

"Almost nothing is commonly known about the origins of Kalda," he wrote. "That a town should spring up in isolation, where no town is needed, may surprise no one; but that such a town should be served by a railway is strange indeed. Many are the forces which compel otherwise solitary people, whose lonely homesteads, devoid of visitors or of any variation in human contact beyond the occasional arrival of an infant, which can hardly be regarded as variation given the inevitable formative influence of its surroundings" (I didn't say the inspector wrote well; only that he wrote) "to build a forum as it were for daily contact and interaction. Some may indict certain romantic or poetical tendencies among these lonely steppe-dwellers, but it is legendary among railway personnel, of whom I am admittedly one, that in the case of Kalda the hermits of a vast tract of interior land were lured, briefly, into one place by precisely one common goal: namely, that of obtaining railway service.

"Records of the railway's initial decision to consider construction of the Kalda line make reference to a thriving market for priceless furs of fisher and sable, where common household goods such as colanders, imported from manufacturing centers, might be exchanged for their weight in gold. That these stories were believed does not bespeak gullibility on the part of the railway company, but rather great skill in deceit and falsehood on the part of the people of Kalda—or rather, the solitary hermits of the steppes who, for several days many years ago, filled the poor gray city they had prepared of mud and lime to welcome the first train, on which, I am strangely proud to say, my father rode as chief inspector. There are no citizens of Kalda, as there is no city of Kalda. To explain how an illusory city might come to occupy a prominent position on the maps of our nation and even, due to its unique isolation, on globes of the world will be one aim of this essay; a defense and, I hope, complete vindication of my father's role will be another, albeit minor, goal."

Here in the margin the inspector had written: "Mary."

The text continued: "The essentially solitary nature of Kalda can be disputed by no one who has visited that city. Yet with what regret must I note how few can claim to have done so! Whatever I write will be dismissed as the word of one man against a thousand, for everyone holds his own opinion of the city of Kalda, and has always held it. I who have returned from witnessing the dread desolation imposed by the vast caldron of featureless sky which oppresses our interior in general and the spurious city of Kalda in particular—unique so far as I know, in that no one who sets foot on the earth of that region can claim to have escaped its"—here I felt all at once like a descending yoke the ponderous self-aggrandizement of his prose, and turned to the appendices. Mary was named only once, as the fifth item in an alphabetical glossary of Kalda's false citizenry: "a beauty whose qualities might, given greater scope, have come to some use, had she not lost the power of speech; but the subject of this book is the little town itself, and the vindication of my father." The book was very dull.

The price was outrageous—"Extremely rare," the bookseller said, snatching it away in distress. My buttery fingers had left a halo of translucency around each word I had touched, and a greasy radiance still emanated from the page where the inspector had written "Mary," underlined many times by my amazed index finger. In the bookseller's eyes I seemed to see the calf, emaciated, his swollen belly heaving, lying on bare ground in a place where the prairie had been parted as if by a comb. A burying beetle paused in a corner of the scene, unsure where to start.

"Did you also know Mary?" I asked the bookseller.

He closed his eyes and faced the back of the shop. A

musky odor, as if he seldom bathed, rose as he turned and his untrimmed nails clicked on the tiled countertop. I sang softly to his reddening ears: "Merry comrades, I belong to you. Swiftly the river flows, carrying us onward together. Never mind where: Has anything a source or destination?" The bookseller fled the shop, and I slipped the book into my pocket and took it back to the boat to read.

While I walked I sang the other song: "Where are you going, little child, in the woods? At home, your parents wait for you. Yet you hurry onward, head down, appearing to seek for something in the carpet of needles. Why do you walk at dawn toward the western darkness?" I lay in the boat and ate buttered rolls. I thought of singing the love song without words, but finished the sack of rolls instead.

I read further. "Once experienced, Kalda's brutal deceptions instantly drain a man's life of all possible meaning. This thesis being difficult to prove without reference to the all-too-personal, I beg you to place your full confidence in me on this point. The sensitive reader will easily deduce Kalda's effects and refrain from further inquiry as to its causes. Respect for my father's memory demands nothing less." Dropped over the side, the book sank quickly. I lay back, admiring the sharp outlines of the clouds overhead. I kept imagining the roar of an approaching waterfall, but there was none. The river was broad and placid as a serving plate.

CHAPTER 18

AFTER TRYING OUT ONLY THIRTY-FIVE
thousand words, I learned that I had, through blind luck,
happened on one utilized by Shats. He writes:

> An albatross features in my *Sailing Toward the Sunset,*
> a specific one named Albert (details: www.zetnet.co.uk
> /sigs/birds/albert.html). Mary mocks the protagonist's
> attempt to use it as a literary symbol of something.

The URL refers to the pathetic story of a solitary black-
browed albatross, a species whose proper home lies in the
far Southern Hemisphere. In Shetland, northernmost of the
British Isles, Albert's chances of finding love and starting a
family are slim, but he returns nonetheless every year to a
cliffside nook from whence he makes clumsy passes at neigh-
boring gannets. He has become a tourist attraction.

Shats has also helped clarify two rather more urgent issues.
Close reading of the excerpt above reveals: (1) that Mary is
not the protagonist of *Sailing Toward the Sunset,* and (2) that
"Zetland" and "Shetland" are very likely the same place. The
translator of Proust, C. K. Scott Moncrieff, also provided the
text for a lovely picture book about Scotland [note that this

is false; the book about Scotland is by Sir Iain Moncreiffe of that Ilk], and when I was still quite small, I memorized its list of the seven crofting counties and resolved to visit each one. They were:

Argyll
Caithness
Inverness
Ross
Sutherland
Orkney
and (suspiciously)
Zetland

Even as a child, I could tell there was something un-Scottish about the name "Zetland." It tainted the entire list for me. I never suspected that it had anything to do with the quaint, rugged, and picturesque "Shetland" of pony fame. And indeed, perusal of the Internet's "Zetland" pages makes clear that the inhabitants are eager to cast off all associations with Scotland in favor of a putative Viking heritage. Yet even the briefest look at the accompanying illustrations puts the lie to their charade: The ships supposedly employed by the Vikings in their voyages of conquest were made of wood. There are no trees on Shetland.

Legends of Scandinavian seafaring have an obvious motive. Readers of authentic tales such as *Hrafnkel's Saga* will recall the monotony of clan warfare as it was carried on by poorly armed louts mounted on horses that came up to their waists. Bravery may be possible under these conditions, but glamour certainly is not. Ambitious young men were well advised to head south in rowboats, returning several weeks later laden with exotic riches such as (I'm guessing now) spoons. Leif

Ericson may or may not have crossed to North America in a Viking ship, but Thor Heyerdahl most certainly crossed the Pacific on a reed raft powered by guesswork, which just goes to show you that any number of failures receives less publicity than a single success, especially if all the failures drown or can't get their books published. After all, it took over a hundred years for the classic Scandinavian adventure "Slow Death by Balloon" to find the publicity it deserved.

From various sources it is becoming clear that a ship in a bottle must soon play a decisive role in my plot. On the cover of Shats' first edition (I assume there will be corrections for subsequent editions), a ship in a bottle appears, perched on a copy of *Lolita*. My assumption, grounded in hearsay, is that some character or another builds ships in bottles as a hobby, and I hereby elect that character to be Zohar. For the past few days, he has been unwinding from the stress of his Himalayan escape at the World Ships-in-Bottles Convention in Honolulu.

Ships-in-bottles conventions, like science fiction conventions, manifest only very tenuous links to ships in bottles themselves. In large hotels on suburban bypass roads, women dressed as figureheads exchange pleasantries with men dressed as old-timey sea captains, through endless rounds of parties and receptions. Downstairs are displays, competitions, and panel discussions while upstairs ship-in-bottle enthusiasts swarm from open bar to open bar, engaging in discussions even more pretentiously formal than those taking place downstairs. As a rule, formality, once undertaken, increases with drunkenness, which lengthens the gaps between utterances, allowing time for exponential increases in ponderousness and gravity. Men in ragged frock coats, with waxed black goatees, debate the merits of competing shipyards, solemnly exchanging business cards that read:

HERMAN GOOCH & SONS'
SHIPBUILDING AND DRY DOCK
17 Norma Court
Indianapolis, IN

and

JIM "ROB" FRANK
Tackle—Bollards—Belaying Pins
445 W. 22nd St., #12P
New York, NY

On Saturday night everyone goes downstairs for the "masquerade," at which the more exhibitionist elements of the costuming crowd come into their own. Waving fluttering white pennants, an ex-Rockette in a flesh-colored catsuit reenacts the first America's Cup race. A line of well-rehearsed children spell a holiday message with signal flags to a standing ovation. A bearded man stands very still while a friend hoists sails all over his body. The bewildered crowd applauds politely. By midnight the rooms upstairs are packed with convention-goers who long ago stopped stirring their drinks. They sip the vodka off the bottoms of highballs through little red straws, and gossip about what happened at the last convention. In one such room, in a corner, out of the way and minding his own business, sits Zohar, listening attentively, through headphones, to a talk radio call-in show. Every so often someone approaches, shuffling and slightly bowed, as though requesting an audience from a despotic czar.

"Your name?" Zohar asks.

"I am Gary Blaine, the chief operating officer of _____

Bank, and Mr. Schmidt told me you might have something of interest to us."

Nodding, Zohar removes his latest work from his pocket and unwraps its protective tissue paper. "USS *Essex* CV-9," he says modestly, letting the tiny ship, built entirely of cardboard matchsticks inside a crack vial, rest in his palm. Tiny P-47s, their wings folded upward, populate the deck, joined by a legion of weary swabbies whose mops really move, in circles too small for the naked eye. The bank officer, sweating, asks for a jeweler's loupe and watches in silence as tiny ensigns oversee routine maintenance on the catapults. "A million dollars. Take it or leave it." Nervously, the bank officer asks for more time. "I have something else really special, for the right customer," Zohar will add, opening a slip of waxed paper with tweezers to reveal the Haganah ship *Exodus* under steam in the harbor of Famagusta, carved on a grain of rice.

"Too rich for my blood," the sap will say, retreating. I always told Zohar if he'd lower his prices a little he might sell something now and then, but he has very firm ideas about art.

Zohar has asked me to put more of his friends in my book, so I will add that at his elbow stood a mysterious, slender figure, thirty years old, ineffably beautiful and sexy, dressed like a French gamine and smoking a wickedly potent cigarette. "Zohar," she said impatiently, "I'll give you a million dollars myself if you'll just give up and come to bed."

He sighed. Though he saw her only at conventions, she was still managing to wear him out with her incessant sexual demands. He thought longingly of the comforts of marriage and home, and then obeyed her, which after all was easier than making a scene.

CHAPTER 19

HAVING ALLOWED A MISSILE WITH
sexual content to penetrate *Sailing Toward the Sunset,* I feel I
should mention *Gravity's Rainbow,* but I won't.

Yigal never liked Pynchon either. He had been traumatized
early in life by his friend Elad Manor, one of those Pynchon
fanatics who call you in the middle of the night to say, "I just
got to page 332!" In bed with a notebook, the pencil in his
hand poised over the word "Swedenborg," Yigal would answer
the phone only to find Elad in the advanced state of mental
decomposition that later became known as "deconstruction."

"Dewey Gland!" Elad would giggle before begging, nay, ordering Yigal to immerse himself likewise in Pynchon's inter-
minable *tableau vivant.*

"Get a girlfriend," Yigal would advise him patiently. "Better yet, see a whore. Rub some coke on your dick and you
might last long enough to get your money's worth." With his
left hand Yigal would smooth out the wrinkled reproduction,
clipped from a newspaper by a distant pen pal, of Picasso's
Guernica and return to his private thoughts.

To Yigal's astonishment, the easily led Elad would later
accomplish several daring media pranks, most notably his

facilitation of Avner Shats' meteoric career as a poet. Back when Amir Or first organized the Mishkenot Sha'ananim poetry workshop, Shats explains, he published this ad calling young, unknown poets to apply. I sent some poems signed 'Elad Manor,' because I was already very famous at the time, or so I thought. . . . In gratitude for his performance in Jerusalem, Shats awarded Manor the leading role in his first novel, *Sailing Toward the Sunset*.

This rankled Yigal, who had received assurances the role was his, but he remembered Manor without bitterness. If Elad Manor, he thought, is the sort of Pynchon-loving soft-butch lapdog these postmodern novelists want, then they can have him. He had never read *Sailing Toward the Sunset,* but based his entire assessment of the situation on his youthful memories of Manor, which over time had become conflated with the feelings of irritation he had experienced from his position in the family as an only son with five younger sisters. The girls, doctrinaire feminists, were passionate about their careers, and it didn't seem to have crossed anyone's mind that Yigal, with the world at his feet, would persist in avoiding anything resembling commitment until, late in the course of his last philosophy degree, a professor took him aside and indicated to him that, with his qualifications, academia was out of the question. "But you really seem to know how to mind your own business, don't you?" Yigal shrugged. "I mean, I'm your adviser and I can't claim to be privy to the subject of your thesis. Have you considered becoming a Mossad agent?"

"No."

The professor grasped Yigal's shoulder and looked deeply into his eyes. He spoke of Rome, of Paris, of Tokyo, of the French South Sea nuclear-testing islands. . . . It was a bit like the scene in *Gigi* where they're trying to convince innocent little Gigi to accept Gaston for the travel opportunities, except that what the professor was describing to Yigal opened up such undreamed-of new vistas of whores, gambling, and cocaine that Yigal was almost dumbstruck.

"Cannibals?" was all he asked, rather cryptically.

"Promise me you'll call them. Do this for me, and for your future. I don't want to see you in ten years living in a tent on the beach." Then he said a special Aramaic code phrase I'm not allowed to share, and kissed and hugged Yigal with the secret kiss and hug before shaking his hand with the secret handshake. Obviously they're all faggots, Yigal thought. But, come to think of it, they must have thousands of telephone operators and secretaries—I'll be like the only straight man in a ballet company. He imagined the Mossad as a gigantic network of girls' boarding schools into which he would be smuggled to be secretly shared and enjoyed by thousands of hungry junior assistants to diplomatic attachés, all fresh out of the army—the diplomats themselves would be flaming queens, agog over clothes and parties, oblivious to the foment taking place in the souls of their nubile stenographers. He imagined an Israeli girl, a kibbutznikit with her hair in braids, on her knees begging him to stay away from the Milanese whorehouses he'd wanted to visit ever since reading *Catch-22*, and his proud refusal.

"Take me as I am," Yigal said aloud by accident, remembering his long-lost moment of puerile grandiosity. He was sitting alone in Café Basel, not far from his apartment, drinking a cappuccino and watching a cat cross the street while pretending to concentrate on a passage from Sartre's *Saint Genet:*

> There is no more effective defense against the
> temptation to have *everything* than to own some-

thing. If you have only a crumb that has fallen
from the table, your life will be spent in defend-
ing that crumb, in convincing others and yourself
that it is the best of crumbs and that, in the last
analysis, it contains the universe.

Yigal's eyes took in the expanse of Basel Street, Tel Aviv's
current *rive gauche.* The scene had aspects of a miniature: The
rife and chaotic antiquarian bookshops of Paris were represented by a single orderly retail store. Its pitchers of Ricard
were replaced by a glass of lemonade, its riot of *caniches* by a
Chihuahua which sniffed at one of two potted geraniums, its
women by a teenage girl perched on a traffic barrier, waiting for her small taxi. In one of these cafés, Yigal thought, a
single anarchist sits reading *Charlie hebdomadaire,* wearing his
one black T-shirt.

He tore off a corner of his croissant and dropped it to
the pavement. A pigeon with a clubfoot walked toward him,
then walked away. A wren-like, striped sparrow with round
black eyes crept out from behind a geranium and began to
peck at the gravel loose on the sidewalk. The Chihuahua
walked to the middle of the street and stood there. If I close
my eyes, Yigal thought, I could imagine myself in a little village where no strangers go, where I was born and which I
have never left.

(A clarification with regard to Yigal's substitution of
"Whores, Gambling, and Cocaine" for a similar list he believed had been compiled by Kafka: Kafka's list consisted
of "Hatred, Envy, Avarice, and Greed." I apologize for any
inconvenience.)

Mary sat in a diner to write a letter to Taylor.

Dear Taylor,

I bet you're surprised to be getting a letter from me, but I just wanted to let you know everything is doing great! I'm still in New York, but maybe I'll go back to Tel Aviv soon. I know you think that's wrong, but there's so much you don't understand. Why would you? I met a man the other day who knows more about silkies than any other human being on earth, except that adds up to just about ZERO. It's like somebody saying he knows about vampires because he read Dracula. When, as I'm sure you know, vampires are really just nasty sacks of gooey icky stuff, like old cucumbers, and they smell totally awful, so the idea of a vampire being sexy or anybody wanting to TOUCH a vampire is like totally beyond me. So anyhow this guy—wait, I forgot I never told you I am a silkie—do you know what that is? If you want the details, I mean the cool fake details which are way more interesting than the truth, talk to a demonologist, but here's the boring facts: Some girl seals turn out to like men—I hope it doesn't hurt your feelings that I didn't like you. It doesn't, does it? Now you're back where you belong and I'm so glad. So being a silkie is an easy life, I think. I don't know what to compare it to. I don't remember being a seal very well, because being a seal is so easy that you sort of lose track after a while, you can't focus your thoughts, and compared to people, who are always after something amazingly specific like "I'm going to become a certified public accountant so I can drive a 500-series Mercedes," your brain turns

to mush. Did you ever think about that? People say
dolphins are smarter, but it's only because dolphins
are always after something. TRUST ME. Seals try not
to be. We admire most the people who are never after
anything, such as: Kelp. Jellyfish. Starfish! Have
you ever really watched a starfish? Some have fifty
arms! They move so slowly, and patiently, and they
are beautiful like flowers. Seals try to sit still but
we were born to play. Lots of people go to starfish
school but I think it's just the dumbest thing—
imagine 20 seals trying to sit still. I am told that
if you ever really sit still you will receive the most
frightening hallucinations, so I am not in a hurry to
try it. Did you ever see a flock of tuna? Their huge
silver sides flash in the sun, they swim as fast as
motorboats. If you get a chance to spend some time
in the ocean, you should do it. I would like to visit
the Sargasso Sea. There are no starfish, but crabs
that walk on the water, and so much kelp it's like
islands, or like the bogs on the moors, where you can
walk if you want but you have to watch and make
sure your foot doesn't go through, at which point
you will be dug up only after 3,000 years—well, I
don't think you can actually walk on the Sargasso
Sea, but I am a strong swimmer. A VERY strong
swimmer. Well, I think I've written enough for one
letter. Say hi to your wife for me!

                              Very truly yours,
                              Mary

　　She began a letter to Yigal and then ripped it up. Then
she leafed through the *New York Post* for a while. What's the

Gowanus, she thought, and who is the Son of Sam? How is he connected with Alexander Hamilton? She read an adorable personal and considered drafting a sympathetic response, even though the person wanted a widowed man in his sixties or seventies, but then she just sealed $10,000 into an envelope anonymously. She read a real estate feature, then some crossword clues, then she wrote in five answers, and then she saw the single-column ad, near the comics:

**ALONE? PREGNANT? SCARED? SILKIE?
ADOPTION IS THE OPTION**
If you are a silkie aged 18 to 35 in weeks 7–28,
your expenses can be PAID IN FULL for the
duration of your pregnancy and you will receive
a consideration of $40,000.

She ripped it out and took it over to the phone. Instead of calling the number on the ad right away, she changed the last three digits to zeroes and tried for their main reception desk. It was the Defense Logistics Agency. That's so pathetic, she thought. The notion of a silkie "alone" and "scared" was too much for her, and she burst out laughing. All the same, she had a sudden urge to fly to London and retrieve her skin. She wrote another letter to Taylor on the plane.

Dear Taylor,
   I know I'm writing you an awful lot, but maybe you'll just have to get used to it. Who else can I write to? I don't have a mom, you know—isn't that sad? I remember her, sort of, except I always got her mixed up with somebody else. They say we all have unique smells and cries, which is all very well assuming we remember what they are. I mean, every

human on earth has unique smells and cries, but could you use them to find your mom in Times Square on New Year's Eve? Because that's what these nurseries are like, imagine ten or twelve bazillion little baby seals all rolling around yelling at one time. They're really cute, humans keep telling me. They're attractive because of some maternal instinct thing involving big eyes and short noses, but what do most people do with baby animals? They EAT them, that's what! Baby animals taste the best, everybody knows, so I think it's just a load of crap that they're always saying they're attracted to them because they look like human babies—guess again! Since when do human babies have big eyes? They have little pinhead eyes. Also, they have no fur. I mean, for example, let's say your choice was eating cats or kittens—well, maybe kittens aren't the best, but I bet they taste better than full-grown cats, who live off garbage. Same with goats. I personally never eat anything but fish. Actually I eat all sorts of stuff, especially sweet rolls, candy and cereal which are not readily available in the sea. Anyhow, I'm going to London now. Then I have to pick: Shetland or Tel Aviv? I know what you'd say. Well, maybe not, you didn't know I was a silkie, so it depends what sort of guy you are. If you're a sort of conservative guy, a Confucianistic kind of guy who thinks everything has its proper place, you'd say, "Mary, return to your home, the sea!" But if you're a conservative guy, you might also say, "Return to your husband and try to work things out!" I saw the craziest ad in the

newspaper: They wanted silkies to sell their babies
to the government. I thought, THIS is fucked up.
Just so you know not to worry, believe me—silkies
never worry. Maybe it's something we picked up from
being seals, but short of killer whales, of which
there are precisely NONE WHATSOEVER in New York
City, London, and Tel Aviv combined, there's not really
much to worry about. If you're ever in a bad mood,
that's something you can think about when you're
walking around New York. Are there any killer whales
here? Then look around, look up, look down. The
answer will always be no!

Your friend,
Mary

She wrote another letter on the plane to Tel Aviv.

Dear Taylor,
    London is so WEAK. First, it's rainy and cold, almost
as rainy and cold as stupid Shetland. That's fine
if you're wrapped up in sealskin and have heal-
conserving ears inside your head where they don't
poke out, but otherwise it sucks. When I picked up
my skin I was tempted to put it on and head for the
water—well, actually that's what I went to London to
do, but then I thought of my nice friends in Tel Aviv,
plus my husband if he shows up. I was going to go
down to Cornwall and put on my skin and eat some
fish, but I didn't. I feel about boy seals now just
about the way I feel about the Runts. Not that it
matters much, because about 98% of the time they
don't know you exist, and neither does anyone else,

*and actually when you're a seal you don't even care.
But I cared, because I wasn't a seal yet. It's like
people being afraid of dying.*

That last sentence was enough to provoke a response from
Taylor's widow, which Mary received two weeks later when
Yigal brought it to her as she lay naked on the balcony, enjoy-
ing the midday sun.

*Dear Mary,
  I must let you know that Taylor has died. He was
struck by a car and did not suffer. The funeral
was held two weeks ago. Please don't be sad. Ask a
grown-up if you don't understand. Happy New Year!*

"Happy New Year?" Mary said, rolling over.

"She means the Jewish new year." Yigal tapped a disposable
pen on the table and added, "Someday I should buy a real pen."

"Taylor's dead—I met him in New York."

"What did he do?"

"He sold toothpaste, I think." She rolled over on her back
again. "Yigal, I'm bored."

"Fine, do something."

She stared up at the sky. "Let's go to the beach."

"I hear there are jellyfish."

"Okay, let's not go to the beach."

"I'm fine where I am." Yigal turned a page in his notebook.

"Let's kill Mr. Pickwick. Nell said the next missile will come
any day now. Missile attacks are so annoying! I hate them."

"We can if you'll let me do it. You shouldn't take risks when
you're pregnant. I think it's dangerous."

"So why would you do it either? Besides, you don't know

how to talk to dolphins. You can't even read Dolphin!" She assumed a superior air. "Nobody could possibly do this job better than me! You know mothers are very fierce. Dolphins are scared of us. You'd probably shoot at them, and then be eaten by a shark."

Yigal looked at his watch. "Can we do it tomorrow? I want to go to this reading."

"A poetry reading? Can I see?"

"Sure." He gave her the notebook, which was filled with random lines and dots.

"Show me how to write 'Moshe Dayan.'" He complied, and she took the pen and copied it several times.

"Do you want a blanket? The sun is making you purple." She wrapped up in a woolen comforter, arranged her pillow and went to sleep. Yigal put on a shirt and pants and walked to the North Tel Aviv art center, where a crowd was already gathering to hear Elad Manor read from his critically acclaimed new work, *South Lebanon Nocturnes*.

Elad had lost most of his hair and was wearing a white suit, flamenco boots, and aviator glasses. Yigal sat near the back and waited for the first poet to begin

A matronly woman tried to introduce her, but as soon as the crowd saw that she was eighteen, with fine, wispy short hair and the body of a twelve-year-old, it burst into cheers and she began.

Kiss of the Spider Woman

Raúl Juliá and William Hurt are together in jail.
William tells Raúl the plots of movies to pass the time.
The prison warden is not nice, he makes William give Raúl
poison.

But William wants to do it because that way he gets to see his
  mother.
Raúl almost dies and then they have sex.
At the end, William gives his life for Raúl.
The end, by Oria.

The crowd was silent for a moment, then leaped to its feet, applauding wildly. She smiled and spoke again.

One Million B.C.

Raquel Welch wears a leather bikini.
What else? I don't know.
The end, by Oria.

This time the applause was more subdued, but the young poet was unfazed and launched into an epic:

Babe, the Gallant Pig

Babe is a cute little pig who has no mom.
He lives on a farm with lots of animals.
There is a sheep, actually lots of sheep, a cat, a dog. . . .

Yigal saw that Elad was beaming with pride and guessed that the current poet must be his student.

Easy Rider

Bruce Dern and Dennis Hopper go riding to New Orleans.
They have big motorcycles, especially Dennis.
Bruce's jacket has an American flag.
They go to a wild party in the desert and meet girls.

They take acid in a cemetery with a different girl.
They meet Jack Nicholson, but these peasants bash his head in.
Look out, Bruce, here come the peasants!
They put the shotgun in Dennis' face and blow him away!
Bruce rides back to check on Dennis and they kill him too.
It's sad because Bruce is so dreamy.
The end, by Oria.

He looked at Elad again. Elad seemed not to know or care that it was Peter Fonda and not Bruce Dern.

At last she reached her climax:

Fantasia

It's really hard to explain but it's nice.
The end, by Oria.

Yigal turned to a woman sitting near him and said, "What is with this girl?"

The woman kept clapping and whispered, "Don't you see? She never allows the sign to obscure the thing signified. She'll surpass anything we've ever done."

Elad took center stage. "I'd like to thank Oria again for sharing herself with us." Oria glowed with a look of gratified lust and took off her sweater. Elad began promptly.

Fifty-Gallon Drum of Toxic Chemicals Lying Forgotten in a
Stream and Cow Entangled in Barbed Wire at the Edge of
a Minefield by Fendi

This year the look is sleeker, more refined.
Gone are last year's fringes and that tattered look in the cuffs.
This time of austerity calls for a narrower silhouette.

Skirts are tapered, over the knee.
Heels are stacked on a medium platform.
Earth textures are giving way to a more elegant satiny finish.
Key colors: russet and celadon.

He gestured, palm down, to hold the applause and continued:

Electrical Fire Still Smoldering in the Disabled
Jeep, Near It, an Abandoned Boot by Chanel

Oversized accessories, interchangeable between outfits
Create a look of funky chic. . . .

Yigal began to squirm. He looked around for a way out, but the hall was too crowded. He did not want Elad to recognize him. The woman he had spoken to leaned over to make a comment. "Isn't Karl Lagerfeld dead? Or was that Armani?"

"Versace," Yigal said. He put on sunglasses and stumbled out into the evening twilight.

CHAPTER 20

WHEN YIGAL GOT BACK FROM THE
poetry reading he knocked on our door. "Hi, Nell, is Zohar
back yet?"

I invited him in. "No, actually. He was called to Chicago for
a musicological emergency."

"What kind?"

"Something to do with the organ at Wrigley Field. The Cubs
are going to the playoffs, so he's helping them develop a new
tuning and some chord changes for their fanfares, and then
there's something with these parabolic disks on rooftops. He
said the Yankees had a similar system in the Bronx, but they
got caught after the super-low frequencies they were using
made one of the upper decks collapse, or something like that.
Coffee?"

"Sure—maybe you can help me."

I ignored him and started some water on the stove. "I think
the Yankees' mistake was being too influenced by La Monte
Young and Phill Niblock, or the CIA or whatever it was—
they were thinking in terms of mind control on an organic
level, when you can do the same thing using musical effects.
Like, if you were in the fifth inning of a no-hitter on a full

count, would you want to be hearing Penderecki's *Tren ofiarom Hiroszimy?*"

"No."

"And the beauty part is, no one but the target has any idea what's going on, and the whole system is passive. What did you say?"

"You're talking a lot. Are you lonely?"

"Not at the moment."

"I have some questions about Rafi," Yigal said. His boss happened to be Zohar's uncle. In compliance with Zohar's request, I am putting him in Avner's book, even though John le Carré already put him in another book. "I'm concerned that he may be disappointed by what I'm planning for tomorrow."

"Do you want a tarot reading?" Yigal shook his head. "Do you want my advice? Asking Zohar won't get you anywhere. The whole family just thinks Rafi is cute."

"Sure."

"Okay, here's the scenario: Rafi Eitan vs. the name of Moshe Dayan. Who wins?"

"I see your point. Thanks, Nell, you've been a big help, as always." He gave me a kiss on the cheek and took his coffee with him downstairs.

In the morning I went along to the port. We were in a festive mood. Mary seemed especially full of life, fidgeting in the backseat of the taxi. Yigal looked nervous. After a long and difficult discussion, he had agreed to hold the video camera while Mary did all the work. She wanted to get a nice film of what went on above the water, in case she missed something.

The seawall was nearly empty. Only a few tired ravers were left, drooling and hiccuping on the concrete, while a cadre of religious men said their prayers. With the sun behind us, we could see the submarine's outline clearly. Yigal and Mary crossed the seawall. He squatted with the camera, out of sight, while Mary took off her jeans. I stayed behind, in my arms what could turn out to be our mission's most important element: a forlorn, threadbare, one-eyed teddy bear known as "Meyer." It belonged to Yigal and might once have been intended to represent Winnie-the-Pooh.

"Rolling," Yigal said, and she leaped into the waves. Barely a minute later she was back, carrying a tiny strip of parchment. "Here," she said, still climbing up the rocks, and gave it to Yigal. He read it ("Moshe Dayan" was all it said), rolled it up, and punched it with his thumb through a hole in the neck-seam of the neglected toy. The effect was dramatic. The bear, Meyer, whom we were later to come to know so well, immediately turned his head, gave Yigal a despairing look, raised his arms, brought his blunt paws together like pincers, and ripped off his one remaining eye.

"Did you film that?" I asked.

Yigal was looking at the wall of a building. He seemed distracted. Quickly he shouldered the camera and aimed at the bubbling sea. Mr. Pickwick broke the surface in a slick of brown ooze. A layer of slime, crowded with bubbles, began to form on the dancing blue waves as the spiral casing of the sub unwound slowly, like one of those long, twisted bagels flipping itself in boiling water. The dowels popped out one by one and floated on the surface. Something like an airplane cockpit rose and then fell, dragged down by the massive osmium skeleton of the Leviathan, which came to rest on the shallow bottom, still oozing brown bubbles. A religious guy tapped on my shoulder.

"What's going on?" he asked.

"I don't know, it's doing something."

He looked over the wall. "Hi," he said to Mary and Yigal.

"Were you swimming?" he said, noticing Mary's wet hair. "Don't swim around here, it's not safe. Look at that—the sewer pipe's leaking again."

"Nasty!" Yigal said. "Let's get you into a shower." We thanked him and moved away. I asked Yigal if he wanted to hold Meyer. "No, no . . ." he said slowly. "I—there's something—I have a feeling he doesn't like me."

"Who doesn't like you?"

Yigal took off his glasses and rubbed his eyes as we crawled into the taxi. "I don't deserve to live," he said, looking far away out the window.

"What's wrong?" Mary asked. "Why aren't you happy? What's going on? Is there something between you and Meyer?" I pulled on her sleeve and indicated the taxi driver. "Do you speak English? No? Okay. Tell me, Yigal, I can't take this. I thought we'd have fun."

Yigal's voice became low and husky as he struggled to speak. "It's Meyer—I think I had sex with him, just once, and then I put him at the bottom of the laundry hamper for . . ." He paused and seemed to be counting. "For thirty-one years. I punished him—I didn't remember it until he looked at me—" Yigal opened his fist and there was the little black button, Meyer's eye. "My mother made his eyes, and his nose, and he used to have this little red shirt that said 'Meyer.'"

"Poor Meyer!" Mary cried, taking him in her arms. He inclined his head against her, and she felt the gentle pressure of his stubby arms. "Poor little Meyer," she repeated, before introducing herself at length.

"I thought there was some sentimental reason I was saving him," Yigal said to me. "I just always thought there was something like that, like I wanted to show him to my kids, I don't know. I idealized our whole relationship. It had nothing to do with reality." He looked at Meyer. "Is he—is he suffering? Should we take the parchment out and put it somewhere else?"

"Yigal, how could you say that?!" Mary cried. "Meyer is going to be fine!"

"Mary's right," I opined. "This is the best possible thing for him. Now he can take an active role in his life. He'll be able to grow and change and recover. He's a very lucky bear." Mary and I huddled together, stroking Meyer's somewhat truncated head and his tattered ears, from which all the plush had worn off.

Yigal retied his shoelaces for no reason and frowned. "I also remember this book I once saw that attracted me very much, and it makes me feel more than ever like shooting myself."

"What book?"

"It was in a bookstore, I only saw the cover. About these little yellow aliens with one eye—"

"*Runts of 61 Cygni C,*" Mary said. "I know that book. I talk about it all the time. I relate it to the way men are fascinated by silkies."

"Maybe," I whispered, "we shouldn't talk about this in front of Meyer."

Meanwhile, Zohar sat quietly facing the chimpanzees in the Lincoln Park Zoo. Near him on the bench were a small electronic keyboard and a cassette recorder. A small child approached and asked what he was doing.

"Musicological research—this is my control group. Have you ever tried to find graduate student volunteers who can demonstrate an authentic lack of musical education?"

"No," the child said.

"Have you taken music lessons?"

"No."

"Can you spare twenty minutes?"

The child shook his head. "No, my dad just went to the bathroom. He said we have to go and ride the train."

Zohar was lucky he had not gone to the zoo with anyone from Chicago. A Chicago native will always point up to a certain tall building from whose roof, one hot Fourth of July, a man fell and was bisected, leaving a vertical smear hundreds of feet long, in front of a crowd approaching one million. Zohar was not fated to hear this grotesque story: His Lincoln Park Zoo trauma was to be of a different order. Packing up, he walked toward the koala house. How he loved the gentle, peaceful koalas. There, a small crowd was admiring a new arrival. "What's he doing?" Zohar asked the zookeeper. "Is that baby koala doing what I think he's doing?"

"Yes, that's why the pouch faces toward the rear. There are also a few burrowing marsupials with pouches opening at the bottom, but that's just to keep the dirt—"

Zohar ran, covering his ears.

Due to my literary digressions—

I should point out, in case the reader has not already noticed, that economy and brevity are not what I value most in literature. I suspect many readers of having been suckered by the high school standard, usually introduced in a reading of "The Tell-Tale Heart" or "Hills Like White Elephants," that there is no idea worth expressing that is not worth expressing in 250 words.

Due to my digressions, Shats has expressed some concern that I appear to have read "everything." I share his concern to some degree and refer the reader to a loose legal-pad page floating in a notebook entitled "Ulan Bator and the New Schemata" dating from around 1987. The page originated as a note from a friend:

Hello—Nell—
came by to
drag a captive
off for breakfast
but there were
no prisoners to
be had
Mary

Three notes in my handwriting surround this amiable
missive.

Sideways:

> Gide's <u>acte gratuit</u> < = > surrealist activity?
> "where abstract potentiality achieves pseudo-realization."

Right side up:

> (24) "Thus Cesare Pavese notes . . . a sharp
> oscillation between 'superficial <u>verismo</u>' and
> 'abstract Expressionist schematism'"
> like in Robbe-Grillet/Joyce static and sensational
> vs. dynamic & developmental (<u>Lotte in Weimar</u>)

Upside down:

> In Hegel—inner & outer world form
> "objective dialectical unity"

With a different pen, obviously at some later date, I have
written:

> Lukács notes, I think?
> —<u>Realism in Our Time</u>, "Franz Kafka or Thomas
> Mann?"

In other words, not only was I reading Lukács for fun, but I was capable of remembering, even after several days, that I had done so. I was passionately attached to Adorno and other thinkers who reasoned carefully and wrote clearly, especially if they managed to mention Kafka, which all the good ones do sooner or later, and the bad ones too. The citation tends to support my claim, which I make at least once every five years whenever I feel I am in the presence of somebody who might give a flying fuck or have any clue what I am talking about, that between 1987 and 1989 I read nothing but Kafka, Kafka-related primary material, Kafka's favorite authors (e.g., Robert Walser), and Kafka scholarship. I fantasized about entering a Kafka trivia contest and coming away with the top prize for naming his Hebrew teacher. My to-do lists of this period bring me nothing but joy. For example:

> Read more Hamsun
> Janz, FN
> Pay income taxes!

I take *FN* to mean *Friedrich Nietzsche.* Hamsun was another favorite author of Kafka's, frequently recommended to his younger sisters. A Scandinavian, he wrote eloquently about things like shooting dogs in the head from close range. Similar lists still play a role in my life. For example, this spring I read Spengler. I expect to go cheerfully to my grave never having met another human being who has read a word of Spengler. The prospect does not frighten me.

Tucked into the same notebook is an unmailed letter to my mother about a class I had attended (December 1, 1987), taught by my friend Alberto Bades Fernandez Arago.

Went to Albert's contemporary lit class yesterday—it was lots of fun, the students were very sluggish, so sluggish that when some of them said very funny things, I was the only one giggling. Reading "The Heavy Bear Who Goes with Me," Delmore Schwartz about the body in general, & A. asks, "So what IS the heavy bear?" Student has a quick answer of which he is obviously sure: "The penis." A: "So how do you explain 'breathing at my side'? How do you explain 'kicks the football'?" Most males in the class seemed sure, at any rate, that it was a poem by and for males, which is like saying that Bambi is a book by and for deer. The penis proponent stuck to his guns for a while, while A. gently urged a more "consistently consistent" interpretation—then a sixteenish blondette in a ponytail says, "It's the conscience." She immediately had a legion of supporters, eager to believe that the conscience is the seat of aggression and lust. The moral I drew from most of this is that these are people raised on ambiguous (a.k.a. meaningless) contemporary poetry who thus have no respect for straightforward language . . . or any poem that isn't a Rorschach blot/riddle.

As well as a postcard from her (November 4):

For two days now I've dashed out when the mail arrived, all set to settle down and enjoy the letter you said you were going to write on Sunday. Have I been put out of mind again? What a blow! If you don't plan to write, say so. Love, I think, Mom.

The notebook contains a single poem.

Your face is like a coin to me
Your feet are like the snow's
Your ears descend like maple seeds
More slowly past your nose

Than diatoms that ornament
The ocean's turgid coils;
Come, delegate yourself to glide
To me on subtle hydrofoils! . . .

I remember how I came to write, under duress, this flagrantly criminal work, reminiscent of the poems composed by robots in the works of Stanisław Lem. I enrolled in a poetry workshop (I have mentioned it before), and at the very first meeting the professor asked each student to write a word on the chalkboard. Then he asked us all to go home and write poems that employed every word on the list.

I can't remember which word was mine, but I remember the white-faced, red-haired boy who wrote "turgid."

To return from these digressions to the topic of digression: Educated people are taught to value prose for its economy and poetry for its opacity, and in this their taste differs so completely from mine that, in fact, I may well have read, in the reading public's eyes, instead of "everything," virtually "nothing." For example, despite my having read the complete works of De Quincey and every word ever published by George Eliot except her translation of *Das Leben Jesu,* I cannot recall ever having seen or touched a book by Raymond Carver. In my mind, he appears as a sodden, terse combination of John Cheever and Charles Bukowski, lifting sketchy tales of cancer and divorce from country and western songs. Where did this impression come from? Who can say? But he is truly famous and popular.

When Mary and Yigal got home they put Meyer to bed and went out to talk on the balcony.

CHAPTER 21

"YIGAL, HE CAN'T LIVE HERE."

"Why not?"

"Can you imagine what it must be like for him? You saw how he responds to you."

"So where will he live?"

"I was thinking of getting him his own place. There are lots of little apartments around here—"

"You're forgetting one thing. He's supposed to protect me from Rafi."

"He will, Yigal, he will," Mary said. She ran her hand along the balcony railing and looked sorrowfully down at the street. "But give him time."

"What if I don't have any time? What about tonight, and tomorrow, and the next six months?"

"I don't know."

Yigal went inside to see if Meyer was awake. "Meyer?" he called. The bear ducked his head and inched under the pillow, trying to hide. "Meyer, I'm so sorry. I am so deeply sorry. I never suspected how you felt. I forgot what I'd done, and the whole thing is one of the most disgraceful episodes of my life." Meyer succeeded in pulling down the near edge of the pillow. Only the tip of one leg poked out. "Mary?"

"What?"

"Can you tell what he's feeling?"

"If you leave the room, maybe." Mary lifted the pillow and peeked underneath. Meyer was quivering and shaking his head. "Leave the room, Yigal."

About half an hour later Mary and Meyer appeared at my door. They stayed overnight, and in the morning, while Yigal went to see Rafi after receiving an urgent summons, we went shopping. We covered a big cardboard box inside and out with flowered contact paper and put it under a table in a corner of the living room. Inside we placed a sofa cushion, a small rug, a doll's rocking chair, and a selection of house-plants. "Meyer?" we called out. "We made you your own pri-vate place, where no one else is allowed to go."

Meyer approached, feeling his way along the floor. "What is he looking for?" Mary asked.

"You know what—it could be his eye. I think it's in Yigal's pocket." Meyer cocked his head at me and began to shiver, rolling over into a fetal position. Mary scooped him up and took him to bed just as Yigal sat opposite Rafi, fingering Meyer's eye.

"Rye Playland was no help at all," Yigal said. "I'm still consid-ering a trip to Iceland."

"What's in your pocket? Souvenir?"

Yigal gave him the button. "Look familiar?"

"It reminds me of—you know, it's a little strange who it re-minds me of."

"Actually, it's not strange at all." He took the button back and held it in his hand. "By the way, the target doesn't exist."

"That's fine, because the committee met last night and we voted to offer you a pension. I wanted to keep you on, but there was a consensus to—to let you go . . ."

Yigal eased the pistol out of his waistband and laid it on the desk. "Any more formalities?"

Rafi started to pick up the gun, then seemed to change his mind. He wiped his hands on his lapels and smiled. "Yigal, you really have done excellent work, and I'm going to ask the committee to double your pension. I'm also nominating you for the Har-Zion Award, and I'm going to name a suite of offices after you, in Dimona. Privately, I'd like to offer you an opportunity to purchase shares in the expansion of the Eilat dolphin reef."

Yigal took the gun back and smiled. "Thank you. My retirement comes as a pleasant surprise. As you know, my wife is pregnant, and I look forward to spending quality time with our child." Rafi was laughing as Yigal closed the door.

Yigal had seriously misinterpreted one of his remarks. The button reminded Rafi of certain pajamas worn by a certain somebody's mother on certain occasions between 1952 and 1956, and not, as Yigal had assumed, of Moshe Dayan. Moshe Dayan's pajamas, Rafi recalled, had large, flat buttons of light blue Bakelite. Then he sighed and returned to work. The Kibbutz Negba pajama parties were legendary, but belonged to a time and a mood that would never return again. He thought of the lines of Luis Cernuda:

Adolescente fui en días idénticos a nubes,
Cosa grácil, visible por penumbra y reflejo,
Y extraño es, si ese recuerdo busco,
Que tanto, tanto duela sobre el cuerpo de hoy. . . .

Roughly, "I was adolescent in a haze of delicate confusion, but the remembrance brings only pain to the body I have now." Soon after, Yigal and Mary began having their big fights about prenatal care. I would hear the door rattling and there would be Meyer, dusty from the stairs, pushing to be let in. From below I could hear Yigal shouting about folic acid and ultrasounds.

Meyer nestled into my arms and looked up gratefully. His new eyes were neatly picked out in blue-and-white embroidery floss, and he had a tiny red line for a mouth. All his ruptures were neatly darned, and he wore a different outfit every day. He lived in the box, which he had rigged up with a washcloth for a door, and spent most of his time listening intently to talk radio call-in shows.

I was beginning to show the strain of separation from Zohar. When he called I found his excuses increasingly thin. Our conversations—at least on my side—became sarcastic. "The Cubs in the World Series? When hell freezes over! Can't you do any better than that? How about some lost Schubert songs discovered extant as microscopic fragments in recycled newsprint papering the ladies' room of a bell tower in St. Petersburg?"

"Actually, Nell, you're not far from the truth—"

I screamed. I heard Meyer's characteristic thud as he hit the floor downstairs and ran to safety on the balcony. Sometimes I wondered if instead of giving him eyes, we should have sewn his ears shut.

"I've been invited to examine a piano that has not been touched since it was played by Chopin. It's been enshrined, more or less, in the drawing room of a mansion in Bydgoszcz. The youngest daughter in each generation is entrusted with ensuring that—"

"That's it, Zohar. Make up your mind. It's him or me."

There was a long silence. "I've been writing some prose-poetry," he said. "About my students. There's a recurring image that haunts me—mechanical cockroaches." He blew his nose.

I was moved by pity and asked, "Did you know Elad Manor is seeing that little nympho you were so crazy about?"

"Elad Manor? He couldn't fuck his way out of a paper bag!" I sensed Zohar's machismo emerging again from the cocoon where it had briefly sheltered, unable to thrive in the touchy-feely, romantic atmosphere of an American sports team. "Elad Manor hasn't done anything worth mentioning since *Sailing Toward the Sunset,* and that was, what, let me see, almost six weeks ago. Elad Manor is washed up. By next week nobody will remember the name of Elad Manor, except maybe that ungrateful minx—she'll remember him every time she takes her penicillin—did you see him?"

"Yigal saw him read at Beit Haomanim."

He gagged. "If I were Avner Shats, I would put out a contract on Elad Manor."

"Zohar, think what you're saying! Avner knew the risk going in. He knew if he let Elad lay claim to his poetry, Elad would probably end up with ten or twelve beautiful teenaged lovers—he told me so himself. Avner knows the seductive power of words, unlike some other people I could name who write obsessively about mechanical cockroaches. Anyway, you should hear what Elad is writing now. I hate it when people write about war. It's such a cheap effect. Of course, everybody worships him. Amos Oz is saying he's going to shoot himself on television so Elad can be the new prophet of Eretz Israel, or something like that."

"I must come home," Zohar said. "My country needs me. Expect me soon. Give my love to the eerie little bear."

"Meyer," I said. "Good-bye, my love! Until tomorrow!"

CHAPTER 22

SUMMER TIDES HAVE STRIPPED MUCH of the sand from the beach below the Roman city of Apollonia, and Zohar and I often walk there now to seek pretty shells and Phoenician mosaic tiles. On Saturday as I skirted the waterline, a narrow black form caught my eye, a digital watch which proved to be exactly identical to Zohar's, but one hour faster. Crusted with salt and worn smooth by the action of the waves, it had apparently functioned in the Mediterranean for three months, since the end of daylight saving time.

As *Sailing Toward the Sunset* flirts ever more promiscuously with satire, I often think of Ödön von Horváth's beautiful novel *Youth Without God,* and its injunction to abandon ridicule in favor of sincere praise of that which is highest. Why then should I hesitate to reveal the brand name of the heroic wristwatch? If it did not in fact survive three months in the bitter waters of the ancient and historic cesspool, it can only have come to us via the Suez Canal. Perhaps a fish coughed it up on the beach, like Jonah; perhaps it fell from an Indian freighter; very possibly, waterspouts were involved. Whatever its origin, I stand in awe of the Casio F91W, our gift from the sea.

As William Blake once wrote,

Mock on, mock on, [Avner], [Nell];
Mock on, mock on; 'tis all in vain!
You throw the [watch into the sea],
And the wind blows it back again.

And every [watch] becomes a gem
Reflected in the beams divine;
Blown back they blind the mocking eye,
But still in Israel's paths they shine.

Mary pulled her beret down over her ears and shivered. We were sitting outside in the shade at the café downstairs. I hadn't seen her in several days. Her nose was red from crying.

"What's wrong with Yigal? Is he crazy?" she moaned. "He wants me to stay here and never leave, and he wants to raise his child himself, and he wants me to get all these tests to make sure it's okay—it's a seal pup, all right? How okay is that?"

"Maybe it's you he's worried about."

"Then he should let me go! It's not me, it's his pup. Ever since I've been pregnant he's so possessive. Except when he ran off, did I mention that?"

"You did."

"He ignores me now. He spends all his time model railroading with Meyer. He never touches me except to do this weird listening, palpating routine like he thinks he's some sort of obstetrician."

"Listen, Mary," I said. "You have to put yourself in his position. He just lost his job, he's in love with a seal, and he's living with an ersatz Winnie-the-Pooh he raped and abandoned. He doesn't feel he has any control over his environment, so he's trying to control what he can, like your diet and the model railroad. Don't you think it makes him feel good, when the little train goes around and around, and he can make it go faster and slower?"

"I guess," she sniffled. "The train is great. Meyer loves it too. You know, Meyer's an odd character."

"Yes?" I encouraged her. I wanted to know what she found so unusual about Meyer.

"What I mean is, he's completely independent, yet there's nothing he can do for himself. If he wants to see a book, you have to open it for him and turn the pages. But if you didn't open it, he'd be fine. He has his house, and his radio. Except that he's so cute, and tragic, and Yigal feels really guilty, so he just sits there all the time, watching him, waiting to see if he wants something, trying out different things to see if he likes them . . ."

Just then, two floors up, Meyer sat on the carpet studying an aerial view of the Temple Mount. He indicated to Yigal that he needed a better map. Yigal opened a file cabinet and found a tourist guide to the Old City of Jerusalem. "Something more detailed?" he asked. "Are you looking for something for driving, or as a pedestrian?" Yigal turned the pages one by one until they arrived at the City of David, at which point Meyer nodded and looked fixedly at the model railroad. "You want to go to Jerusalem on the train? It's too late to go today. Is tomorrow all right?" Meyer nodded again. As Yigal lifted the phone to call for the train schedule, he added, "Are you sure it wouldn't be okay to drive?"

Then he saw, stuck to the bulletin board with a pin, the Order of Har-Zion. With a flash of insight, his brief psychogenic fugue ended as it had begun.

He turned and stared at Meyer. "Mind if I look in your

house? Yes? Well, I'm looking anyway." Yigal lay down and lifted the washcloth. He felt around inside until his hand encountered something heavy and rectangular. "Meyer, what the hell is this? Is this, or is this not, the box of Kalashnikov cartridges I thought I had lost?" Meyer looked at the floor. "Meyer, you have been a very bad bear, and you are not going to Jerusalem tomorrow." Yigal kept feeling around inside Meyer's house until he found a shiv, several lengths of wire, a perfume bottle, a disposable camera, and almost three thousand shekels in cash. He opened the bottle carefully over the sink. It contained ether. "Bad, bad bear," Yigal repeated, placing Meyer unceremoniously in a briefcase and locking it shut.

We saw him come out the front door. "Yigal, over here!" Mary waved cheerfully. "Where are you headed?"

"I wasn't sure," he said, sitting down. "We have some serious Meyer trouble." He told the story and concluded, patting the briefcase, "He's in here."

Mary was outraged. "How could you do such a thing?!" She snatched the briefcase from Yigal. "What's the combination? Meyer, Meyer, everything's going to be fine!"

"No," Yigal told Mary.

I held her arm to keep her from running. "Wait," I said. "What if it's like this: What if this isn't Meyer at all? What if Meyer doesn't get any benefit from being animated this way? You say all he does is sit and listen to talk radio, right? Well, what if what he'd really rather do is live on a shelf and be played with every so often? What I'm saying is, maybe this has nothing to do with Meyer."

She sat down. "Ask Meyer."

Yigal opened the briefcase and put Meyer on the table, after taking away the letter opener he'd concealed in his tiny underpants. Meyer looked around nervously, then sat down by the sugar. "You ask him, Mary," Yigal said.

Mary picked him up and he snuggled almost violently against her, trying to lose himself between her breasts. "Poor little Meyer," she said. "Is this really hard for you?" Meyer nodded. "Would you rather rest?" He nodded again and actually made a sort of tiny whimpering sound, God knows how, but we kept our distance.

"Is it Yigal?" He shook his head. "Is it Moshe?" He nodded. She loosened a thread at his neck and found the edge of the parchment. "Tell me if this doesn't feel good," she said, drawing it slowly from between two lumpy wads of cotton batting. Meyer kept nodding and nodding, and then, suddenly, was inert.

We were all silent for a long time. Mary held the name in her hand, reading it over and over, and then said, "That was the saddest thing I ever saw." She gave Meyer to Yigal, who hugged him, sobbing. The waitress finally noticed him. "Double espresso," Yigal said through his tears.

"Another large cappuccino," I added. "Can I see that?" Mary handed me the all-powerful name of Moshe Dayan. "Now what do we do with it? Eating it or rolling a joint with it are definitely out."

"Do you think it could be improved?" Mary said. "Like, if we tucked it into a good book?"

"What languages do you think it can read?" I asked Yigal. "I like Mary's idea a lot. I want to start it on some Robert Walser right away."

"I think this is a case for a demonologist," Yigal said, "but after what I've heard about their general level of expertise, my proposal is as follows." He stirred his coffee. "First, we need to see what the smallest effective dose is. How big a piece of this name is needed to animate objects? In fact, I don't think we should be touching it without gloves. It could be influencing our thoughts. There's some basic information we need before we can formulate an effective disposal plan. Actually, thinking about it, I'd rather just assume that even the smallest particles could be dangerous, which inclines me to favor sealing it in a concrete block and—Nell, didn't you say your brother has a job dropping things into deep trenches in the Gulf of Mexico?"

"He sure does," I said proudly.

"Well, that's my plan," Yigal concluded. "Concrete block, ocean trench."

"Except what if the concrete block rises out of the ocean, flies through the sky, and lands smack-dab on the Dome of the Rock?" Mary asked.

"Oh." We were silent again.

"And at first everybody thinks it's a bomb, and then a meteor, but then they crack it open—"

"We get the picture," I said. "This is a tough one."

"We could bury it in a mine. Except then it might animate the whole earth." Yigal was pensive. "We don't know where it would stop."

"Maybe all the oil from Saudi Arabia would flow to Tel Aviv and start gushing out of the storm sewers," Mary suggested. "And it would rain once a week, all summer long. And then giant volcanoes—"

I suddenly thought of a different tactic and interrupted. "It needs to go somewhere where there are safeguards already in place. A political group, say, that's already frustrated and under surveillance. Make sure it gets into people we know are inept, instead of some heavy object that could prove dangerous."

They both looked at me and smiled. "Nell's right," Yigal

said. "That's genius. And I have a brilliant idea to go along with it."

"I don't want to know," I said.

"Is it that soccer team you hate?" Mary asked.

"I don't want to say," Yigal said. "Hey, where's the parchment?"

We looked all around. "I guess it blew away," Mary said. Yigal jumped up and ran down the street while I scoured the sidewalk. The name of Moshe Dayan was nowhere to be found.

Mary shrugged. "So what? It's best of all this way. What can a name do to hurt anybody?"

CHAPTER 23

ALREADY I SUFFER FROM NOSTALGIA and vain regrets, a personal Anxiety of Influence: How can I maintain cohesiveness and unity without falling into pointless rehashing of subjects and characters already flogged to death? I prefer not to think about chapters earlier than yesterday's, yet I cannot help recalling vaguely an early lament on the attitudes of certain academics toward the ancient Greeks. How I long to rectify my failure to mention the pre-Socratics!

The pre-Socratic philosophers were favorites of Heidegger's and of all those who believe that when the world was new and fresh, ultimate truth lay floundering on the dock, and all you needed was a bucket. Sophisticated language, you see, tends to obscure our view of things-in-themselves, creating lifetimes of thankless labor for the philosophers of today. Luckily some languages are less obscurantist than others. Pre-Socratic Greek, the theory goes, was chock-full of stunningly accurate common nouns. Only German (Heidegger wrote) can hope to rival its ontological precision.

I took a semester-long course in Greek philosophy and a year's seminar on Heidegger. Our education in pre-Socratic philosophy consisted of the following statement:

EVERYTHING IS MADE OF WATER.

The professor, a big fan of both Heidegger and the pre-Socratics, said this proved that the pre-Socratics were way beyond Einstein. I tried to rediscover the mysterious statement in a book on the pre-Socratics belonging to Zohar's sister and lifted from her by Zohar without permission many years ago, but I failed. Although the book was published in 1981, the primary texts are rendered in a vaguely Mishnaic turn-of-the-century Hebrew that mystifies even Zohar. However, I did find a poem by Empedocles in which the words "Zohar" and "Meyer" both appear.

Of Heidegger I learned, not from the hagiographic class discussions but from reading *Being and Time* in German, that he was an idiot. His etymological curios, so bewitching in translation, flaunt in their transparently moronic original an air of validity on the order of: [Insert here impromptu Heidegger imitation of choice, e.g., "Seattle, we see, is a fine place to sit," or "The word 'boring' suggests a drill-like, twisting action; you will recall from our discussion of 'screwing' . . ." or "Poodles come from puddles"].

I was a little sorry, when Zohar returned home late one night, having attended a department meeting on his way from the airport, that he had missed Meyer's period of activity. Even Meyer's house was already gone from the garbage pile—

American readers may not realize that when I refer to a "garbage pile," I am speaking of a literal pile of literal garbage sitting in a shallow pit created by its usual means of removal (a municipal combination dump truck and backhoe). Why these piles are allowed to exist, on conspicuous street corners and in the entrances to public parks, it is not in the purview of this work to say. Leaving its pile, garbage makes a short trip to one of the picturesque "Garbage Mountains" that dot the Israeli skyline. These are conveniently located next to major intersections so that no tourist can miss seeing at least two or three.

—and Meyer sat dimwittedly on a shelf, doing service as a bookend. Zohar threw down his briefcase and embraced me passionately.

"My dear Zohar, you are so cute," I said.

"Give me a minute. I have to print." He ran to the computer and inserted a diskette. "My Chicago epic will revolutionize Israeli poetry and chart its development for the next hundred years. Of course, I can't say it's about Chicago, and I'll have to put a naked woman on the cover. I'm thinking of calling it *South Lebanon Nocturnes*. What do you think?"

"That's the name of Elad's new book."

Zohar fixed me with an angry eye. "Curse him! That scoundrel will pay for this." From his T-shirt pocket he pulled a half-moon-shaped knife. "Do you know what this is?"

"Darling," I said, "would you like a chocolate sandwich instead?"

"You don't know? Here's a hint: It's Mongolian—but were you referring to a frozen pita carefully defrosted in a warm toaster oven, split, halved, and stuffed with a generous portion of the ersatz chocolate crème made famous by the native industry of Be'er Sheva in the hallowed year of 1961?" Zohar pulled up a chair and sat down at the kitchen table. "Already I feel my bloodlust melting away. I pardon you, Elad Manor. You will live to write again; your egregious poetry will spatter its blots of shame, which cry out to heaven, upon the Hebrew language without my interference." He bit the sandwich and turned to me. "Elad Manor," he added, "owes you his life."

With that he opened his briefcase and began preparing to teach the next day's music analysis class, pausing only to extort a promise that he will be assigned no more lines of dialogue, especially ones like those above, from now until the end of the novel.

Just then Yigal appeared at the door. In his hand was a page torn from a spiral notebook and marked in a childish, almost unreadable hand. He gave it in silence to Zohar. " 'What the Serial Killer Wants,' " Zohar read aloud.

What the Serial Killer Wants

The serial killer wants everything to be love.
Like an egg, he explains.
What isn't love must be eliminated, says
The serial killer, filed smooth, like
An egg. There is no place, he
Says, for what is not sufficiently smooth,
Round and
White.

"Whoever wrote this," Zohar added, voluntarily breaking his self-imposed ban on speech, "is perhaps the greatest living Israeli writer."

"It's Meyer's," Yigal said.

"Wow, Yigal," I said, reading over Zohar's shoulder. "It's just like in *Star Trek II: The Wrath of Khan,* where Khan says, 'From hell's heart I stab at thee.' Also it's a little bit like the episode with Nomad." Zohar had already started typing the poem on his computer.

"I've been turning the house upside down, seeing if there are any more of these," Yigal said. "But I can't find a thing.

I wish we hadn't lost that little parchment. This can't be the first and last thing he ever wrote, can it? It's so powerful. I never thought of myself as a serial killer before, and I never thought what it meant to demand that Meyer love me."

"Don't whine," I said. "You have to learn to let things go."

"That's your New Age crap," Yigal said. "It's like telling me I have to learn to say, 'Who cares?' when everything worth having stands on a foundation of memory, responsibility, and sacrifice."

Zohar looked up with a pained expression, then went back to typing.

"So what are you doing for Meyer right now?" I asked. "Remembering him? What have you sacrificed, besides what was probably a better mood?"

Yigal grabbed the paper and ran off.

Since my friend David says I should write my memoirs, and Zohar is always saying I should write a book about my parents, I thought I would take this opportunity to tell the story of:

THE MAILBOX

The American tale of a father's struggle against adversity is a genre in itself. Generally, following the model of Lear, the father harms no one more than himself, and comes to see his folly only after alienating no one more than his beloved ten-year-old daughter, the light of his life. The story typically begins when the father, a white-collar proletarian who works long hours, is sitting one evening in his La-Z-Boy before the picture window, looking peacefully across the shaded lawn to his vegetable garden/bird feeder and sees the deer/squirrel that will become his nemesis. It ends when the father understands that he must submit to nature just as he already submits to his boss, his wife, and his ten-year-old daughter, the light of his life.

My family did not work quite like that. Also, the challenge facing my father was urgent, practical, and expensive. Our house sat one hundred yards from a narrow but busy country road. Our mail came by Rural Free Delivery to a large mailbox on which I had painted, on one side, a sixteen-inch disappearing gun hurling a projectile and, on the other, a koala. The mailbox bore the rubric "PREPONDERANCE," which, as our school bus driver often told the assembled children, was a dirty word in Spanish. My father had protested against my mother's naming the house "Banner Acre" in memory of the Banner Chinchilla Ranch on which his father had spent the family's savings in the early 1930s, so we chose the name "Preponderance," which refers to a mounted cannon's weight at the breech. Once the chinchilla farm folded, my father's family stayed on the land, and it was there, as a child, that my father learned to use dynamite. Dynamite plays no role in the story of the mailbox, but my father and his father used it to blow a barn door quite a few feet into the air while excavating a basement, and many years later, when my father visited the farm again, he felt compelled to point out to the new owners that most of the dynamite was still there, its paper casings nearly rotted away, on a shelf in the garage.

One morning we saw that our mailbox was dented. It is well known that young men like to hang out the windows of cars and hit things with sticks. We fixed it. A week later, it happened again, and then a week after that, and so on, almost every Friday night for months. After the mailbox was knocked right off its post, we asked a sheriff's deputy to sit all night in his car watching it so he could make an arrest.

Strangely, he agreed, but he must have taken a nap, for in the morning, our mailbox was gone.

We bought a new mailbox and started again. The deputy staked it out again. Nothing happened. New players, or at least new equipment, seemed to join the fray: Our mailbox was now regularly peppered with buckshot. But it continued to function, receiving mail, and my father's grief was held somewhat in check, until it vanished completely, post and all. We set the post in concrete, but late that Friday night, we heard a sound, ran outside, and saw that only a hole remained where mailbox number three or number four or whichever it was had stood. At this point it became clear to us that my father had sworn a mighty oath, for, apparently fearing an interruption of mail service, he had mailbox number four or number five on reserve in the garage, and now comes the truly amazing part of the story, which I still remember vividly and viscerally.

The new mailbox went up on a metal post attached to a "deadman," that is, a pipe buried horizontally several feet below the ground. It went up late that summer night (I remember holding the flashlight), and then the watches began. From that point forward, whoever attempted to put a load of buckshot into the Zinks' mailbox would find himself confronted by a child, aged approximately nine, ten, or eleven (there were three of us), armed with an Instamatic flash camera.

The two-hour shifts were supposed to be carried out from a clump of honeysuckle that covered a rotting stump about thirty feet from the road, but I recall putting myself a little farther out of the line of fire, up the hill a bit, behind an ornamental spruce tree. My usual shift started at midnight in a pastoral silence broken only by the hooting of owls, the creaking of dead pine trees not yet fallen, and the sound of

animals moving about in the underbrush. My feelings of terror were generally low and constant, thus manageable, except
when a car came by and seemed to be slowing down, or just
before two when my older brother, who took the last shift,
would make a game of stalking me.

At some point came the quiet denouement. My father must
have submitted. I don't know anymore. When I try to remember how it ended, I think only of how I used to scream when
I felt my brother's hand on my shoulder, materializing out of
the darkness and silence like a ghost's. I admired him for it.
Tarzan himself, I thought, could not have approached more
silently.

At home, I was a stranger to the learned helplessness of
well-brought-up children. When I felt hungry, I would make
a fried bologna sandwich, garlic toast, or a meringue pie. If
my parents wanted me, they knew how to find me: My father
had installed a buzzer system, and two short beeps was my signal to appear "front and center," standing at attention in the
living room. Breakfast was my responsibility. If I missed the
school bus, I would run as fast as I could the three-quarters
of a mile to a corner where the bus would pass again after
making a loop through a housing tract.

At ten I was already a competent roofer, but my first love
was digging foundations. I remember the odd impression
things like this made on my classmates. They preferred to
play things like "Barbie Is Constipated," which generally involved putting things in her pants. Mudpies? Is this a joke?
I would think, invited to crouch behind a house with a girl I
admired in school as some sort of unapproachably cool and
popular superwoman.

How I suffered. I suffered constantly. My classmates were

compelled to appear in plays I had written, horrible, tasteless plays. How I long to know that every copy of these plays has been destroyed. I destroyed my own long ago. I am sure everyone despised me. One by one, all my personal deadlines and challenges slipped past, unmet. I could never climb from tree to tree, and as my ninth birthday passed steeped in sin, I realized I would never be a younger saint than the Little Flower of Jesus. I then pinned my hopes on being the Second Coming of Christ, or at least His mother, but realizing the cards were stacked against me, I chose to become instead the first female cadet at the U.S. Naval Academy. To my horror, they began admitting women when I was twelve. A new idol entered my life, giving Tarzan some breathing room: Sarah Bernhardt. I searched for, but could not find in our local library, La Fontaine's fable of the two pigeons, the piece with which she won entrance to the Comédie-Française. I memorized the soliloquies of Hamlet, noting that it would have taken Sarah no more time to do so than it took me just to scan them. I read a biography of a contemporary California genius who escaped to college at age twelve, and noticed that I had nothing whatsoever in common with him—I had not gone to kindergarten prattling of dolomitic marble as he had, nor did I learn the alphabet in my cradle. "Your brother is a genius," my mother explained. "You are merely very bright." All my attempts to seem supersmart impressed no one. My idea of learning Latin from a book ended in emotional collapse after I discovered that, in addition to acquiring new vocabulary, I was expected to develop some sneaking suspicion of what noun cases might be. I noticed once and for all that George Gamow's *One, Two, Three . . . Infinity* lost me around page 30, and despite all my efforts to please my mother on the tennis court, I had no backhand, no serve, and an inconsistent forehand. I played both the fife and the bosun's pipe too poorly to merit a public performance on either. In other words, I realized, I was a fool. School was constant torture—my pants were all too short—and I would sit under my bed reading the Psalms, trying to befriend the God of the Old Testament who would be with me to help as I looked down upon my foes, their brains dashed out against assorted rocks.

"Let it go, let it go," my friend Ms. Jumbo Loopy Chenille would say to all this, and she would be right. People today are often heard to remark that I am articulate. Why should they be made to suspect that my verbal skill, such as it is, originated not in a habit of speaking, but in a lifetime spent preparing a single essay (any length, as long as it might hold the wandering attention of the listener from start to finish) on the subject "Why are you crying?" By the time I first heard the question at age fifteen, I had already reasoned that there might be an inverse proportion between a given subject's willingness to ask it and his or her ability to understand the response. Therefore, over the years, I prepared and presented many heavily edited, audience-specific versions of the essay. I suspected that the original would easily fill a book, but who would read it? In November 1996, at age thirty-two, I finally succeeded in communicating the essay in its entirety. I wrote it all by hand, and mailed it away. While I wrote it, I lived in a state of angelic peace. When I imagined the recipient reading it, I saw him bathed in golden light. Sometimes I wonder what it said.

Having delivered myself of my own magnum opus, I was at last ready to turn my attention to the great works of others, such as Avner Shats.

CHAPTER 24

THE PLOT OF *SAILING TOWARD THE Sunset* seems forced and dry after the lurid glory of the mailbox, but being a novel, it must march on. October turned to November, the leaves fell, and the first snow spangled the tree branches—in Vermont I mean—while in Tel Aviv the summer continued unabated, but somewhat less like an oven. With December came the jelly doughnuts of Hanukkah, not unlike those which John F. Kennedy claimed he resembled so closely in his famous speech *"Ich bin ein Berliner."* The weather cooled by several degrees, and Mary began to look pregnant. January: A time of frosty chill on Mount Hermon, where Shats sat placidly fulfilling his military reserve duty. February, month of Israel's arbor day and the cruel holiday of Purim, arrived just as the weeds of the Galilee hit nine feet in height, fueled by the turgor pressure of constant rain on saturated ground. March brought with it huge poppies, daisies and anemones, swarms of birds, and mushrooms. In April four storks passed over, heading for Holland, and Mary had her baby.

She was perfectly beautiful, downy soft and white, with

huge black eyes and long whiskers stiff as nylon. They named her Rakeffet, after a potted plant. Mary bought a cat brush and saved all the fur as it fell out. She never did quite decide what to do with it, and it's still in the top of their closet in a transparent plastic bag.

Little Rakeffet was Yigal's pride and joy, so it was no big shock to anyone except Mary when, at the age of eight weeks, she was found following him around the kitchen with her skin hanging by one leg. "I don't really want to consider the implications," Mary said, "but it's fine by me." A month later she came upstairs with Rakeffet and the skin, looking upset. "Help me get her into this," she begged. We pinched and squeezed until Rakeffet squeaked and moaned, but it was no use—we couldn't get it over her head. Yigal's parents then materialized and insisted on having a party called a *brita*, i.e., the feminine version of a circumcision. (Rakeffet emerged unharmed.) Yes, those were lively, entertaining times, but now I should get back to the really rich stuff: "My Memoirs and Parents." Come to think of it, I should leave my parents out of it, since they might read this far someday, so I'll just call it: "My Memoirs."

"MY MEMOIRS" BY NELL

When I was eighteen, my mother and I took a trip to Greater Detroit, where my elder brother was in school. After two years on a tuba scholarship at Valley Forge Military Academy, he had chosen to attend the University of Michigan at Ann Arbor. He was majoring, of course, in mathematics, but had elected, in his first semester, to study both elementary Hebrew and elementary Arabic, and his grades were suffering. In the second semester, after our visit, he accepted his tuition money from our mother and used it to buy a very large and even mysterious stereo system. I remember the amplifier well, a silver cube with a vertical row of red LEDs and one knob. His record was *The Velvet Underground and Nico.* I bought him *Songs of Leonard Cohen,* and he played them both.

Together we went to visit a very nice and charming woman whom we all like very much. She had visited us in California in 1966 to bear an illegitimate son, so she had known my elder brother and me from an early age. As we sat in a festive circle around her Christmas table, she turned to David and asked, "Do you remember Nell's imaginary friend you killed?"

He did not. Neither did I. She went on to tell how I had possessed, as a very small child, one friend. This friend was small enough to fit in my hand, and no one else touched him. I carried him in my pocket, and when I sat down, wherever I was, I always placed him carefully next to me.

One day, David and I were playing with a wagon, and in the commotion David saw that my friend was alone. He picked up my friend with two fingers and raised it over his head. I stood petrified in terror, my mouth like an O, the woman said, as David slowly parted his thumb and forefinger and watched my friend fall to the concrete. I remained motionless with my hands on my cheeks for a few seconds, and then I began screaming. I continued screaming for hours, and I never had another imaginary friend, at least not until November 1996.

After November 1996 I reorganized my priorities along lines suggested by Montaigne's "On Some Verses of Virgil."

The little slip of parchment flew on the dry wind. It flew right over the Ayalon Highway, and over Ben Gurion Airport and the monastery at Latrun and Zohar's sister's apartment and the walls of the Old City, and eventually it flew right into East Jerusalem, and then across the Jordan, still heading east, at which point everyone lost sight of it as if it had never existed, though it was to undertake several interesting confidential projects.

Meyer went to live with Yigal's six-year-old cousin in Kibbutz Be'eri. A year later, he lay on top of a water tank, disintegrating in the sun. He turned to lint.

Zohar and I lay in bed and I told him about my next novel, *Volvox*. "Remember *Vox*?" I asked. "This is just like that, except it's about unicelled flagellates." There were clear echoes of my novel #0—the novel before my first novel (*Sailing Toward the Sunset* is my second novel)—which I always assumed it would be my life's work to write. Titled *Autobiography of a Radiolarian*, it showed the influence of Solzhenitsyn all too plainly: The protagonist, a small diatom, is caught in a deep ocean current that will take two hundred years to cross the Atlantic and release her off the coast of France, but meanwhile she is forced to confront the globigerine ooze, a vast graveyard of near-infinite numbers of her friends and family. I never wrote a word of it, until in 1993 I decided that the first issue of my punk rock fanzine should include a work of fiction. Modestly, I titled the piece "Fiction."

"FICTION" BY NELL

Rfmx left the sea at the age of four. . . .

The next few sentences concern her efforts to get drunk in New York City with no money. Eventually, frustrated, she resolves to seek the company of other radiolaria. Rescued from them by heroic baby lambs, she becomes a professional shepherdess, drinking brandy on her back in the Sheep Meadow and watching them frolic and play until her death at age six. The lambs say the same line over and over: "Baa!" I.e., they are difficult to understand, but it is clear that everything they say is positive and that all their intentions are good.

I realize now that I forgot to explain what I meant by Yigal's lofty feeling of superiority vis-à-vis the sexuality of American men.

Israeli men maintain:

1. That American men are obsessed with large breasts.

The grass is always greener on the other side of the fence—it really is, because you can't help trampling the grass on the side where you are, but anyhow, perhaps those American men would enjoy visiting Tel Aviv. I attribute the absurdly large breasts of some American lingerie models to internal competition in the industry, the same force that supposedly led a Nevada strip club in the 1960s to advertise a "topless nursing mother of six" who was a dachshund. The glamor of dominatrices arises in a similar way—submissive men are not actually very picky, but with so many doms jockeying for the submissive dollar, a competitive subculture arises on its own. The top echelon comes to function as a cartel, bringing some assurance of decent pay and safe working conditions to its members. Like the possession of a dentist's chair or a cattle prod, absurd breasts function for the model, in marketing terms, as a "point of difference."

2. *That American men are obsessed with blow jobs.*

This is quite true. I blame it on estrogenic drinking water and the "growth hormone" in American beef. Together, these have reduced the median American penis by 35 percent over the last fifty years (I base my estimate on anecdotal evidence and on drawings and tables found in a strangely comprehensive hygiene manual of the 1920s, property of the University of Pennsylvania), while the American woman has become a giantess. If you can't see the connection, just forget I said anything at all.

3. *That American pornography is perversely clinical.*

I have seen two American porno films, which is two too many. As everyone admits, they are all the same: the beige bedspread, the stock footage, Ron Jeremy. Only once did I catch a glimpse of foreign smut. A French movie featured a character addicted to pornography, and in the video he was watching, two very attractive young people went to a beach, parked their motorcycle, and began to make out. It was actually sort of romantic—compared with American porn, it was *Pride and Prejudice*—so I think I know what the Israelis mean.

There is no Israeli pornography. Zohar showed me the explicit passage in *A Baby Comes into the World* that got him through adolescence:

> And here's how the thing happens: Father and
> Mother lie down together, close to each other,

and the penis enters into the vagina. The sper-
matozoa in the semen come out of the penis and
swim. . . .

Yigal, Mary, and Rakeffet went for a walk on the beach.
They sat down to watch the sun touch the horizon and
seem to melt and flatten to it, making a hot-pink Krembo
shape. Then they bought ice cream. Rakeffet dropped her
ice cream and ran very fast on the sand with her arms out,
saying, "I'm a bird!"

"You are not a bird," Mary contradicted.

Then she and Yigal looked at each other and kissed tenderly, for they noticed that the novel had ended. The time for
reviews had come.

SAILING ONE MORE TIME TOWARD THE SUNSET, AGAIN
by Elad Manor

Under the pen name "Nell Zink," critically acclaimed author Avner Shats has rewritten his commercial failure *Sailing Toward the Sunset* as an easy-to-read, palatable, and naive
spy thriller, set in a small glass booth above the falls of
the Rhine. The Swiss setting hints at involvement in the
struggle to recover lost Jewish assets, and before the novel
ends we see that the hero has definitely come into some
money somehow. But *Sailing Toward the Sunset* is not merely
a legal procedural on the intricacies of Swiss banking
law—it incorporates elements of romance, horror, and a
revealing look backward at the historic moment of Israel's
victory in the Six-Day War. The technical details regarding
the use of dolphins in contemporary submarine warfare

are fascinating. On the negative side, Shats underestimates the importance of science fiction in English literature (I, for one, would never have learned English without it), but, all in all, *Sailing Toward the Sunset* is the perfect Israeli thriller.

NEW FOR AGES 13–41: NELL ZINK GOES SAILING
by A. Oz

Readers of *Swallows and Amazons* and *The Wind in the Willows* will recall the pleasure of "messing about in boats." I am pleased to say that at last Israel can boast an author willing to gratify our long-suppressed national desire to float, both physically and mentally. Too many writers have succumbed to the large bribes offered by manufacturers of military hardware, and have applied their energies to international spy thrillers designed to promote a sense of urgent paranoia and a renewal of Cold War–style tensions. Zink bucks this trend, turning inward in ever-smaller circles until at last her plot assumes the form of a very small and unidentifiable animal which appears to be sleeping soundly.

MEMORIES OF A POND
(unsigned)

Nell Zink's first novel, *Sailing Toward the Sunset,* takes us on a nostalgic journey to the rural Virginia of her early youth, where she was in possession of a small green wooden boat, somewhat like a punt. Although it leaked and had to be bailed constantly with a margarine tub, she was able to spend hours floating in it on a large eighteenth-century millpond hidden in the woods behind her house. This experience functions more as a scar or a burden than anything else, and there is no better argument for the common practice of raising children without privacy.

EUROPEAN STORY
FOR AVNER SHATS

AUGUST 25–SEPTEMBER 22, 2005

THIS STORY WILL BE COMPOSED IN

bad English, the up-and-coming lingua franca of the European Union and, with any luck, the world. Bad English incongruously pairs transparent simplicity with high-flown academic jargon. Willful misapprehension of everyday words and ignorance of cliché make bad English a forceful vehicle for literary expression. Precursors and predecessors to this work include the classic novelette *Heart of Darkness*. A self-respecting native English speaker would shudder at his own bathos as he penned the phrase "heart of darkness" and laugh at anyone who suggested he make his villain's last words "the horror"—after all, who can actually say it? Available options include Brooklynese ("the hara"), "the whore" (what always happens when I try to say it), and a solemn precision not really suggestive of a dying man who's not playing a vampire. Other masterworks of bad English include the romantic era. So as you can see, you don't have to be a European like Joseph Conrad to write in bad English. I am still, as I write, arguably American, but I feel that seven years' absence, along with a lot of practice talking pidgin to foreigners, have qualified me to write as poorly as he did.

Every sentence in bad English is short, short, short. Individual phrases may be dauntingly terse, even inherently paradoxical, but constructions are stripped down to the point of blank tautology. Argumentation has no place in what is essentially a prose style originated by American high school teachers. Where someone hoping to bring an effective argument might expect to be permitted to save his conclusion for the end where it might seem more convincing, Americans know that conclusions belong up front as "topic sentences" and even *en détail* as "abstracts." By the way, anyone who thought that last sentence was a long one is already so inured to patois that he wouldn't know high culture if it bit him on the butt—which in its turn might indeed constitute a topic sentence for this story, which is about high culture.

"Oh no," you are surely sighing, "this is going to be a story in a kitsch language about kitsch and I refuse to read it." Well, guess what—you have no choice! How many centuries has it been since Western culture peaked? Two, maybe three? Do you really expect anyone, not just me, but anyone to write a story in 2005 that will tell you something you didn't know about the human condition? Maybe I will, but only by a sin of omission on your part; I could rehash everything from Pushkin to Platonov, and who would notice? Nobody. I don't mean that you don't have a choice but to read this story, just that any story you pick up is going to be kitsch by the time it hits your consciousness, if not before, so you might as well get used to it.

Yesterday a German student told me all about how much William Blake loved Jesus. The German student in this story is a bit more sophisticated than that. For one, he's been studying art history intensively for almost nine years, and for two, he's one of the best postdocs at his university and was given a scholarship to spend three months in an exclusive villa on the outskirts of Florence while working on a project that could give his career a major jump-start. His name is David (pronounced *Dah-veed*).

David lived in a villa that the artist Max Klinger had willed to Kaiser Wilhelm. An immense mansion in toasted marshmallow color with green shutters, it was shaded by a high and crumbling garden wall bordering the old road to Siena. The garden's many blue and pink mirror balls reflected tall cypresses and occasionally late roses, which were still, in November, blooming. David's room was on the fifth or sixth floor (the stairs were very confusing), high up in a corner, not quite under the roof, in a bare but largish stone cell that must have been built to house a whole bunch of maids. His room had two windows.

Across the hall was an aging Israeli writer who seemed generally disappointed by life and was writing some sad book about something, possibly a socialist embittered by the failure of communism (David wasn't sure at all, but he happened to have seen big reference books about Russian history in the room). Next door was an extremely good-looking girl. She looked very young. She told the Israeli writer she was nineteen and from the Crimea and a lesbian, and he told David. David believed it, because she would go to the shower wearing only a smallish towel. To get to the shower, you had to go down the hall, down a spiral stairway to a larger hall, through a public area to a really big staircase in an atrium, and down another spiral stairway to the shower, which was on a landing. Looking down from the gallery in the atrium, you could see the real inhabitants of the villa come and go—the artists. The writers and scholars in the little stone cells were some kind of afterthought. The other people living on the hall were a German novelist in his sixties and an English art historian. David studiously avoided the art historian. In a place as picked over as Florence, it would be some kind of miracle if you met someone in the same field who didn't feel he was competing with you directly. In this case, the competition was right out in the open. David got as far as the word "Giotto" before the Englishman rolled his eyes back in his head and moaned. He avoided the German novelist because he was German, and who goes to Florence to meet other Germans? Besides, the novelist was famous, and he didn't want anyone to think he was sucking up. He was more or less terrified of the beautiful girl, so his main conversational partner, when rain led him to settle in early for the night upstairs, was the Israeli.

"What does she make?" David asked.

"That is not entirely clear," said the Israeli. "I like to think she's a poet, probably because she has no books at all, and she doesn't paint or do anything else downstairs. I talked to Siegfried about her." That was his name for the regal (as in flowers and string quartets going into rooms where David and the Israeli weren't welcome, discreet laughter as they walked away, condescension whenever they spoke) German in a green suit who ran the place. "He said she's here as a favor to an old friend who knew her mother, something like that."

David laughed.

"Okay, I know what you're thinking. The old friend is Siegfried's wilting, forgotten dick." David laughed again. "But I swear I believe her. She is a lesbian. Otherwise the Earth is a cruel planet devoid of hope, and I'm not ready to accept that yet."

"For me, it's better when she is not a lesbian," said David.

"Then you are a great optimist," replied the Israeli. "To me, she is the world's most desperate heterosexual slut, who became a lesbian overnight to avoid sleeping with me." David laughed. "That is, just in time to avoid rejecting me on some concrete personal basis of which there is all too abundant proof. An unregenerate nymphomaniac, until she met me and I healed her. Now she thinks only of spiritual values and the delicate love of a like-minded girl who is probably even more beautiful. I am quite sure she is a poet, now that she dreams of this girl, even if she was not a poet before, but a nymphomaniac slut. I am her savior."

"I will ask to read her poetry," said David. "This we call a win-win situation. If she is a lesbian, she will like it. If she is not a lesbian, she will like it. Every poet likes it."

"But it's in Russian. I see her taking notes in the garden."
David sighed.

David was both an art historian and a chemist. Right off, you can see he's from the wrong side of the tracks. An influential art historian from an established family of professors can see an ear tacked up on a wall a mile off and immediately say, "Rembrandt," but David would most likely take a week to think it over before he says, "I like the ear, but it's recent. Still, it's a great ear, one of Rembrandt's best ear designs ever, honestly, even if it was painted by a restorer in 1951." It's an unwelcome new discipline. It used to be you could say, "Painting X was ineptly restored." People like David force you to admit that it was obliterated. David wanted to be the type who gets to proclaim works authentic on aesthetic grounds alone, but that kind of deep sensibility can only be inherited. Or at least, art history departments work as though it can only be inherited, which boils down to the same thing. So he took up chemistry.

His project in Florence was, generally speaking, a deep, dark secret. There was no media presence. A bulldozer ripping out an old rail line had hit rocks that turned out to be the tops of the walls of something Etruscan. They put up a high fence and called in an American team (except for the ultra-specialist David), which was slowly digging and making drawings. He had a lab in two containers on the site and it was all terribly exciting. When people at the villa asked what he was doing, he said, *"Affreschi di Giotto."* It had to be kept quiet because, no matter what they found, the high-speed magnetic-levitation rail line was going right through the middle of it come hell or high water.

It wasn't all Etruscan. It was a very solid structure and had seen a lot of use. There was something for everyone, from Byzantine graffiti to broken glass. It was tucked into a ravine next to the river not far from town. There was some discussion as to whether it might have been buried deliberately and not merely covered by erosion, and many were intrigued by the evidence that a tunnel had been dug to it from the river at some point before the 1920s. (That was the date of the newest condoms.) (Explanation: rats.) In slow increments, David was working his way through samples and scrapings. A picture was emerging of an ancient and unglamorous granary, or possibly a temple of Artemis in a sacred grove, or perhaps just one of those places you drop off an infant you'd rather not see again. Or at least there were plenty of small bits of human bone in the dirt covering the floor, all pretty much ground to dust by archaic mass tourism of some kind, or maybe pigs or cattle. The place had once been surrounded by trees. All were cut down on the same day in 755 B.C. Around the same time, someone had hammered quite a few pegs into the interior walls—all at the same height, but at irregular intervals, as if to hang crepe paper for a party while drunk. David kept his distance from archaeologists. His specialty was analyzing lint.

There were five artists living downstairs in palatial apartments, according to the German novelist:

1. A Macedonian guy who pretended to be Iranian. He sketched male nudes, beautifully, from memory.
2. A German of the Leipzig school, painter of schematic architectural exteriors.
3. Another German from Leipzig, a copyist of advertising circulars.
4. A Swiss sculptor in cheese.
5. An elderly Dutchwoman whose turbid landscapes recalled prowling archangels in the angry coalescing of their impasto skies.

"Sculptor in cheese?" said the Israeli.

"In Switzerland are many, many cows," the German novelist replied. "The government gives a subvention for every way to use more milk." They were walking together across an open plaza downtown on their way to an art performance. One of the more significant central churches, with a small pietà by Bernini and an irreplaceable inlaid agate floor, had been half filled with scaffolding and a collapsible aboveground swimming pool into which a world-famous video artist was about to jump naked. Since the local cardinal was to give a

benediction first, in Italian, and they had tickets from Siegfried for a VIP area up front, they were walking very slowly.

"Why cheese?" mused the Israeli. "I suspect this artist. Where
cheese is made, there are two smell possibilities. One is fungus,
the other is a penetrating smell of vomit, a smell that flings a
person to the floor in involuntary contractions."

"It is not only cheese," the German added. "At times, there
are other products of Swiss and French agriculture in his
work." He stumbled against a low step leading to the portico
of the church. "Owa, the leg. I am telling you, Eyal, I have a
problem with my knee." He sat down on the steps.

Eyal, the Israeli, paused in front of him with his hands
in his pockets, looking up at the heavy bronze door of the
church, which was slowly closing, pulled by invisible hands
from inside. A group of young students of both sexes raced
past them and through the door at the last second.

The German, Ingo, stretched out his leg and groaned. "Go
in, go without me."

"No, why? It's a nice night, here outside. Perhaps it's better
here than there." They could hear the hugely amplified dron-
ing of the cardinal. "You have a bad knee?"

"In general, I never walk. Kierkegaard either, or, you know
it? Either I never walk and everyone knows I am old, or I walk
and everyone knows I am old."

The humid air seemed to be staining the marble a cool
shade of electric blue, and the Israeli had no urge to enter
the cathedral. He sat down next to the German. There was
scattered applause from the church, then a monumental syn-
thesizer chord that rose to a muffled wailing. "Let's go," Ingo
said. They both stood up.

The church door opened and a woman of about fifty-three
emerged. She stood facing them, wearing high heels, dark

tights, and a short red overcoat, and said clearly, in English, "It's unbearable. It's awful. Don't go in there."

"We do not plan to do this. We only rest a short while on the veranda," said Ingo. He stopped leaning on his walking stick and stood precariously upright. With great graciousness, he removed a cigarette case from his inside breast pocket and added, "Pleased to meet you. Cigarette?"

She waved off the cigarette and said, "The guy is so hairy. Jesus Christ. He looks like some kind of German left-wing nudist from the eighties. I always thought that was him in his other videos. It must have been a model. Good God."

"I am German left-wing nudist in the eighties," Ingo said. "I had long hair and a beard, but no more."

"Ingo is right," Eyal elucidated. "Body hair resists cultivation."

"You don't look that old," the woman said to Ingo.

Ingo leaned on his cane and looked at the ground. His feet were clearly visible. "I never eat," he explained. "I live for my art, the art of drinking well."

"Ingo is a brilliant young prodigy, preparing to do his best work," Eyal added. "Until now he has been overrated. One sees this only in retrospect, as there are no adjectives remaining to describe what he will soon accomplish."

The woman was silent. "Do you need a ride somewhere?" she asked finally. "My car is in the garage right under here." She pointed down at the cobblestones.

Eyal expressed sincere gratitude, and several minutes later, they were rolling quietly up the Via Senese in a red BMW.

She was from Bowling Green, Ohio, and her name was Amy. She knew the villa well and said she never missed an art opening there. She said she had studied art and got stuck in Florence because of a guy and got married and ended up as a real estate agent. Ingo compelled her to reveal that she was divorced. She assured them that she would attend the opening of the group exhibition at the villa on the coming Friday.

When Eyal came downstairs to the opening, Amy was already deep in conversation with David. Ingo was sitting on a high couch upholstered in silk, drinking coffee, and staring at her. A string quartet was playing something that could have been Franck or Ravel, very loudly, and there was an overwhelming odor of vomit. He turned around and went back up the stairs.

David was telling Amy that he would rather like to rent a small apartment somewhere other than the villa—perhaps something in a hip neighborhood with many attractive single women. She said, "I know something perfect for you. There's this crazy retired sea captain with an apartment near the Boboli Gardens that I'm trying to sublet furnished month to month, but it's just impossible because he was a compulsive collector. The place is totally jam-packed with junk, but his daughter doesn't want me getting rid of any of it to make space, because he's still alive. He's in a nursing home, and when he gets out, he's going to want things just the way they were. But the home is so expensive that she wants to rent the place out. It's basically a beautiful apartment, and really cheap, for what it is."

David was intrigued. "Boboli, very nice. Is there hot water?"

Upstairs, the lesbian was sitting cross-legged on her bed and Eyal was watching her from an armchair. "Jenny, I revere you," he said.

"Hmm," she replied. "Did I ever tell you why I am in Florence?" she asked. "Truly stupid story. We have family anecdote.

My great-grandmother, princess from Voronezh, has small bronze copy of *David* of Donatello in her bedroom. She goes to Baden-Baden and tells another princess, from Spain, that this statue is not copy or souvenir but original of Donatello and worth money. When she gets home, her statue is stolen away, and her parents tell her it is true statue of Donatello. Her stupid boast is true. My cousins in Paris are always looking for this statue, but it never comes to the market. It is symbol of my family."

"How is that?"

"A lie. What part of this story is the lie? It is simply not Donatello. It is plaster. Or it is Donatello, they wait until she is on holiday, then they sell it. Probably there is no statue. Probably it is teapot of Meissen, maid breaks it, and then it becomes teapot of Sèvres, then vase, then statue, and maid becomes princess of Spain. And is my great-grandmother truly a princess?"

"You are a radical critic."

"I am radical." She narrowed her eyes and leaned back on her arms. "Now tell me, Israeli writer, what you are doing in Florence."

"I'm not sure," he said. "I was fully intending to write a novel about Siberia in 1942, but something about you makes me think I should write a tale of hopeless unrequited love."

She seemed pleased. Girls like flattery, he thought. He was getting ready to pour it on when she said, "I am not true lesbian. I am married to impotent billionaire."

David had rented the retired sea captain's apartment without showing any particular signs of excitement. It had been difficult. Now he removed a framed picture from the wall, slit open the back with a pocketknife, held the paper up in the dim sunlight, and squinted at it through a jeweler's loupe.

It was a fantastically precise small gouache of a man receiving mild discipline from a naked lady in black stockings that came up just over the knee, presumably executed by Félicien Rops. In a broad, flat drawer of the kitchen table between sheets of wax paper were four unknown pastels by Odilon Redon, and framed on the wall facing the bed was a letter from Goethe to Franz Schubert.

"Dear Mr. Schubert," one might have paraphrased it, "I received your settings of my poems and found them to be the reprehensible, abysmal, heinous moltings and preenings of a would-be peacock at the expense of literary jewels which have done nothing to deserve abuse of any kind. For your information, a song should put the text first and foremost. Melodies should be simple, with two or maybe three notes at the absolute outside, with no modulations and not too high or too low so that anybody can sing them and so everybody understands every word in real time as it is declaimed without having to read along. But my views on song are well known, so I'm surprised you had the gall to defy them, and frankly shocked at your effrontery in sending me the rotten, dangling fruits of your entirely superfluous labors. Also, may you rot in hell for leaving out verses. I wrote them all for a reason, and you can bet your buttons it wasn't so bootlicking wannabes like you could decide that only the first and last verses are keepers. But it would be churlish of me," etc.

Understandably, David had visions of a professional breakthrough. No longer will I scrape lint in an echoing biscuit tin from faded relics of the homely dead, miraculous as its survival might be, he said to himself. In truth, beauty is an absolute, and these works of Redon are eons advanced beyond—go on, dare to say it out loud, he thought: Redon leaves art in the dirt. He laughed bitterly, drunk with excitement.

The Rops interested him only slightly. He had seen many such drawings; it was pretty generic, as Ropses go. The letter from Goethe was certainly worth some money to a library somewhere. But he needed to bring home some lab equipment somehow, to authenticate the Redons. He resolved not to say anything to Amy, then not to anyone, and suddenly he was gripped by fear: Of course the daughter knows these things are here, and she will sell them all. But on the other hand she can't possibly know, or she wouldn't rent them to a penniless art historian. He walked slowly around the apartment, examining things, picking them up, putting them down, and musing vaguely. The beer cans displayed in the china cabinet were clearly American, 1980s. The plastic models of songbirds on the bottom shelf had been painted and varnished with great care. The top of the buffet was taken up with collections, sorted by color, of glass marbles and cocktail stirrers. He opened the buffet's wooden doors and saw a perfectly preserved wooden panel by the Master of the Three-Quarter Figures depicting, in meticulous perfection of line and radiant color, girls playing virginals, contrabass, and *viole bastarde*. He sighed. He had found the Redons by accident, just looking for a fork. He suspected that if he searched the apartment systematically, he might find all sorts of things.

He called Amy and said, "I want to tell you only that the place here is also full of nice art, not only junk. So be careful that the owner does not ask for a company to come and take away rummage. Even if the old man is dead. I am an art historian, I will help you."

She scoffed. "If you mean the Depression glass candy dish, it's the last of eight or ten they had in there. The daughter's had to sell off some stuff. Don't be surprised if there's a little something missing every time you come home from work. This home they've got him in is pricey. But trust me, with that much junk you'll never notice."

"She comes in while I am at work?"

"She's the landlady, she's got a key."

David unzipped his portfolio and tucked the Redons inside very gingerly. He was not going to bring home lab equipment for the daughter to see; he would take them along to work. As a sort of deliberate afterthought, saying to himself that it didn't really count, he put the Rops and the letter from Goethe, still in their frames, in a plastic sack from the grocery store. The next morning before going to the containers to do the molecular analysis that would bring him international renown, he made a few high-quality color copies at a copy shop.

It was late. Ingo and Eyal were drinking brandy in the library after dinner.

Eyal said, "I have not written since I arrived. Everything is too interesting for me, and I have no wish to concentrate. I am terminally distracted."

"Often a great genius never succeeds to write one single word," Ingo replied.

"You apply for a fellowship and win, and always it is to live the lifestyle of a young student with artistic types in some artist colony where everyone is bored and randy, or it is a university, with thousands of women all twenty-one. Only if you are already very famous, then you get the really big cash prize, so you can stay at home with your wife to write out of loneliness."

"These young women, I don't give a fuck about them anymore, as they say. Or is it the opposite? I have become invisible."

"I looked you up in the Internet," Eyal said. "You published five novels before you were thirty. And me, one novel with thirty-seven. You are industrious and devoted, and I am not." Ingo demurred, but Eyal insisted. "You know Price's law describing the distribution of success in the natural sciences? In a field of scientists numbering n, half the papers will be published by the square root of n. You have twenty-five scientists doing work on a subject; five of them will publish half the papers. One hundred, then only ten. But in science there is a big difference to literature, in theory. A scientist writes many papers he has never seen. His admirers invite him to add his name, so a top physicist publishes a word every two seconds, twenty-four hours a day his entire life. Now compare a composer. Bach is discovered after his death, and they find he has written twenty pages of music every day from birth. Isn't this a little bit like the True Cross? Tens of thousands of little bits of the True Cross, enough to make a good-sized forest?"

"Eyal, my dear, I must disappoint you. I wrote my novels myself, even when I was a hippie and totally crazy after women. And Bach is truly a great genius."

"Sorry, that was not my intention. I intend to apply Price's law to myself alone. That is, if there is only one writer working on a certain aspect of literature, he will publish in his lifetime a grand total of one-half of one book."

"Is this Price's law true for literature? I doubt it."

"No, strangely enough. For literature, the curve is even more hyperbolic than for composers and painters. Top famous writers hundreds of years ago, they have an output that is completely unbelievable. Of course, they all dictate to some amanuensis, some fan scribbles down their plays during the performance, students are taking shorthand in the lectures. They never write themselves. Some are blind. They can't type. But no problem, they have secretaries. Even now. Borges is blind. Nabokov also is dictating to his wife."

"What's your point?"

"Maybe this thing that I attempt, this lonely sitting at my computer staring at the metaphor of blank paper, is a perversion born of poverty and isolation. Before, only women write this way, between housekeeping duties, secretly, in silence, for a maximum two, maybe three novels in a lifetime." He sighed heavily.

"You are breaking my heart, Eyal. What do you want me to do? Invite you to live in a villa in Florence, so you have time to write? I have worked hard in my life, always writing every morning, drinking every afternoon."

"Not only women, perhaps also the insane and prisoners. Your Hölderlin—"

They were interrupted by the entrance of David. He showed Ingo a copy of the letter from Goethe to Schubert.

Ingo said, "Yes, very interesting. This letter is well known." He was confused by the fact that Goethe's views on song really are well known, and it is also well known that Schubert sent him some songs at one point, neatly copied in his own hand. We know this because Goethe saved them. But he is not known to have replied to the young upstart in any way, so the letter was in fact priceless.

"Well, I find it and I just think I show it you. I know you admire the great heroes of our discredited German bourgeois culture."

Ingo said apologetically to Eyal, "He laughs at me a little, but he is young. Everyone with a love for art, regardless of politics, must adore Goethe and Schubert. How not to admire

Goethe? His language, impossible to imitate, impossible to translate. And Schubert, the antinomies of rhythm and song, ultimate joy and ultimate tragedy walking together hand in hand! Ah, Schubert is divine! And you must know Goethe's translation of Hafez, *West-östlicher Divan?*"

"There is an orchestra in Ramallah of Daniel Barenboim's by this name," Eyal said. "The Brit Kipling says, 'East is East and West is West, and never the twain shall meet.' Probably Goethe forgets Mesopotamia is the start of Western civilization, not Eastern. But this way of thinking is how they make now Jewish studies section of Oriental studies in universities. Germany is a Celtic forest outlying district of Lapland that must fight to resist the foreign threat of monotheism coming from Jews and Turks and Voltaire and so on, such as Hafez. Goethe's literary output was very big, wasn't it? His secretary is always taking notes. Isn't it true that the most famous aphorisms of Goethe are all from the memoirs of his secretary, Herr Eckermann?"

"Not really. He wrote hundreds—"

"I can see him now, extruding great works like a sausage grinder in a nonstop monologue from day to night. Probably he spends his whole life drinking only espresso straight from the thermos." Ingo tapped the floor with his cane. David laughed nervously. "I'm drunk, I think I'll go to bed," Eyal added.

"I'm never drunk," Ingo replied, pouring himself another glass of brandy.

Eyal went upstairs to David's old room. It had been cleaned and tidied in preparation for the next tenant. Eyal's own room was a bit of a mess, with dirty laundry on the chairs.

He lay down on the white coverlet with his shoes on, then sat up and took them off. They dropped to the floor with a thud. Jenny appeared in the doorway.

"But soft, what light in yonder doorway breaks," he said. "It is the east, and Jenny is the sun."

"As you like," said Jenny. "I hear this clanging and think someone new has come to live in David's room, but it's only you." She sat down next to him on the bed. "I miss David. He is only innocent man."

"This is because he has a very literal mind. He is a chemist. He thinks, Combine me, David, and a lesbian, this will produce no reaction whatsoever. The lesbian is inert, like the noble gases."

"You are not a chemist."

"Even if I were a chemist, I would not see you as a single element. Perhaps one of these rare diamonds possessing an odd color through impurities." He put his arm around her. "Or inclusions, like the insects in amber. Don't flatter yourself that I am a famous writer. In actuality, I am a zero. I work in public relations."

"Fame is a matter of no interest whatsoever. My husband is film director who is worshipped by everyone. Big stars are kissing my ass."

"Then I propose a deal with him," said Eyal. "I sleep with his wife, and in return, he films a script, which I will write, to immortalize the affair for general delectation, starring all your ass-kissing stars."

"That is difficult. To make any deal I must contact him, and now he does not know where I am. Soon I will go to him for money, but not yet. Also, you ignore what is central. Who would marry an impotent man?"

"A lesbian, maybe?"

"Wrong, wrong, wrong," she said. "A bitch greedy for money. I will not last long in this poor place of stone cells with a kilometer to walk to the shower. Watch me, Israeli writer, I go now, and tomorrow, I am gone."

"But I am your savior," Eyal called, closing his eyes as she stood up and backed away.

"What? My savior?"

"I offer you redemption," he said, opening his eyes. "And nothing more. What can I give you? I am poor and ugly, and I am entirely certain that I am impotent as we speak, if only for the alcohol. Listen to me, Jenny! If you abandon your husband for a rich and good-looking young man or for some ass-kissing star, the world will say you are a venal tramp and a whore! You will be defaced with base motives of lust and cupidity. But on the contrary, when I assist you in destroying your marriage, no one sees any motive other than the purest and most respectable hatred for your husband! They will think, What a monster that billionaire must be, if his Jenny leaves him for this miserable writer."

"This is not too far from the truth," she said, sitting down again.

David's conversation with Ingo in the library returned to the subject of Schubert. Before long, David had promised to come to the next private concert of chamber music in Siegfried's suite in the villa, and to bring the original of the Goethe letter with him. In honor of the occasion, the program would be all Schubert. The quartet playing the French music at the opening had been Japanese, and the Japanese, Ingo confided to David, should be kept at a safe distance from Schubert.

The quartet qualified to play Schubert called itself Gli Dere-
litti, after an orphanage with an excellent all-female orchestra that had been active in Venice in the eighteenth century.
The two original members were forty-five-ish twins, a former
sex bomb on violin and her envious sister on cello. The first
violin was the violinist's ex-lover, a Romanian Gypsy in his
seventies. Viola was supplied by a melancholy young Russian
composer.

The musical salon gathered for the Schubertiade after dinner. Present was a cross-section of the local elite, both German and Italian. The hum of voices, the glow of candlelight,
the elegant clothing, the yellow velvet wallpaper, the women
who seemed stunning until you got close enough to see they
were fifty-six—David felt deeply unsure of himself. It's like a
harem in the Vatican, he thought. He wore clothing that had
cost a combined total of forty dollars and carried a plastic bag
with the framed letter. Siegfried greeted him with an enthusiasm and friendliness he'd never suspected possible, and Ingo
nodded benevolently. After the small talk wore down, they sat
down on the Louis XVI chairs and listened. The music was
wild, controlled, redolent with sincere feeling and irony, filled
with inevitable and unexpected harmonies, just as Ingo had
promised. The musicians were working hard. You could hear
their heavy breathing and see them sweat. Ingo sat leaning
forward expectantly, his mouth slightly open, while Siegfried
leaned back, nipping at a glass of Scotch. The audience was
attentive, and its final applause was heartfelt.

David felt a hand on his arm. *"Jetzt lassen Sie Ihren Brief mal
ansehen,"* Siegfried said to David. He read the letter quickly,
nodding. *"Faszinierend, von großem akademischem Interesse,"* and
passed it to Ingo.

"*Goethe ist immer genial,*" Ingo agreed. He turned to the Gypsy, who had packed up his violin, and said, "Perhaps you are interested. Our friend has found a new letter from Goethe, very critical of Schubert's songs. It's all common knowledge, but the letter is perhaps quite interesting for scholarship, as you can see."

The Gypsy agreed that it was quite wonderful and passed it to the Italian twins, who confirmed his opinion before passing it to the absent-minded violist, who alone among the musicians could read German.

He began to read and, simultaneously, to sway back and forth and turn red. He moved over to lean on the mantelpiece, wiped his eyes, and kept reading, then lowered the frame and bellowed to all and sundry, "This is shit!"

There was general silence as everyone stared at him.

"Arkady, what happens?" the cellist asked.

"It is—unbelievable!" Words failed him. "This stupid, stupid, no aesthetic sense, this false god of a godless Nazi barbarian, this son of—" At some point during the middle of the penultimate phrase, he had begun smashing the picture frame against the pale fawn of the firebricks and, alternately, on a rack of wrought-iron fireplace implements. Slivers of glass were flying down to the rug and clinging to the front of his suit. Everyone backed away. After prying the letter from its bed of splinters and cardboard with his fingernails, he tore it in half, smashed it into a ball, and dropped it into the fire with bleeding hands. "Philistine!" he said, addressing the fire. Trying then to wipe his hands on his suit, he cried out in surprise at the pain. "I must wash my hands," he added with an air of great innocence, looking around for a glass of water, which he dumped unceremoniously on his hands, now pink with blood, to form a puddle on the rug.

"What is this paper they show us?" asked the Gypsy, eyeing Siegfried with suspicion. "What sort of place is this?"

"The greatest German," the violist replied, "writes to Schubert, and I hope Schubert does not get this letter. It must kill him. How he loves Goethe, who hopes to destroy him like a worm!"

"Well," said Siegfried placidly, "there's no evidence whatsoever that Schubert received the letter. That's why I had rather assumed it was priceless, or at least worth several hundred thousand. I wonder who was the owner. David?"

"I made several facsimiles," David said. "So I suppose I should thank our viola player for sparing the frame, more or less."

"Surely someone must be compensated after a priceless artifact is willfully destroyed," said Siegfried.

"But not you," the Gypsy said. "Pay us. We go."

"This is all my fault," Ingo said.

David repaired the frame, inserted a copy of the letter, hung it on the wall over the bed, and thought, Well, no harm done. He was tempted to do the same with the Rops. There are good color copies of etchings by Dürer hanging in the Albertina in Vienna, after all, and no one seems to care that they're not originals. Of course no one goes to see them anymore, or in other words, once they can be copied accurately, hares and praying hands are of no interest to anyone. The fading aura of the work of art in the age of mechanical reproduction, etc. A copy is like the naked emperor in the fairy tale. If there were some accurate way of reproducing the swirling, platitudinous, piebald paintings of van Gogh, no one would care about them either. But, David thought, if there were a way to re-create the luminous, pure, semitransparent colors of Redon, he would conquer the world.

Maybe photograph them with a soft-focus filter, the way soft-core pornographers photograph girls under the age of consent, he pondered, walking around the apartment with a cup of coffee in his hand. Accuracy is not everything. One must capture the spirit. He was glad to be out of the villa. He needed privacy to think, and the apartment seemed to expand his mind. It was filled with objects that had meaning to him and seemed to work in concert, like an elaborate riddle: an ivory statuette of an elephant, an ancient clay figure of Anubis, and a ballpoint pen from Las Vegas, all grouped carefully on a tiny Navajo rug. What does it mean? he thought. Nothing? Impossible. There are no coincidences.

His work at the dig intrigued and bored him at the same time. It was intrinsically spellbinding, but he didn't much care for Etruscans. The stuff is dirty, fragmentary, nothing to look at until the restorers are done with it, but the restorers can't sign their names or take credit. Nor can they do anything the customers don't expect and want. Restorers could create whole new genres, if they had the nerve— polychrome Greek sculpture, for example, a historical fact on ice, its resurgence repressed by connoisseurs who fancy they have better taste than the Greeks. With a few weeks' time and a mass spectrometer he could supply the pigments to repaint it all. Why not? You'd have to wash it first, or at least the beautiful figures of young people with that patina of waxy fat from eons of fondling, that secret habit of everyone with private access to a museum of feeling the muscle and bone under the smooth, cool skin of figures carved from marble 2,500 years ago. What makes everyone depict Pygmalion always falling in love with his creation by contemplating its perfect proportions from a distance? He imagined telling the restorers that these particular Etruscans had employed luminous pastel shades like Redon. He could say he was finding flakes of such color in the scum on the floor. Couldn't he? Probably not.

The most interesting thing they had found so far was the holes in the walls. He guessed there had been tapestries hanging there. He was looking hard for lint, but not finding anything good. The Etruscan structure refused to give him what he wanted. In the apartment, on the other hand, everything seemed to have been lying in wait for him. He walked slowly, distracted, staring at whatever was hanging on the walls until he came to a small cabinet he had never opened. It was filled with little hooks on which were hanging a few keys with labels: "*sous-sol,*" "*cave,*" "*trésor.*" Something about the first two intrigued him. It sounded to him as if there might be wine lying around somewhere in the basement.

He took the keys and went down for the first time to the cellar. It was dry, and had electric light despite its earthen floor. It was certainly the sort of place where one might store wine. He began to feel very jolly and optimistic. After trying a few doors, he found one that fit the *cave* key. Unfortunately, the large wine rack was empty. From one corner of the floor to the other extended, of all things, a two-man kayak. It had been painted a dull shade of matte black. Two paddles in dark brown were leaning on the wall. Immediately he thought of Jenny. Jenny is so young and *sportlich,* he thought. Any lesbian would surely love a kayak trip. It is so easy to transport, tied to the roof of a taxi. He lifted it with one hand to confirm its lightness. I can take it to work, he thought. I work by the river. From there we can start. It is almost winter. There will be enough water. He regarded the kayak with a sense of passionate urgency.

Eyal, deeply absorbed in an online chat, was very surprised a few mornings later to hear luggage being kicked. Someone was clearly pushing a very heavy box down the hall with his feet. He opened the door and looked out. A man with large, fluffy bandages instead of hands was frowning furiously, clutching a viola case like a little girl clutching a teddy bear close to his chest with both arms, and pushing a cardboard box in the general direction of David's old room. "Hello," the man said. "I am composer from Florence, Arkady. I do not play viola."

"They call me Eyal. I can see that you cannot play viola at this time. Let me help." He carried the box into the room.

The composer took a look at the bed and cried out, "They tell me this is my room, my new room, clean! This is very bad and shameful!"

"Sorry," Eyal said. "I have a special friend and we think perhaps it is better to meet on neutral territory. I will organize new sheets."

"Thank you, friend. Perhaps you hear about my accident."

Eyal shook his head.

"String quartet, big soiree with director down in salon. I hurt my hands. Now I live here. I write a bagatelle for him, so I pay my rent. I cannot work. This is very bad. Also very good. I hate to play the viola. Except German romantic music. I write this bagatelle, stay one month. For the bagatelle I need maybe one hour."

"Excellent deal," said Eyal.

"Thank you." The composer began to unpack and Eyal left the room.

This is very bad, Eyal thought. Also shameful. This dingbat composer speaks Russian like Jenny, plus he's sort of cute in this lost-orphan-child way—no, face it, he's handsome,

probably, when he's asleep or otherwise failing to say something blatantly egomaniacal. Jenny will get a crush on him
and then I am screwed, over, finished, unless I can get rid of
him posthaste. What can I do? Help me, precious Lord! Eyal
was not especially good-looking, and he tended to be insecure.

He went back and asked, "How long will you be wearing
these bandages?"

"One week, maybe two weeks. Until then, you will not hear
me play viola, also rest in peace." He laughed at his own joke. "I
still will not write. I will compose in my mind while I have the
bandages, song cycle on texts of Fedor Tyutchev. 'Silentium'!"

I have one week, Eyal thought. One week.

Late that afternoon Eyal walked out the door to go into town
and saw Jenny and the composer sitting together on a bench
in the garden, talking animatedly. He stood very still for a
moment. Then he walked straight over to them and said,
"Hello, Jenny! Arkady, I see you have met my special friend."
The Russian immediately moved a foot farther away from her
and took his elbow down from the back of the bench.

Why didn't I think of that before? Eyal thought. I just spent
seven hours plotting everything from death to maiming to
discrediting him in the eyes of the world, seven hours nursing a gemlike flame of hatred that was slowly condensing to
a kind of inner creosote that threatened to poison my entire
existence, in the hope that this spiritual substance alone
might suffice to kill him or me or both of us. But all I had to
do was say, "Get your hands off my girlfriend," and only once.
Is it that easy?

The composer said something to Jenny in Russian, and
she giggled. "You need anything from town?" he asked them
both.

"Vodka!" said the composer.

In your dreams! thought Eyal, bouncing away in a youthful manner.

When he returned with a bottle of Frascati, Jenny was waiting for him in her room to inform him that she would be moving in with David. Her husband would soon think of looking for her in the villa, if he hadn't already, she said. "And the innocent David has a kayak at his top secret place of secret work. We will take this kayak to the river. Such great fun. And you will visit me always. Okay?"

"Okay. I will visit you. And this Russian guy?"

"No good for you. He knows nothing of Siberia, only Petersburg. Also, he is injured to the hands through spontaneous application of violence to expensive golden age relic not his own. Crazy man. I move to David to escape him." She nestled up close to Eyal.

"This is the most beautiful sexual affair of my life," he said. "I hope it is very shallow and meaningless. In any other case, I should not like to go home."

"It is excessively trivial," she assured him. "Please open this wine."

There was a knock at the door. It was the English art historian, with whom no one mentioned in this story had as yet spoken a word voluntarily. He was apparently a hard worker, in libraries or something, from just after breakfast to late at night.

"Sorry to disturb you. Could I bother you for a glass of that?" he said. "I'm a bit shook up." He sat down on a chair.

"So what's up?" Eyal asked.

"There's about eight feet of bloody bandages on the floor of my room." They both laughed. "Stop laughing! I'm serious! I think it's that mad Russian, the one who's always charging about like a singed rabbit. I have to get out of this place. It's driving me mad. No one here ever speaks to anyone. It's bloody eerie."

"What?" said Jenny.

"I will explain," said Eyal. "You believe that you speak English, but this is not an accurate estimate of your powers. I struggle most pitifully to understand your rapid, inflected speech. This is very hard work. You are a hard worker, but no one else here is a hard worker, except David. We are lazy artists of life."

"David. That's the bloke with the *affreschi di Giotto.* We didn't hit it off. He told me about the Giotto and I thought, They're still giving stipends for Giotto? I should be German. I believe I looked a bit skeptical and he took it personally. Seems nice enough."

"David is just brilliant," said Jenny. "He's very innocent."

"He may be a hard worker, but innocent? I suppose that's why he's robbing the library blind. Wandering about with letters of Goethe and belle epoque erotica in a shopping bag. Really! Where can he have got them? I've half a mind to call him on it."

"Erotica? It's not possible. He's innocent," Jenny said. "You admit you have never spoken to him. How can you call him a thief and a pornographer? Get out of my room. You are bored, but we are not your interactive television."

The Englishman, who was making a great effort to overcome months of antisocial reticence, continued down the hall to chat, for the first time, with Ingo. Ingo quickly became very effusive about Giotto, Goethe, and the gifted young Russian composer who displayed all the behavioral eccentricities traditionally attendant on genius, short-circuiting everything he had to say, so he gave up and never spoke to anyone in the villa ever again.

Compared with the other men in the neighborhood, David was virtually immune to Jenny. His work with symbolist drawings had given him a great deal of practice in looking at things he was not allowed to touch. An oil painting, you tap it with your finger just to make a point, and does anybody care? No. But a pastel is as delicate after a hundred years as fresh spray paint, and it's all painted with cans they're not selling anymore. Touch a field of solid color, and you'll be working for days to match the tint and build the surface back up to where no one sees the depression. Smudge charcoal into white paper, and you might as well have taken a knife to it. It will never look the same. David had in fact spent a lot more time with symbolist drawings than with girls, so he was conditioned to think anything attractive should be left alone. Probably that was the unconscious reason he had written his dissertation on Etruscan wall hangings: It didn't upset him to rip them apart, fiber by fiber, with tweezers.

David was always at work centrifuging slurries of our irreplaceable cultural heritage or whatever when Eyal came to his apartment to see Jenny. It was only the landlord's daughter who dropped by once while David was away.

Eyal came out in his shorts to see who was puttering around the living room. "You must be David," she said. "Pleased to meet you."

"Yes, I am David," Eyal said.

"I will not stay long. I am here to pick up something. Ah, yes, I see it." She stood on tiptoe and extricated a scrimshaw seal from between two highball glasses on a shelf. She placed it carefully on a table, then reached up again for a cracked tortoiseshell hand mirror propped between Snoopy bookends. She blew the dust off the seal and mirror and tucked them into her handbag. "Cheerio!" she said.

"Can I please see this ivory?" said Eyal. She took it back out and handed it over. "Nice work," he observed, turning it over and over in his hands. "Old."

"My father is a great aficionado of the sea," said the woman. "He ask me to bring things from the sea for his room."

"Is he very ill?"

She laughed. "Of course he is ill. To be ninety-five is a sickness! But he refuses to be cured. He is only having the knees replaced, with titanium. In two, three months he will be playing football."

"I too am quite fond of the sea. I work for a shipping company, and once I was on merchant ships."

"You are not an art historian of the *quattrocento*?"

"Yes, I studied art history, and now I am the art historian of an historic shipping company."

"You are perfect! I tell Amy, I need this art historian to help me with the inventory. So many things in this apartment! So many rare and wonderful things my father is collecting. I fear that some things may be valuable. You are exactly the perfect man!"

"I have noticed some interesting items here. Also some high-quality copies. Of course the copies are worthless, but very interesting as well."

"Did you see this?" She pointed to a framed certificate in French. "My father is the last surviving captain of the Amicale Internationale des Capitaines au Long Cours Cap Horniers."

"Impossible! Amazing!" He read the certificate and shook

his head. "I would like to meet him. I must meet him. This is astounding." He was sincere.

The woman was flattered. "How about Saturday? I will come here and take you to see him."

"Monday is better."

"Then Sunday perhaps?" They agreed on Friday.

Eyal was unaware that Friday was a holiday, the Feast of the Immaculate Conception. David would not be working. But he knew all about the *amicale*. It was a professional society of merchant sea captains who had managed to get around Cape Horn under sail. The last time a commercial vessel had done this was not, as you might think, before the advent of steam and the Panama Canal, but rather in 1949, when the *amicale* still had two hundred members. Eyal was highly susceptible to the romance of sail. You could almost say he was susceptible to anything that floated, including air mattresses and pontoon bridges. His novel and most of his stories involved boats. He often considered trying to write for *Mare* and other upscale yachting magazines, but the stubborn pariah status of bad English gave him pause. Until bad English received official recognition, Hebrew was still his strongest language, and he would go on attempting great literature. It was this urge to turn away from the abysmal English that was engulfing the world, and from its metonym, the sea, that had led him to set his latest novel in Siberia. Again and again he was tempted to relocate his story ten years into the future and let global warming melt the polar ice so he could give Siberia a vibrant port city on the now fruitful delta of the river Lena, but he was determined not to write cheesy science fiction. His story, set in 1942, would be based in its entirety on real, actual incidents involving real human beings with real longings, routine misfortunes, and subtle character flaws.

So it was not without discouragement that he read that a
Scottish journalist fluent in the worst English imaginable had
sold in advance the film rights to a true-life adventure novel
in which cocaine-addicted Czech partisans led by a sixteen-
year-old female sadist, weary of fighting first the Hapsburgs
and then the Whites, desert from the Russian civil war only
to clash lethally with a band of religiously motivated castrati
in a remote Siberian village. The events of the novel and any
movies to be made and even the action figures were all drawn
straight from life. It wouldn't be expensive to film. Siberia
is low-rent territory, and castrati are cheaper than aliens.
There's no makeup involved. You just point at them and
say, "Castrati." The viewer's mind does the rest. Eyal sighed
heavily.

Still, a recent Austrian road movie he had seen on TV offered a glimmer of hope: It had been outfitted with subtitles
for Russian and German, but whenever the characters spoke
bad English, it was apparently assumed that audiences everywhere would understand. Twenty years ago, he remembered,
things had been different. Back then, it was French that was
regarded as a universal language like music or mathematics.
Plus ça change. The English of the castrati had surely been very
poor. The script would reflect that and perhaps even capital-
ize on it, assuming they were cast as villains. He sighed again,
and Jenny came out to see what was going on.

"She is gone?"

"Did you hear what was said? It's really quite interesting.
Want coffee?"

"Tea, please," Jenny said.

"Russians are fabulously exotic and strange, as well as im-
mensely perverse and odd," said Eyal. "Imagine, in Italy and

not drinking coffee! Tell me, are there really castrated fighting monks in Siberia?"

"Yes," Jenny replied. "The Old Believers take baby boys and squeeze in hot bath water until they go away. It is not painful. Then they are priests, also good singers, with long dresses, long hair. Very aggressive fighters against evil. Not strong like men, but clever, and angry all the time."

"Bitter, perhaps."

"Yes, very bitter, and with swords. Soviet animation is selling them to Japan, now Japanese to Russia. Old Believers do wonderful magic."

"I am certain Old Believers are a schismatic sect that separated from the Orthodox because they want to cross themselves with two fingers, not three."

"And so? Their anime is cool. They rule Siberia with an iron fist!"

Amy and Ingo sat in a chichi bar near the villa and drank vividly colored aperitifs. Ingo had been telling her about his experiences ca. 1968. He had helped found one of Germany's first communes. The founders had hoped that their well-publicized liberal notions about free love and psychedelic drugs would attract people who could provide such things, but mostly they were left to themselves, drinking beer. "The name is commune 'Morning Dew,' but soon we call it commune 'Always Drunk.' In German, this is a rhyme."

"I'm not that much younger than you are, but I missed all that stuff," Amy said. "I knew some weirdos in grad school at NYU, but you couldn't found a commune in Manhattan, not in 1985. The real estate was too expensive. The closest you could get was maybe refuse to move out of the dorm."

Ingo nodded.

"You're the first lefty I ever ran into in the villa, you know? They're all pretty straight. The guy who makes the sculptures out of cheese, I'm not sure about him. I mean, is that political? Obviously the European Union is producing a lot of surplus cheese. In America we call it government cheese. They pay the farmers to make too much of it, and then poor people that are on like food stamps come and pick it up by the kilo."

"I never talk to him. Also he is Swiss, not European. But I'm afraid you will not like my politics now, or even then. We were not political. We only wanted to get laid."

"But getting laid was a political act in 1968!"

Ingo laughed like a seal barking, shifted his weight, and coughed. "Oh, I don't think so. Sex is a constant of human life. When unattractive men rise up in revolution and say, 'We too will sleep with beautiful young students in free love if volunteers can be found,' this is not political, but merely sad. The sexual revolution is a mass hallucination suggested by a revolution in women's clothing."

"I don't see it that way. When I was coming up, girls still had reputations to protect, and by the time I was twenty-five, everybody was living with a guy."

"Everybody, everybody," Ingo said. "No matter. I marry my revolutionary comrade. We do not have sex. Always everybody is naked, but never make love. I start to write because to work is reactionary. Nothing to do but drink coffee every day, then beer, then maybe move, take over an empty house and sit there drinking coffee and beer. In winter we freeze almost to death. Then comes the German autumn, 1978. The police always search through our houses. They overhear the telephone. It is hell. Always fighting to release people from jail, and always they are imprisoned for idiocy. They go to the atomic power works with a sign saying no to atomic power. They climb over the fence. Then for half a year we work to make money for lawyers so this person can come out and do this again, and this we call political action, not self-slavery. Then twenty years ago I inherit a little money, so good-bye. Lucky my wife is a radical feminist. She does not think for requesting half of the money, does not want to depend from me. Very lucky!"

"There was one squat on East Seventh Street," Amy said. "But the scene was pretty much in Jersey. The problem was, this was way later than '68. Nobody had a political thought in their heads. Everybody was just a runaway. I mean, there were like five of them that had positive goals, like to build up something different, like a commune. The rest was just misfit kids calling themselves anarchists. I remember this one kid said his name was Adolf, and I was like, 'Adolf! Hitler is so not an anarchist!' And he says, 'Hitler was radical and an outsider and nobody liked him, so he's my role model.'"

Ingo laughed. "And he is not a neo-Nazi?"

"How can you put that label on somebody who knows nothing about anything? He hooked up with these neo-Nazis because they're like his role models, and he gets a swastika tattoo and starts writing in gothic script, but he's a chatterbox and drives his new best friends up the wall, so they kill him with a hammer, roll him up in a rug, and stick him out on their front porch in Morristown, and then—"

"Stop, enough about Adolf," said Ingo.

"I thought you were a writer. Aren't you people always looking for material?"

"Adolf is too interesting for me. If I did not inherit this money twenty years ago, I will be taking notes now. But I am a literati. My writing is obligated to be intensely boring. Only in this way can my excellent style and form be seen by everyone. If I bring interesting, funny content, I am over as a writer, finished. Tell this story to the Israeli writer, Eyal."

"Are you kidding? Not in a million years, with Adolf and all that. Is he really a writer?"

"He has published a novel about boats once, and works as a literary critic and PR agent, so you could say he is a writer. But sadly, he is wasting all his strength on an affair with a nineteen-year-old bisexual."

Amy frowned.

"I myself prefer a woman with wisdom and experience. Also mature beauty."

Amy smiled. Maybe it was because she liked Ingo. Maybe it was because any woman, generally speaking, will flirt with anyone at all, regardless, just for the feeling of power she's going to have later when she's making fun of him for misunderstanding her.

On Friday the weather was good, and David invited Jenny to go kayaking. On the bus to the archaeological site where he had the kayak stashed inside the fence, they got to talking about their lives. Jenny told a touching story about her difficult initial emigration via Riga and Macau to Hawaii in 1989 and the nondescript existence as a hotel bartender that had preceded her full-throttle transition to the international jet-set.

"There's something I don't understand," said David. "Now we have the year 2006. You are nineteen years old, right?"

"Who tells you I am nineteen?"

"Eyal."

"Probably he is also saying I am lesbian from Yalta."

"You are not?" David was very intrigued.

"Why should I tell him what is true? Writers hate all stories. Private stories are only competition for their special public stories. In people, they interest themselves only for character. This is their raw material. They are imperialists of the inter-personal. We are their third world. So I tell him I am inno-cent virgin, also married, also lesbian, and he is very happy all the time. He asks no questions. To believe impossible ex-otic mysteries is religion. The essence of religion! It is just the same. Happiness is same as not caring. Indifference is joy. Details, he will be disappointed. To invent details by himself, this is his profession."

"So you are not lesbian? Are you Russian?"

"Shall I tell you the truth? I could tell you the truth."

"Please!"

She was silent and thoughtful for a long time, and then the bus driver accelerated through one last curve, shifting down, double-clutching, and grinding to a halt at their bus stop. David led her through some underbrush and down an eroded gully to the site by the river, camouflaged with green nylon netting and an opaque plastic fence. "My place of work," he said. "I get the kayak." She insisted on coming inside.

The stone building was now freestanding. Its foundations had been uncovered, and the floor inside was down to a fourth-century mosaic of the risen Christ wielding a sickle against goats with breasts, Abraham sacrificing a male fig-ure clearly labeled "Ishmael" in Greek, Adam and Eve in flagrante delicto, and any number of fly agaric mushrooms. An artist was making detailed drawings that would allow the mosaic to be reassembled for viewing, should such a project turn out to be in the public interest. Under it were at least two more layers of mosaic. No relevant lint had been found as yet, but from among the wall and floor scrapings David had been given quite a few wooden splinters with remnants of brightly colored wax. He had succeeded in piecing five or six of them together to create something that suggested half of a prosimian face—something along the lines of a lemur, with round, nubby ears. But there was nothing for Jenny to see. The floor was covered by a tarp, and the lemur was in the lab.

"Not much here," Jenny said. "Before the railroad comes, we make radical, secret art event. Invite graffiti artists to decorate this ugly thing. I will make video."

"Please no. This is big trouble. I have something like a career. I will not like to lose it."

"Shame," she said.

As they paddled back and forth across the Arno in the cool sunshine, David brought up the subject of Jenny's background again. She swore him to secrecy, then informed him that she was the love child of Ali MacGraw and the Dalai Lama. Her vain and uncaring parents had abandoned her at a young age to the tender mercies of the Chinese, who hid her by secret arrangement in an underground Anglican convent in Prague, where she was sexually abused by the nuns and forced to practice the piano nine hours a day. Escaping via Cuba to Texas, she had met Quentin Tarantino on his ranch and married him at sixteen to keep her parents from having her committed to an insane asylum. But the relationship was on the skids. "It will not last," she concluded. "He must give me a divorce. We are Muslim, and now no sex for four, five months. It is written. He must set me free."

David thought it over, then asked, "Will you someday become god-queen of Tibet in exile?"

She shook her head. "No. A lama is my father's spiritual follower only, always a small boy. But I reject it. In my ideas there is equality and classless society, also no sex discrimination." She rested her paddle, looking peacefully downstream. "What a nice day."

"Are you playing sometimes as corepetitor?"

"What?"

"Accompanist for singing. I sing baritone. Schubert."

"No!"

"And Schumann, *Dichterliebe*."

"You are completely insane! Who is doing this in twenty-first century? Are you bananas?" She laughed.

David felt absurdly happy. Of course, he still hadn't found out anything about her, but as someone who was very tired of priceless antiquities, he appreciated anything at all that could be valued for something other than its authenticity. In her case, he had no choice.

"I tell you what, David. I talk to Arkady. We get his songs of Tyutchev. Perform them in the villa. Behind you is seen video of destruction of Etruscan house by skater punks, then petrol fire. I will dance. This is the fucked up art event of the century."

"Only if you invite your husband and your parents."

"A deal!" She offered him her hand. They shook hands with vigorous solemnity, looking straight into each other's eyes for about a minute. David thought that he would like to kiss her, but as the idea was quite impracticable in the kayak, which confined them to two separate little holes, he decided against it.

"I like my idea," she added. "Art event series, name is *Good-bye*. We buy unique works of art, then on video we destroy them. Good-bye! Then video is sold for same price we pay for artwork. One work replaces another."

"The artifact is replaced by information of equivalent monetary value. This is a highly postmodern, fabulous idea," said David.

With David and Jenny away, Eyal was able to meet the landlord's daughter in David's apartment as planned. She drove him to the nursing home.

The old man was sitting up in a wheelchair by his bed. After a few abortive attempts at communication, it became clear that he and Eyal had no common language. The old man dated from the French generation, and Eyal's French was limited to greetings, integers, and pop songs. *"Moi Lolita,"* he hummed disconsolately. The daughter agreed to act as interpreter.

She didn't seem to translate everything. Once, for example, when he heard the old man say the words *"ivoire"* and *"Esquimaux,"* she turned to Eyal and asked how he was enjoying Florence. Actually there were quite a few sentences she seemed to ignore, as if she were using Eyal's presence to pump her father for information without passing it along.

But generally the old man seemed pleased to meet the art historian of a shipping company, or to have a visitor—Eyal wasn't sure. He claimed, the daughter translated, that he had been around the Horn sixty times under sail before 1935, though not always as captain, and began to list the ships by name. Eyal tried to write down all the names. In the end, bored of repeating herself and spelling things out, the daughter asked the old man to write them down himself.

The name of the eleventh ship, between *"Anne Shirley,* Prince

Edward Island," and "*Netochka Nezvanova*, Vladivostok," caught Eyal's eye. It was "*Come Back Alone,* Tuesday."

David and Jenny sat in the evening twilight in a park near the apartment with a cigarette lighter and two heavy sheets of paper. Jenny wanted to rehearse, so David had made her rough copies of two famous Redons from memory, with pastel and charcoal on heavy watercolor paper, just to see how they would burn. Would it be slow enough to look dramatic?

He thought, This is very forbidden, though I'm not burning anything of value, not even information. Of course, if the originals were gone—but I drew these from memory, so you see, the information would remain, even if every exemplar were to vanish. With sufficient training, the most perfect picture can be something like those short poems which everyone knows by heart, or music. Still, to burn a Bible or Koran is a small thrill even today, and how many Bibles are there in the world? Lots.

He could tell he was on thin ice because he hadn't been able to bring himself to copy the Redons he had found in the drawer. It's a lot easier to burn a copy of something that's already reproduced in thousands of books. His Redons were both unique and unusual. Neither were they lost, stolen, or strayed, if the registries could be trusted. They were free to begin a new life as the propellant that would take his career to the high castles of the stratosphere. In the meantime it was chilly, and his down jacket was collecting dew.

"The air is wet," Jenny said. "Good." She held up a picture by one corner and said, "Good-bye, take one." Incidentally, they were pretty drunk, so that when David then attempted to come closer and kiss her without disturbing her arm or the sodden picture, which refused to catch fire, he knocked her over. "Pay attention!" she said, propping herself up on the arm holding the cigarette lighter. "Take two!"

"It's no use," he said. "Too wet. Also, I am in love with you, but I am too stupid to do anything about it."

"Good," she said. "I am in love with you as well, and slowly we come together, like innocent children."

"Nice idea," David said, "but for you it's easy to wait because you are sleeping with the Russian Arkady, I think. I am not jealous, but it is getting on my nerves."

"Stop! We have only one pointless one-night stand, sentimental about Petersburg. Nothing important. He is a catastrophe, in bed as well. I am sorry. It is over. And not to worry, he will still deliver song cycle of Tyutchev for good-bye to Etruscans."

David sat looking for a moment mournfully at the clumsy and lightly singed reproduction of a work whose memory he treasured, then got to his feet and went upstairs singing "Gute Nacht" from the *Winterreise*. If she had bothered to ask how he knew she was sleeping with Arkady, which of course she wasn't, he would have replied that it was a random guess. Although an art historian, he was still a man, and not really much for noticing trivia. So he never counted towels or coffee cups when he got home from work, nor did he see Eyal's hair in the drain, nor think she would sleep with a guy like Eyal if he were the last man on earth. An art historian learns a certain tunnel vision: to see past details to the essence. So he had no idea what was going on. His powers of observation had been schooled and channeled into near uselessness. But he was old enough to know Jenny was too cute to be alone.

Eyal knocked and entered the old man's room. *"Bonjour,"* he said. *"Ça va?"* He knew that was supposed to be the French version of *"kak dila."*

"Thank God you're here, David," the old man replied. "Sorry about the other day. It takes some explaining, but I don't trust that woman."

Eyal wanted to say yes, or no, and then decided to limit his response to a noncommittal nod.

He sat down on a chair and put his hands on his knees. "She's my wife's daughter, not mine. Wartime and all that."

Eyal nodded.

"I neglected her education, deliberately, I suppose. I didn't want her knowing too much and stealing. There's a reason you're in the apartment, you know. That's to keep her out. She likes to poke around. Her mother had a habit of telling her I was a collector. Horrible woman. She may have told you I'm here for a new knee. Not true, I'm dying. I need some help with a little business matter, and I think you might be just the man."

"Me?"

"You're an art historian and something to do with shipping, she tells me. I do have quite a bit of experience with shipping myself. Not as a sailing captain, good Lord no. There are things one doesn't tell one's family. What one did in the war, or before it, for example. But I can see you're an educated, respectable sort. You're German?"

"Not only. Also Poland."

"Yes, they call it Poland now. Well then, you'll understand the situation. I'd been in Bilbao since the summer of '37, just doing some import-export. After you boys marched into Paris, there were quite a lot of communists and so on wanting to get to America, some fairly well-off, but on their last legs where cash was concerned. Well, I helped quite a few of them find a spot on a ship going somewhere or other. I was never much for ships, but in the import-export business you do get to know people. In the end I had quite a little collection of European art and manuscripts."

"And now you want to return the lost Jewish treasures to their rightful owners?"

The old man laughed, and Eyal laughed along with him. "An amusing sort, you are! Very funny. It was all payment for services rendered and perfectly legal, but I've kept it quiet all this time, thinking prices had nowhere to go but up. Which is true enough, but I'd forgotten the little matter of my mortality. And now that I'm ready to do something about it, I'm stuck here in bed with a greedy, conniving bastard for a daughter! I fob her off with ashtrays and knickknacks, but at some point she's going to start opening cupboards, and when I'm gone she'll clear out my bank vault without batting an eyelash, and what's worse, she's sure to find the really valuable stuff sooner or later. Which would be all very well if I wanted her to inherit, but my plan is a bit different. It has been all along. I want to sell the items at auction, a prominent house like Sotheby's because it's some very good stuff, and start a scholarship fund for young people from the Channel Islands to study in Japan."

Eyal twitched, but said nothing.

"I'm from Jersey myself, and my one regret in life is that I never made it to Japan."

"I will help you," Eyal said. "I have excellent connections at Sotheby's and other great auction houses through my academic work, and we will get a mind-blowing sum for every piece in your collection. The auction will be a huge news story, and the scholarship foundation will foster international understanding and peace between the island nations. I am your humble servant, proud to become involved in this worthy operation."

The old man relaxed, smiling peacefully. He reached over to turn up his morphine drip. "Can you give me a hand with this?" he asked. Eyal obliged. "Thank you so much. By the way, I don't want a lawyer skimming off percentages every time money changes hands. Vultures. Can you organize one who's discreet? Maybe offshore somewhere."

"Certainly. One thing. If you are not a sailing captain, how do you get this certificate of the Amicale des Capitaines au Long Cours—"

He laughed weakly. "For a historian, you don't know much about shipping! But how could you? The Cape Horn was a bar on the road to Laibach. Very spoiled boys, midshipmen so to speak, from all over. You know, Ljubljana, Yugoslavia, near Trieste. The East Bloc Taormina. I don't think it survived the war."

"Ah, yes," Eyal said. He could see that the old man was lost in thought. Nostalgia, he supposed. He excused himself, promising to come again soon with a lawyer, then bounced off down the hall and straight to David's apartment.

Time was running short and David's team had picked up the pace. The next layer of mosaic was, to David's relief, scattered with bits of really good lint. They documented it with especial care but destroyed it like the layer above, since it stemmed from a historical period—the height of the Roman Empire—when not really a lot was going on that we don't already know about. The only exception was a motif that a few of the archaeologists were quite excited about: Cain, depicted as a stooped and beetle-browed Neanderthal, turns away from the dead Abel.

"This explains the story of the mark of Cain, on Cain's forehead," one of the archaeologists explained to David. "The mark was that he didn't have a forehead. Get it? *Homo sapiens* settled down and learned agriculture, but his black sheep brother kept on hunting and didn't make it through the Neolithic, even though it was forbidden to kill him. Of course no law bothers forbidding something that isn't common practice. Neanderthal man dies out. So this is the first graphic example we have of a story as ancient as the Flood. I mean, it's plain that the competition with Neanderthals was going to be reproduced culturally."

"But Cain is not the hunter. Abel is keeping sheep. Cain is the farmer, and children of Cain become musicians, nomads, and makers of iron tools. This is more like tinkers than Neanderthalers. And why is your Abel blue like Krishna?"

"Asphyxiation," the archaeologist replied. "Cain strangled him with his hands, because he didn't have any tools, so he's blue from lack of oxygen. Really, David! Krishna in Florence in A.D. 30? I thought you were a historian!"

"Cain and Abel are no more belonging here in the western Roman Empire than Zarathustra. This picture is something else." He was convinced of it. He rather thought it might be a scene from a comedy by Plautus, especially since the revoltingly vulgar and banal scenes they had already disassembled and packed into crates appeared to depict scenes from Plautus. He figured that quizzing a single scholar by phone for two minutes would tell him who turns blue in which comedy and why. But the archaeologists on the site were convinced they had a trendy breakthrough that would get them TV time and better funding, once the maglev train was up and running and the gag order was lifted. "Look, your Cain's head is pretty close to the edge here," David added. "Maybe when they take away some of his head because of this border decoration, now he looks like a gorilla." The archaeologist snorted in contempt and they parted in open disagreement.

David left work very frustrated. Idiots, he thought. But he was happy to have his few scraps of lint. They confirmed the presence of tapestries, as suggested by the holes in the walls. There was only about a week more of work to do, and then he could spend some time off with Jenny. She didn't seem to have any other plans.

Eyal had arrived that afternoon more or less intending to ransack the place, steal everything that wasn't tied down, and find the key to the vault. No one knows what's there but the old man, he reasoned; it's just a bunch of random stuff; finders keepers, property is the whole of the law, etc.

Jenny, who was taking a nap when he arrived, had other ideas. She suggested that David was the one who would know both which things could be sold without causing trouble, and what they might be worth. "He will help us," she said. "Only innocent person like David can steal in way that no one will discover." Eyal saw immediately that she had a point. So they stuck to looking for the key. Since it was labeled *trésor* and hanging in a special cabinet for keys, they ended up having sex and drinking a pungent south German white (Pfefferle) from the exceptional 2003 vintage instead. They cleared out before David got home, but Jenny left him a note saying she was visiting in the villa garden and that he should stop by.

When he arrived, he saw Jenny with Eyal, Ingo, Arkady, and the sculptor in cheese, all sitting on benches around a mirror ball in the center of the garden. Arkady was berating the sculptor for filthiness, and everyone else was smiling.

"Cosa succede?" David asked Jenny.

"Arkady says he can't go on making art always with the same cheese. He must buy new cheese."

"He must leave this place!" Arkady added. "With the cheese is impossible for me to write. Look at him! Covered with fat, with fat hands." The sculptor wiped his hands on his shiny pants.

"It's brilliantly insidious," said Eyal. "His studio is air-conditioned. He always works to the opening. By the time the cheese is an affront to the senses, he has said good-bye to it forever. Only our atrium bears the aesthetic weight of this extremely ripe cheese. You should see it. Around each piece is a lake of grease. The artworks are blue-green fuzzy with fur, and shrinking every day."

"I am a guest of the villa myself, do not forget," the sculptor said. "I never before live with the display of my works. I am also surprised from its revolting character. I have seen it before only in photographs. But I will not buy new cheese!" he added, addressing himself to Arkady. "I have no plan to duplicate these works. First, the expense. Each piece is almost one hundred kilos from the French Jura."

"Sad," Arkady remarked. "All my life, I never taste such fine cheese, and now a kiloton tortures me like a martyr who is burning alive!"

"My current work is very cheap," the sculptor reassured him. "I make it of saffron-color factory cheese slices contained in plastic. It resembles the Christo and Jean-Claude *Gates* of Central Park. Environmentally doubtful, yet, at the least, demanding no refrigerator. Eternal art for temporary installation, not for sale. Then a mountain of garbage." He laughed. "This is a pointed and massive irony. You get it?"

"And my songs?" Arkady demanded to know. "Are they to become a mountain of garbage to your irony? I cannot work in this smell. I have no money to be always writing in cafés or changing to personal apartments like a German."

"Arkasha," Jenny said, "stop worrying. The *finissage* is Saturday. Your trouble is over. The cheese goes and the nice smell of oil paints returns to your life."

"A shame about the cheese," said Ingo. "You could see it was the delicious one from the Franche-Comté with the ashes." There was a long silence.

Then Jenny said, "Ashes makes me think of my own art. I never speak of it until now."

Suddenly everyone was paying close attention.

"You are a poet!" Eyal cried. "I knew it!"

"I am performance artist," she corrected him. "Outside Florence is old Etruscan house to be destroyed next week, when archaeology is finished. I hope one time to destroy it, but no chance. It is heavy stone, all of it. But now I think to burn the cheese there, to film it, of course, also to dance to songs of Tyutchev. Name of project is *Good-bye*."

"There is no way to film the pestilential smell that will arise from this horror," Eyal said.

"The songs are not finished," Arkady said. "Only the bagatelle for solo viola."

"Why the project is called *Good-bye*?" Ingo asked.

Jenny turned to him with a smile and said, "Because I wish to draw attention to transient nature of nonliterary art. More exactly, I believe all art is forgotten immediately, except for poets with many rhymes such as Heine and Mandelstam."

"I give you all my old cheese for this idea," the sculptor said. "Unless a piece will sell before Saturday. Sometimes one is selling on the last day."

"The idea is very bad," David said. "The art historians and others who hope to delay the destruction of the Etruscan house will be angry. Cheese will not burn without a great addition of wood or benzene."

"I don't care," said Jenny.

"There will be great damage to the deepest layer of the mosaic floor from this fire."

"And bulldozers do not make damage?" she countered. "Dreamer!"

"You are joking with this idea."

"I am earnest and determined," Jenny said resolutely.

"She is correct and very brilliant," Ingo added. "The concept functions on many levels. My highest respect to you as an artist, Jenny."

"The concept sucks," David said. "Now I am crying inside, that I ever showed you my workplace."

"Sunday night," Jenny said.

"I call the police," David replied.

"Stop it now!" Arkady said. "Let the beautiful poet work, you rich German freak! You call the police, I rip out your heart!" He brandished his bandaged hands.

David went home. Ingo called Amy to retail the story. Eyal went upstairs with Jenny, and Arkady stayed in the garden, humming. He was hard put to compose without a piano, but without hands it might not have helped.

David was putting in long hours, so Eyal and Jenny could take their time plundering the apartment. They decided to move things to the vault, since it was large and not full and they had the only key.

The vault contained a number of canvases that they couldn't identify beyond that they looked old, cracked, and discolored, rather as if they had never really dried out after the 1966 flood. They found the Master of the Three-Quarter Figures in the buffet right away, along with a Ribera of the beloved disciple, something like a Constable or a Corot with cows, and a packet of love letters from Henri Matisse. The Rops (still the original) was right in plain view on the wall. Under the bed was a plaster bas-relief of the calling of Martin Luther in the outhouse in Wittenberg by Rodin. Eyal dropped it and it broke into nine pieces and a little hill of dust, but as Jenny pointed out, it was a worthless copy.

They missed the Redons. That is, they found them, but Jenny said they were things David had drawn to rehearse for the performance from which he had now distanced himself so decisively, so they put them back in the drawer. They also missed the epic manuscript in Sappho's own hand sealed with wax into a tall glass jar under a floorboard along with nearly $60,000 in U.S. dollars and British pounds, much reduced by inflation, but you can't have everything. The old man had forgotten it completely. After a lifetime of light drinking, he was suffering from progressive atrophy of the cerebral cortex and had fallen into a habit of making poor decisions.

Eyal was somewhat surprised that Jenny saw no need to rehearse, but he didn't say anything. The glamour of her illegal undertaking thrilled him. With perfect aplomb, she identified, contacted, and persuaded the waste disposal firm scheduled to remove the cheese from the villa on Saturday afternoon to transport it to the remote site on the river. No bribe was necessary, since the company would save the municipal dump's substantial fee for accepting a ton of cheese.

David would have pleaded with her, but was silent and huffy and spent his evenings at the villa. He felt unhappy. The deepest layer of mosaic had been revealed to be plain gray, without even a decorative border. The archaeologists claimed this might be one of the earliest known monotheistic depictions of God, but David found it merely disappointing. To save time, they ripped it out with a backhoe. Underneath it was nothing in particular. The soil was undisturbed. They knocked the remaining stucco off the walls with geologists' hammers, but there was nothing hidden behind it. David sat in his lab, looking at 1,700-year-old rat shit through a microscope with sodden eyes.

By Friday the stone structure was little more than a dusty ruin. The researchers had nearly finished the work of destruction begun by the Romans. Soon it would house a rivulet of hot animal fat dripping into the Arno, and soon after that, heavy earthmovers would cover it with fill. What had it been? No one knew.

The trucks came early to take away the containers, and David had to rush to clear his lab into the bus. The archaeologists reached a consensus on which bar to celebrate in. David lugged the kayak to the water's edge and paused, looking back. The sun, setting early on the winter solstice, shone through a number of gaps in the stones of the roof that they had taken for bad workmanship, since it leaked rain, and traced on the dirt the image of a woman whose oversized head had two conspicuous horns. He called out to the archaeologists, but by the time they came back down from the road, the image was gone. Still, standing where it had appeared, you could look up and see it in the roof.

His boss yawned. "Okay, so it was a tophet for some kind of female Moloch. But she didn't last long, right, David? There was next to no soot on the wall. Because who wants a female Moloch? It was just a fuckup in personnel. You can bet your ass she got fired."

"She got her pink slip on day three," his assistant added. All the archaeologists snickered. "Either that or David's discovered a new religion."

"What I mean is, she's a one-shot deal, no historical interest, just like the rest of this shit. Are you ready for beer?"

"And the trees?" David said. "All these baby bones? Artemis with her bow, the big horns on the head of this feminine Moloch you say, the destruction on a single day, the lint, is this not a little bit interesting?"

His boss rolled his eyes. "You saw the ground under there. Fresh as a daisy. There's nothing left to dig here and I, for one, am thirsty." The archaeologists laughed. "You got to understand, Dave, the big-headed girl Moloch and fifty cents will get you a cup of coffee. So you publish it. So what? Who wants to see it? Right now she just looks like a clerical error. So let them cover her up with dirt and build a railroad over her head. By the next time they dig, maybe the science of archaeology will have advanced to where she fits right on in to some discursive context we never even thought about. Right now she hasn't got a leg to stand on. Let it go, babe. Let some great-great-grandson of yours be the star and get the extra credit." He turned and addressed the group as a whole. "You guys' problem is, you always think everything you find is something you already know about. It never crosses your mind that something you find might have nothing to do with anything. You act like history is some kind of jigsaw puzzle! But what is it? It's a bunch of stuff! And leave David alone! He's a good man."

David turned away mournfully after asking again which bar. Then he pushed the kayak out into the river and glided gently around an oxbow for a good three hundred yards before he got stuck on rocks. He carried the kayak almost half a mile through stagnant mudholes swarming with bugs to where a dam formed a sort of narrow artificial lake upstream from Florence. After another mile he hid the kayak in some underbrush and walked up to the road to look for a bus stop.

Sunday afternoon around the time he thought Jenny must be finalizing the crowd control arrangements for her performance, David heard the key turn in the lock and she came in. "You, here?" he said.

"Yes, and I must go again soon," she said. "My plan was perhaps not so realistic." She sat down heavily on a kitchen chair. "Bad two days."

"The cheese does not burn?"

She laughed. "Oh, my dear David, I think I must flee from Italy as a refugee. You go to Freiburg now?"

"To my parents' in Trossingen for the holidays."

"I go to Freiburg," she said. "I will stay in your apartment there and do nothing. Now I tell you why. Yesterday I go with the garbage men to take the cheese. I am not thinking about this before. What kind of truck they use? Garbage truck. Not so clean. We drive to your work place. You know it is far down the hill to this house where you are researching. Truck is very big. I make this story short. One ton of ugly cheese is by the road, and from the truck it is so dirty, ripped open, smelling of bad amputations. I cannot describe it. Screaming and yelling at these men, it is no help. The cheese stands alone. Back to villa, there comes to me Siegfried, says reporters are calling him. I suppose this is because Ingo is telephoning the bitch Amy and she is telling all newspapers about my beautiful performance art. And all the time, my idea is not to burn cheese! I think, Burning will be a disaster of the environmental kind. My piece is for the future archaeologists. They will think, Wow, twenty-first-century culture of ugly cheese."

David laughed sadly. "Probably so."

"But now cheese is dumping by the roadside. Dumping one ton of ugly cheese must be an illegal secret, not a news story. It is not permitted. I will pay and pay. I must hide myself. Help me, David, please."

He went to his bedroom and returned with a key. "This is the key to my place in Freiburg. You can go there and wait for me. But you must promise me you will do nothing strange or ridiculous. Just wait. Read a book. I give you the address."

"Oh, David!" she cried, getting up to hug him.

"Stop that," he replied. "I help you because you are cute. I do not trust you. One thing you must swear to me. You go alone to Freiburg. Tell no one. You understand? Do you have money for the train, and for some food?"

"Oh, perfect David," she said. "I will go alone, right now." And she did. She climbed aboard, found a seat, and fell asleep.

The doorbell rang. It was Eyal. "Is Jenny home?" he asked.

"No."

"Where is she?"

"I don't know," David said. Strictly speaking, he was being precise, as he didn't believe in her ability to go anywhere in particular and stay there.

"You must help me," Eyal said. "I am desperately in love with her. Even after the vile cheese disaster, I adore her."

"Have a beer," David said. "I cannot help you. You must know that I, as well, have a certain interest in Jenny, but love is not enough to get a girl."

"It was not only love. It was amazing hot sex. I am crazy for her and she worships me. But I know nothing about her. Now I am afraid she is poor, because she is hiding from paying for dumping the cheese."

David drank beer and said, after a while, "I see."

"It is not so expensive, maybe eight hundred euros for the cleanup. Please tell her I can pay this. She can return to me. With all the stress, I think she forgets that I have money."

"Listen to me, Eyal," David said. "Of course she has money. It is the police she doesn't like. She is a thief. She has taken every work of art from this apartment, including a valuable Rops and the Master of the Three-Quarter Figures, and from the vault of the bank she has also stolen the key. I am nice to her, hoping I get this art back. I move out soon. The landlady will accuse me. You understand?"

For a second Eyal felt guilty because he had the key to the vault in his pocket. Then he noticed that David's gaze, while he told this story, was directed downward and to the right. From reading about police work he knew this meant David was lying. Possibly cohabitation had reduced David to regarding not only everything Jenny said, but also everything she did, as fiction. "Surely you are joking," Eyal said, making direct eye contact. "This cannot be! The little slut!" They both shook their heads.

"I like her too much," David admitted. "Otherwise, I would betray her to the police." His gaze rested on an uninteresting gouache by Tanguy in the upper left-hand corner of the opposite wall, indicating to Eyal that he was telling the truth. Eyal, confused, drank up his beer and went grocery shopping.

Actually, David assumed it was the landlady who had run off with the art. Her having left the Redons in the drawer assured him that she had no notion of their authorship or value. He packed them up with a clean conscience and flew to Friedrichshafen on the twenty-fourth. His parents picked him up at the airport.

His mother was a vocal teacher and mezzo-soprano with his father accompanying on piano. They had a concert on the twenty-sixth and were busy rehearsing, so he had plenty of time to drink eggnog and brood over his misfortune between phone calls to his apartment in Freiburg. He believed Eyal's claims of hot sex, because he couldn't remember Eyal's ever having lied to him, and also because hot sex with Jenny had been Eyal's main goal in life since before they had met, so it seemed only logical that he might, with a little luck and no competition other than a weird Russian and a bunch of guys who were convinced she was an unapproachable lesbian, eventually succeed in obtaining it. His conversations with Jenny were cheerful and superficial. She thought Freiburg at Christmas was lovely and begged him to come home early and share it with her. He heard such requests, it seemed to him, from an infinite distance, as if he were some kind of benign onlooker watching her through a telescope from another galaxy.

The concert was a success and the inner circle landed, as usual, in the kitchen of his parents' home for the postmortem. Several colleagues from the academy in Trossingen were there, along with a music theorist from Tübingen and a disaffected violinist, once a power monger in Moscow, who had ended up concertmaster of a provincial German freelance orchestra staffed with brawny Poles. After four glasses of vodka David told them all about Arkady, leaving out the Goethe letter. The musicologist, the concertmaster, and a horn teacher assured him that Arkady was a respected composer, the winner of several notable prizes. His parents declared an intention to premiere the Tyutchev songs, if possible.

David went to bed with an acid feeling of despair. He felt how the small, small world was attempting to close in around him. All the loose ends were striving to connect. But life is not a jigsaw puzzle, he thought. It's a bunch of stuff. Why then, if I am doing my best to avoid a composer, must my mother sing his songs? There is only one possible answer: I am to blame.

He came back out to the kitchen in his pajamas and told his parents and the violinist, who was still there, that he'd remembered all wrong: the composer's name was Kostya, the song texts were by Akhmatova, and he'd seen the first three songs, which were pathetic kitsch. His parents laughed, and the violinist named Arkady's publisher. Back upstairs, he leaned far out the window and glared up at the stars. The windowsill was ice cold. He thought of Florence with longing and returned to bed.

Ingo had finally begun to fall for the lamentably elderly Amy on that Sunday as she braked the convertible and lowered her window, randomly addressing a crowd of photographers and art maven friends that had formed on the shoulder of a greasy secondary road bordered by a long, low, rank wall of festering cheese adorned with tread marks and black gravel. Without a trace of embarrassment, she declaimed a welcome in several languages and that she would be right with them. Parking the car, she said to Ingo, "Thank God for digital in-stallations. People are so used to everything crashing, they'll cheer anything that doesn't just freeze up and turn blue. But I'd say there's been some kind of glitch if the cheese is up here by the road. Isn't it supposed to be down in this like Etruscan granary?"

"No problem, Jenny will reboot," Ingo said.

She got out of the car and announced loudly in Italian that the artist would require several minutes to reboot the cheese. There was a long silence, then sighs of deep insight as the photographers gathered, holding their breath, along the road to photograph the cheese in loving close-up. Then she led them, after a false start down the wrong ravine, past the old lab site and down to the building. Once a dank and fetid cave, it was now a bare half-cylinder of stone open on one side to the river. Jenny was nowhere to be seen, but a reporter announced his recollection that the site would be obliterated by the route of the new train.

To say that the articles in the paper on Tuesday were lauda-tory would be a misleading understatement. Jenny, it turned out, had linked the "wet" automatons (gynecological mod-els incorporating fluid masses, Frankenstein's monster, the famous defecating duck) of the eighteenth century to the multivalent destructive power of technology in a stunningly original way. The cheese represented time, life itself, and our own weakness as threatening qualities that constantly threaten to engulf us. With the bare and symmetrical Etrus-can structure, the past (and with it aesthetics) was shown as it was, bereft of relevance and vitality, yet possessing all the elegance of a machine. And through it all roared, by impli-cation, the maglev train which, itself an invulnerable robotic phallus of steel, carried a soft, yet brittle, cargo and would reduce anything in its path to something resembling the cheese. With one brilliant stroke, she had illuminated three centuries of technological progress and horror like no one before her, despite being a mere nineteen years of age and from the wrong side of the tracks.

I must meet her, thought the philosopher Peter Sloterdijk as he was catching up on *Corriere della sera* in his living room in Karlsruhe a week later. He resolved to invite her to perform something in the ZKM Center for Art and Media, where he had a comfy sinecure thinking up installations and letting his

students build them. He called Siegfried, who was feeling a
bit sensitive since the sculptor in cheese had stormed into his
office claiming he'd been duped. He had donated his works
to be burned on film during a dance performance, not to
be crushed to pulp by passing buses, and Jenny was a ruth-
less and exploitative art-world star posing as a dated, deviant
feminist minor. Siegfried managed to calm him down, but he
couldn't find Jenny and was a bit surprised to learn from Arkady that she had moved out weeks before. He told Sloterdijk
he would give her the message.

Eyal liked David's apartment in Freiburg. It was modern and
spare, easy to keep clean. He saw that the clutter in the apartment in Florence was none of David's doing. David's own
place was as efficient as a space capsule.

It hadn't taken him more than a week of brooding hostility
and wandering the streets inwardly calling her name to think
of looking for Jenny there. David was in the phone book, so
once he got started, his metaphysical redemption took a matter of seconds. He was surprised not to find David there as
well, but after all he had gone to the trouble of impressing the
animality of their relationship on him, so he figured it would
be at least two weeks before David got over it enough to make
a move, which gave him a week to work with. He also figured
a week was the most he could persuade his wife to accept as
the duration of a little holiday tour away from the telephone
at the villa. He had told her he felt inspired to rent a lonely
ski hut in the mountains where it was quiet and he could write
and chop wood. She had approved, and he had taken a night
train to Freiburg.

He knew that David might appear at any moment, but he
didn't care. His apathy toward David was truly complete. Jenny

treated him with the utmost consideration while he counted down the days. He knew that David would inherit her. He was torn between two metaphors: that she would be his cast-off, i.e., that whoever had her first was better off; and that he was losing her to a better-looking, younger, more single man, i.e., that whoever got her in the end was better off. He knew there was only one way out of the double bind: He had to go on having an affair with her after she was with David and preferably married to him. Then David would never have anything more than his leavings as he skimmed the cream of her youth, beauty, etc.

As his family's being in Israel rendered such a satisfactory solution impossible, he took refuge in denial. He brought her a plate of small pears, neatly cut and cored, poured her a glass of chilled white wine, and said, "David tells me you are afraid of the police. Don't you expect me to keep a secret with our little art heist?"

"I must keep always underground. I am wanted! And you know why? I am material witness to huge gray-market crime ring, smuggling overpriced shampoo of major American producer from Chinese market to Italy. In China, four cents. In Italy, three euros fifty-nine. Siegfried, he is the ringleader and financier. Now I am also guilty of blackmail—"

He interrupted her for a change. "My love, tell me the truth, just one time. Be kind to me. We will be separated soon. Is my solitary future to contain nothing but memories of fantasies?"

"Okay, I tell the truth." She paused. "I am turning tricks with my girlfriend. She is blowing cop and I am watching street, then comes his friend mister *guardia* and says he rapes me or takes me under arrest. I fight against this. My friend helps, but she is shot in head by her trick. Then I run. I am shot here." She raised one knee and pointed to a small, pitted scar on the back of her thigh. He had never noticed it before. "Management of whorehouse has my passport, but I do not go back there. They are friends of police. I will be arrested and they will beat me to death, before or after or sometime. So no passport!"

"If you have invented this story, it is in very poor taste."

"And if not? Is it then good story?"

"If you mean what is more horrible, nature or naturalism, then clearly fiction is worse. It shows not only the shortcomings of life itself, but also the depravity of the human mind." He ate a piece of pear.

"This is very cerebral thinking," she protested. "In reality my friend dies and I get shot in the leg and bleed like a pig. In fiction, I am lying in soft bed eating pear and thinking thoughts in poor taste."

"Let me see your leg again." He drew it close, but all his many years of service in the somewhat irrelevant Israeli navy had not taught him what a gunshot wound looks like. "When was this?"

"In 1998. But, Eyal! It didn't happen. I lied. I show you my passport." She wrested her leg from his grasp and got up to take her backpack off the dresser. "See? My passport."

"Your name is Alla Bauer?"

"So what? But something small is missing with this passport. You see? My tourist visa is long time expiring. So police are not my favorites. Lucky Switzerland stops checking the passports last year." She lay back down. "So nice here. So clean and tidy in this apartment, like Switzerland. I really like David's way of living."

Eyal decided, all other things being equal, to initiate sex

before it was too late, as he did many times in the course of the next three days. Then it was too late.

David didn't visit Freiburg. He had another three weeks of work left in Florence, and was eager to spend eighteen hours a day at the university grinding his brain to powder.

He had lunch one day with his boss in the student cafeteria next to the cathedral. "I think a lot about what you said," he said. "History is a bunch of stuff. You are right, especially now that I work with this lemur. No antecedents, and the law of causality looking over my shoulder and making fun of me." He took a gulp of wine and added, "Forgive my bad ontology."

"Don't sweat it," his boss replied. "To you, it's a lemur. To the guy who painted it, it was his little sister. It has no reason to be part of art history as we know it. You think those people had art? Did they even have authorship? Somebody digging in two thousand years, if he finds the face of Captain Crunch from a cereal box, all the art history in the world isn't going to help him."

"So you mean it was pop, or folk culture?"

"I wouldn't even go that far. Maybe it was a neurotic symptom. You just don't know! Stop beating yourself up for not knowing. What is it with you guys? You want to know everything, and what you can't know you extrapolate, as if human history were some kind of climate model. You ever think seriously about this notion that everything is interconnected? That everything affects everything else? You know what I mean. Hegel and chaos theory and whatever."

"You mean as in Marxist economic analysis?"

"I mean everything right up to and including Luhmann, as in every philosophical system that's been advanced in the last two hundred years since the—the what? You tell me! This is a test!"

David struggled to think of an answer.

"The industrial revolution! You get a world knee-deep in identical products with identifiable supply chains and a limited number of producers, colonies feeding factories feeding railroads, and all of a sudden, everything is interconnected!"

"Sure, yes," David said, hesitating. "Freudian theory is an epiphenomenon of capitalist imperialism. Why not?"

"Now it's globalization, which is even worse. Now every idea is a global phenomenon, democracy or youth culture or whatever, like there's one big universal mind. At least the de facto Platonism in modernity was limited to producing bazillions of identical artifacts, not bazillions of identical thoughts."

"You are right that there is a universal ideology which is crushing us like an insect. And since, as you have pointed out, rationality was a side effect of rationalization, there is no way to criticize it. This means, for example, that without division of labor it is hopeless to struggle against the Internet. It has the heads of Hydra. Like a field of identical flowers to which the identical bees go happily, thinking they bring home sweet nectar. But they are only pollinators making possible the seeds of more identical plants, which soon cover the earth like the triffids."

"I wouldn't go that far, but there's a real material leveling going on since maybe A.D. 1300, and the pace of cultural leveling is beyond anything anybody ever expected. But now think about the ancient world! It's a patchwork of villages. Cultures and artifacts just come and go, like quantum anomalies. Every priest is a prophet and every craftsman is the Unabomber. People are always taking Occam's razor the wrong way, trying to reduce the total number of objects in the world instead of reducing their complexity. Now they're to the point where a butterfly flaps his wings on the other side of the world and I get up out of bed and shoot the president. I can't just be a freak of nature anymore, or out of my mind. It's one seamless web of causation, but you need all the silicon in the known universe to model it. That's the theory. Care to prove it? Step right up, but don't forget your unknowable quantity of silicon. Know what I'm saying?"

"And what if it's true? What if the butterfly is flapping right now?"

"What good is uncovering a conspiracy if the guy pulling the strings is a butterfly?"

"So there is just this one guy whose little sister looked like a dog, and no trade with Madagascar, and therefore no lemur picture in Italy?"

"Of course there's a lemur, if you can get somebody to buy it. Go ahead and try. You just might pull it off."

"Everything and nothing, just like always." David sighed. "Why work? I am saddened. Although, what you say reminds me of the argument against evolution. Science depends from believing that no fossil is a freak. Without the imperialist dialectic, I am a mere taxonomist. Yet for personal reasons I resist determinism."

His boss swore to himself to avoid postdoc art historians in the future and to stick to humble artifact artists who would faithfully catalog and reproduce the finds and shut up. That reminded him to ask David if by any chance he knew the artist who had done the critically acclaimed but disgusting thing with the cheese on the bluff above the dig. "They said she lives in the villa where you were living for a while. What's she like? Is she cute?"

"She is cute," David said. "I catch her one time in my room.

Probably then she sees the map marked with the site. Then I move away. She is a perfervid lesbian." The boss suggested that David was putting in too many late, lonely nights. He agreed to take the afternoon off.

David rode the bus out to the villa and found Arkady and Ingo sitting in the library drinking sherry. "Have a sherry," Arkady said. "I invite."

"What's the occasion?" David asked. He noticed that Arkady's hands had healed.

"I am rich," Arkady said. "In 1985 I am little child. I write ballet-opera of *Finnegans Wake* for fifty singers, two orchestras, one of them baroque with period instruments, also two pianos and organ in the best Soviet style and with great sincerity. To perform this work takes eleven hours. Now I receive *tantième* of thirteen thousand euros."

"Why?"

"It is performed! Nothing else. So many musicians, even one movement is making big *tantième*. And they perform this not in a hall. It is outside, big park, place for many thousands! Even more *tantième*! And I am so happy. Now I can pay for premiere of songs of Tyutchev."

"My mother—" David said, before pausing to remember that he had resolved to cease functioning as an informational node forging actual contact among things he had hoped to link in his mind alone and by distant association if at all.

"What about your mother?" said Ingo.

"My mother is interested. She knows your work. She is a mezzo-soprano, teaching in Trossingen."

"Songs are for coloratura, flute, piccolo, and muted triangle," Arkady said. "Like cries of mice. Pianissimo."

"Well, then."

"You want to read them? I hear that you are musician. You are singer."

David denied it and poured himself another glass of sherry. "Sherry glasses are very small," he remarked.

"I agree," said Ingo.

"The director has message for Jenny. She should call philosopher Sloterdijk."

Ingo and David looked fixedly at Arkady. "What?" Ingo said. "Peter Sloterdijk?"

Arkady assured him that this was the case.

"Small world. I spent a weekend with him once at a conference."

"Stop now," David said. "Because you had a coffee with him does not make the world small. He is a famous man, always traveling. Many people meet him."

"Many people of a certain class," Ingo said. "Not so many if you take an average. You don't know him. But your mother knows Arkady, it seems, because they are musicians."

"They say if you follow the chain of people knowing people, there are only six people to separate you from any person on earth," said David.

"This is called in English six degrees of separation," Ingo added.

"Probably an old idea. Now everybody knows someone knowing famous people, so it's three degrees."

"Since the Reformation there is only one degree, since God knows everyone and everyone knows God," Ingo said. "A flat hierarchy, basing on a team structure. No chain of command, also no individual responsibility. There is one boss for all, and He forgives everything. So you see why the world is going to hell."

"I don't know famous people," David admitted. "And I do

not wish it. I have decided to stop making new synapses for this cybernetic universe."

"Well said," said Ingo.

"My method will be to speak to each person only about himself. For example, if I find another letter of Goethe, I do not rush to find someone who is interested. This was only a way I was trying to make myself more interesting, by borrowing the famousness of others. An art historian knows many famous people, but they are all dead."

"But this is the only solution," Arkady said. "James Joyce is my friendly helper, gaining for me gratis attention and thirteen thousand euros. I never get this money by myself. Tyutchev will help me also, I hope. The dead artist holds the ladder to money."

"Who is Tyutchev?" Ingo asked.

David was distracted by sudden thoughts of the Redons in his closet in Trossingen and interrupted with a different question. "Where's Eyal?" he asked.

"Writing in the hills alone," Ingo said. "Now that his time runs out, he remembers his novel about Siberia in 1942."

"You see?" Arkady said. "He is same like me. Without Stalin, he is nothing."

When Eyal got back to Florence, he went to see David. He confessed to everything he hadn't confessed to already that didn't involve Freiburg. It had occurred to him that there were probably records in the apartment that pertained to the bank vault, or possibly an inventory, and that these might be found when the old man died, and that there might be trouble.

His actions were not strictly justified by logic. Mostly, he wanted to include David in the plan, or at least get David's attention, perhaps only because of Jenny, or perhaps for reasons unknown to anyone including himself. It may have been that he merely wanted to tell the story. After all, he couldn't fit it into a novel about Siberia in 1942, and he preferred not to tell coworkers anything he wouldn't tell his wife. He had no compunctions about serving as a data node. Any novelist habitually walks the slack rope over the boiling oil of David's deepest anxiety. More than a data node, he is a virus-infected file server, churning out intimacies at random to an audience whose size and attributes remain objects of the loftiest indifference.

David was amused by the idea that Jenny had stolen everything on principle without even going to the trouble to sell it or take it along. He and Eyal searched the apartment as it had never been searched before. They leafed through every book. They dismantled every framed print. In the end they had hundreds of millions of (devalued) lire, a woodcut by Emil Nolde, an almost complete set of the plates to Diderot's *Encyclopédia* masquerading as three decades of *Jane's Fighting Ships,* several old passbooks to empty savings accounts, and a hand-drawn map that marked a spot on an island in the Arno with an X.

"This explains the kayak," David said.

Eyal vaguely remembered Jenny's having mentioned a kayak at some point.

"I hid it on the river with a small tree. Maybe it's still there."

They went out together for coffee on a windy plaza and to a bookstore to buy a detailed hiking map with landmarks and all the best rollerblading routes and so on. They found where the island must be. It was too small to be on the map, but the site was unmistakable.

Then they rode out of town on the bus. The kayak was still there.

The cabdriver who showed up refused to have anything to do with it, so they paddled downstream. Eyal kept track of their progress on the map. The banks became increasingly built up, but it was a nice day to be on the river. After an hour and a half and two portages, they were still solidly outside town, but approaching it through a suburb. There was plenty of water, often enough to fill the walled-in riverbed from one side to the other. The children playing on the banks were only mildly curious. Occasionally they would come out onto a bridge and try to hit them with a gob of spit. Otherwise, they were ignored.

It gradually became clear that something was missing. Eyal showed David the maps. "Look. Here is the stream coming into the river. Here is this church tower. Everything is here, and we are past it now. Where is the island?"

David paddled slowly, looking down through the water. It was not, to say the least, transparent. He poked down with his paddle and eventually, just about where the island was supposed to be, he hit a ridge of gravel. "There's something here."

Eyal said, "Then I suppose I shall search. This is so sad." He took off his pants without taking off his shoes.

"What are you doing?"

"I go waddling."

"Wading," David corrected him.

Eyal, having served for years on the Dead Sea and in Egyptian lagoons, was unafraid of murk. Sliding on sharp stones, up to his chest in water, he poked, kicked, and trampled his way back and forth across the unseen river bottom, screaming only once as he tripped and went under. "A grocery wagon," he remarked. "I believe this box"—he gasped as if to himself—"for it is certainly a box, is heavy and watertight. It stays where it is, even if the sand of this island is vanishing in flood of 1967 or whenever along with trees and landing places and all other features of this precious map. To date, no one has found it, and I will find it. Who will venture into such a desolated place? Not even the stupidest, most ornery child would play here. Yet here I am. But I will not find this improbable and lyrical lost treasure. And not only that. I will not even succeed to sell the story to newspapers, because I am too embarrassed by it. And that's not all. I will never publish an account of my time in Europe, nor will I even be empowered to draw on it for literary material. It will resist my every inroad, like the green hell of the Amazon which can only be explored through harvesting, burning, and grading to a flat immensity resembling the lunar seas. It is not only the little photons. It is absolutely everything that cannot be perceived. Especially not with the feet, with shoes on, in one and one-quarter meters of this filthy water. Still, I am afraid of tetanus. How good that I have shoes."

Meanwhile, David had seen something like a jug of fabric softener half buried in plain view on a nearby sandbank. He paddled over to it, parked the kayak on the sand, and retrieved it. "Okay, I open this now," he called out. He looked inside. In the relatively clear water that filled the dripping bottle, something could be seen glinting through a black mass. He poured the buried treasure out on the sand, spooking a swarm of fleas.

Eyal waded over to peer down at their meager haul. He was tired. "You tell me," he said.

"These are settings for pearls, French, sixteenth century. This is a cheap Victorian ring. And this"—David extricated something resembling the hair that collects in a shower drain, something he had never voluntarily touched—"was a brooch of hair."

"Where are the pearls?" Eyal asked.

"They dissolve in acid rain." He poured off the water. "Yes, they are gone."

"Pity."

"You expect diamonds or emeralds. But these stable stones, nobody has them before. Pearls are the jewel of history. And what is a pearl? Chalk. The touch of skin destroys it."

"An excellent investment."

"You know these modern stones, they are all industry products anyway. They change the colors. This is why old jewels look so boring."

"Gold would be all right."

David rearranged the forlorn necklace and earrings on the rock and flung the hairball into the water. "The ring may have some platinum." He held up a dark green bead. "What is this? Ivory?"

"My eyes hurt," said Eyal. "Also my legs, and my ass itches like crazy."

"I hope it is only the fleas," David said.

As they marched to the Ponte Vecchio, Eyal said, "Why didn't the old man put this stuff in the vault and save me the elaborate self-torture?"

"What is in the vault? You are telling me before."

"Cracked and dirty paintings rolled up like carpets."

"And the key is labeled '*trésor.*' This is the answer. The vault is for the daughter, filled with garbage."

"He connives to humble me. He is the puppet master to my willing marionette."

Back at the villa, Eyal showered until the hot water was gone. His eyes and the cuts on his legs kept itching. When he got to the bank the next morning, the vault was empty. He tried to call the old man. He knew enough Italian to understand the relevant part of the answer he got: *morto*.

David got a call from Amy, praising his timely plan to leave at the end of January. The old man had died of complications from knee surgery. "It's best to lose the weight while you're young and save the surgery later. Trust me on this one."

When it came time for Eyal to fly home, Ingo and Amy drove him to the airport. Ingo allowed that he looked forward to staying in Florence for a while yet. They gratefully received Eyal's best wishes. Eyal was still swollen and slathered in antibiotic cream and cortisone. He told his wife it was frostbite.

Jenny called Sloterdijk. He wondered politely if she might not be interested in coming up for a performance on very short notice at a weekend *vernissage* in mid-February. The exhibition was something about democracy. She said she had no technical requirements beyond thirty square meters of space, a hotel for six people, and a thousand euros an hour. She prepared for her performance by reaching Arkady on the communal villa telephone just before he moved into a two-star hotel with a private bath.

David stayed wrapped up in his work each day, then took the train home to bask in Jenny's radiant presence. That was about all he got from her. She was preoccupied with reading Verlaine. It was his fault (they were his books), but she did little else. Occasionally she took some money from the jar where he kept money and went grocery shopping, or just walked around Freiburg. It had a Gothic cathedral and little brooks in the streets, but it was freezing cold and damp outside, and he lived on the edge of town in leftover temporary student housing from the 1960s. Occasionally she worked on her stringently formal Russian poetry. She looked forward to the trip to Karlsruhe, and eventually she told David about it.

"And again you will dance?" he asked.

"Oh, yes, just wait until you see this dance. All the time I am practicing. This becomes the dance of the century. I am in the center of large exhibition about democracy or something. There I burn not cheese, only hair. This makes very special smell. Hair is extremely morbid. No one will be ready to criticize hair. Okay, I am lying. It is not hair. It is a surprise."

David was indeed surprised when he saw Arkady standing in a circle of people that surrounded an inaudible group of apparent musicians. The murmur of hundreds of art fans milling around the floor of the huge four-story atrium was compounded not only by their heavy winter shoes but also by a series of electronic sound sources that included mechanized exhibit narrations, interactive audiovisual components, and many strange-looking conical loudspeakers that appeared to be glued to the floor and had no other function than to produce a deep, unsettling roar at intervals of two minutes. The general effect was bedlam. Under a spotlight, a soprano mouthed Tyutchev's text, accompanied by an industrious flute and piccolo. You could see that a triangle player occasionally touched his triangle, but there was nothing to be heard in the chaos. David's eyes rested gratefully on the brightly lit ensemble in their somber black outfits, since almost everything else was adorned with strobe lights or reams of vanishingly small text or wouldn't stand still. A film crew had two cameras trained on them, as well as, hung discreetly over their heads, a single stereo microphone. It was entirely possible that the video, if nothing else, would include music.

"Arkady!" he said. "Doesn't this make you crazy?"

"Dear David!" he said, kissing David on the cheek. "It's perfect!" he said. "All my life I am dreaming of this. First time, contact with my work is purely free. People are not sitting chained down to chairs. They are drinking, talking, living! This is real Schubertiade of Schubert, not private salon haute-bourgeois religious-event concert thing."

"You think they hear anything? I cannot hear."

"If they don't, they are themselves guilty! All are standing six, seven meters away! I hear everything. 'Silentium'!" Next to them a cell phone suddenly played *Eine kleine Nachtmusik.*

David went looking for Jenny. He found her with Sloterdijk and the composer Wolfgang Rihm. She was explaining to them that she had no wish to study with either, and like any true artist she refused to write on commission or accept prizes. What she would like is a prize for Arkady, since he was a man and thus always in need of money. And not some little piss-ant prize either: a big prize, perhaps a Nobel.

"There is no Nobel Prize for music," Rihm said. "Unfortunately."

"Why not? I make one," she said. "Nobel is dead for over seventy years. He has no copyright. There must be great deal of money in this prize, for the winner. I will create and award prize, and you will recognize it. This is like when state declares independence and other states recognize. We will have diplomatic relations."

"Hello, everyone," David said. "Come, Jenny, let's go and take a little walk outside. I buy you a drink."

She smiled gallantly and took his arm. "Good-bye, Peter and Wolf! Ah, David, my art is truly not so bad. They are right. It is brilliant commentary on production of living art in universal mechanical context. I do nothing. I only turn on machine by introducing money into aperture for coins. Then

I am producer, artist, genius of work no one can hear!" She threw back her head and laughed.

"Are you drunk or insane?"

"No, I read too much in winter in Germany. This phase is not lasting forever. Let us go to hotel. You are so nice to me, David. Maybe I sleep with you."

David thought it over. He liked the word "maybe," since he wasn't sure it was a good idea, plus he was hungry, so he suggested they go out for dinner. They went to dinner, ate too much, and fell asleep early. He wondered how long it would take him to get over Eyal, and regretted that this was somehow his problem and not hers.

David's life was one of perfect peace and harmony. He spent most days in his office at the university in acerbic preparation for a seminar on symbolist drawings that he planned to add to the curriculum in April. Changing the theme of his *Habilitation* (a sort of postdoctoral thesis Germans have to write before they can become professors) to symbolist drawings was a potential act of fatal hubris entailing the abandonment of years of promising work on Etruscan tapestries, but he wasn't really worried. He saw that he would be compelled to leave Freiburg for Paris, and started shopping around for a stipend. In his evenings at home, he cooked, cleaned, and read the newspaper to relax.

Etruscan tapestries had always been a frustratingly meta-analytical exercise. A diligently acquired expertise on motifs and color preferences, in combination with precise chemical analyses, had allowed him to make highly sophisticated guesses about what might or might not have been the original themes of the putative pictorial sources of certain pieces of lint. Those results were accepted with enthusiasm by the scientific community. Whereas every time he had the pleasure of producing some concrete evidence of a particular motif that wasn't just lint (e.g., a stray lemur), he was not encouraged to present a paper at every leading conference but rather shot down in flames. He saw that with little effort he would soon be the world's leading expert on Etruscan tapestries (in a sense, he was establishing the field), but he wanted more. If, as Arkady said, the dead artist holds the ladder to money, then no one was more dead than the Etruscans. But as he looked across the room at Jenny where she sat silently reading Bourdieu on photography with her legs tucked up under her, he felt that he was not interested in leading a stable, predictable life. He felt like doing something wild. "Jenny," he said. "We could go see a film."

She put her feet down and said, "We could have sex."

"No," he said. "I have no sexual feelings for you. I know this now. My feelings are those of a father. I like you to live here quietly, giving you food and rent. You eat nearly nothing. You are looking thinner all the time, like a little boy. I worry about you. This is paternal feeling. So I wish only to care for you like a child, not like an incestuous pederast."

"Absurd liar," she said. She came over and kissed him. "I write many poems about you," she whispered. "They are Russian, very formalist with short lines, totally impossible to translate, sorry. Always about you, the innocent with eyes closed." He closed his eyes.

Later he was forced to admit that he had, as was often his wont, made a virtue of necessity. His false consciousness collapsed like a house of cards, and he began observing Jenny with more attention. She seemed less contradictory than before, possibly because she spoke much less. She was too busy reading. Eventually she began borrowing his university library card and taking out books in Russian. She began cooking, greasy things like fried patties of flour and cottage cheese, and gained a little weight. She dyed her hair auburn, pointing out that all the girls in Freiburg were doing it. When David suggested they visit his parents on Easter weekend, she agreed immediately. A week later she opined that her life had become so stable and conventional that it might be time to send for her son, who was living with her parents in Novgorod, but before David even had a chance to ask how old he was, she admitted he didn't exist.

On Holy Saturday the family gathered around the piano, where David's mother performed *Frauenliebe und Leben*. Slightly high on a frizzy local wine, David sang his favorites from *Die schöne Müllerin*. His mother said that as always he was terribly lazy, and that despite his near-perfect taste and intonation, a lack of resonance condemned him to mannerism. His father kept quiet. Jenny said, "This is nice music. What's it about?"

"This journeyman has one friend, the stream. Following this stream, he meets a girl. But the girl soon likes a hunter instead and leaves him alone."

"Bitch," Jenny said.

David contradicted her. "She is no bitch! He is always happy with his friend the stream. Also the stream has better music than this innocent girl who likes aggressive hunters. It is not her fault. She is only a young girl. The stream is flowing since the last ice age, and she is maybe sixteen."

David's father said, "You are trying to flatter the older woman your mother. Of course the young girl is more interesting, even if she is a bitch. She takes everything this miller has got and leaves him to die in the brook. The brook cannot save him. But it is always singing nice singing-piano songs, archetypes of Schubert." He played a few measures. "You see?"

"Arkady is always telling me of Schubert."

"The same Arkady that David knows, the composer?" David's mother asked. "Tell me, Jenny, you know him also?"

"Yes, we are together in villa with David."

"Did you know him before?"

"He is my brother."

David's parents were delighted. David was mildly annoyed, since he didn't believe her and was sure he would never know the truth. When she went on to tell a thrilling tale of a familial exodus from the imploding Soviet Union via reindeer sled through the taiga, he felt relieved. It was obviously a lie. He resolved to challenge her on it later, on the way home.

His mother was not quite so shy around beautiful women. "You are inventing this, are you not?" she asked, turning her head to one side to glare at Jenny with one eye like a hungry bird.

Jenny laughed. "Of course! I am only trying to frighten David." She looked at him fondly, suddenly seeming to be really a member of the family as she laughed aloud at him and was joined by both his parents. "I like you people," she said. "In truth, I have no family. My parents are dead of illness when I am teenager. This is sad, but it happens sometimes. Only in Paris I have some cousins. I never meet them. Maybe we go there. David will study French symbolist painting in Paris, I think."

She went upstairs to bed while David's mother was still berating him for abandoning his *Habilitation*. She fell asleep to the sound of his father playing Schumann's *Kinderszenen,* though she didn't know what it was.

On the train David declared that he would not change the focus of his work. Consequently, he would not be going to Paris. Instead he would continue the pioneering studies of ancient lint that would gain him wide respect and a secure academic position.

Jenny said she would go to Paris anyway for two days to meet her cousins. The cousins were surprised and delighted to see her, seeing as how they had been looking for her ever since her mother died and she left home with a woman and started living under an assumed name. She refused their invitation to move in, saying she was quite content in Freiburg, but was happy to accept her share of the proceeds of the sale of the Donatello, which had turned up on the market in 1997 and been declared their property in 2002.

Try as he might, David couldn't think of a way to publicize the Redons without getting into trouble. Ten years earlier maybe, but not now—institutions were under too much pressure to know where their collections came from.

The next time he visited Trossingen, he discovered all four of them framed on the living room wall. His mother explained that she had found them in his room. She thought they were beautiful. He could see that she was proud of him, perhaps for the first time. Her son the embarrassingly boring academic and lousy singer had turned out to be an exceptionally gifted painter. He thanked her and resolved right there never to tell anyone of the pastels' true provenance, except maybe his heirs.

Siegfried invited Ingo and Amy to the premiere of Arkady's bagatelle. Arkady never played his own works in public, so he had enlisted the former twin sex bomb to slum by playing the viola for a change. After a Beethoven piano trio and Prokofiev's Violin Sonata op. 80, the stage was set. The audience drew closer with a sense of special anticipation.

She began to play. Then she stopped. Arkady looked around expectantly. She bowed, and a few people applauded. "Encore!" Amy shouted. She played it again.

"It is very short," Ingo remarked.

"Very short indeed," replied Siegfried.

Arkady stepped forward to accept a bouquet of flowers.

"I like it that way," Amy said. "Sink or swim, you know? I don't like people beating me over the head."

ACKNOWLEDGMENTS

I WISH TO THANK AVNER SHATS FOR writing this book's foreword; the still untranslated novel *Lashut el Ha-Shkiah*, which inspired *Sailing Toward the Sunset by Avner Shats;* and the specifications to which I wrote *European Story for Avner Shats:* "I would go for Florence, with a fifty-three-year-old real estate agent and a young art history student. She is rich but hates her job; the student is young and thinks he is sophisticated. Some piece of art should be involved, as well as a kayak, the last living member of the Amicale Internationale des Capitaines au Long Cours Cap Horniers, and, of course, a 19b [nineteen-year-old bisexual] who is desperately in love with an obscure middle-aged Israeli author." Now I'm the one pushing fifty-three, and Avner is old enough to find androgynous women of nineteen disturbingly childlike, but it's still extremely fun publishing these things. My sincere thanks to Megan Lynch and Dan Halpern of Ecco Press for being so brave about it.

ABOUT THE AUTHOR

NELL ZINK grew up in rural Virginia. She has worked in a variety of trades, including masonry and technical writing. In the early 1990s, she edited an indie rock fanzine. Her books include *The Wallcreeper, Mislaid,* and *Nicotine,* and her writing has appeared in *n+1.* She lives near Berlin, Germany.